WILDLIFE
WAYS

Animal Ark series

LUCY DANIELS

Wildlife Ways

Illustrated by Ann Baum

*Hodder
Children's
Books*

a division of Hodder Headline plc

Special thanks to Tanis Jordan and Bette Paul
Thanks also to C. J. Hall, B.Vet.Med., M.R.C.V.S., for reviewing
the veterinary information contained in this book.

Animal Ark is a trademark of Working Partners Limited
Text copyright © 1999 Working Partners Limited
Created by Working Partners Limited, London W12 7QY
Original series created by Ben M. Baglio
Illustrations copyright © 1999 Ann Baum

First published in Great Britain in 1999
by Hodder Children's Books

A Catalogue record for this book is available from the British Library

ISBN 0 340 73655 0 (HB)

Typeset by Avon Dataset Ltd, Bidford-on-Avon, Warks

Printed and bound in Great Britain by
Clays Ltd, St Ives plc

Hodder Children's Books
a division of Hodder Headline plc
338 Euston Road
London NW1 3BH

Contents

Foxes
– on the –
Farm

One

Mandy Hope saw the note as soon as she came in through the door. It was propped against a bowl of daffodils on the kitchen table. 'Ring Michelle Holmes,' she read out loud. Her mother had jotted down the number and added 'URGENT!!' to the bottom of the note.

Mandy frowned. Dumping her schoolbag on a chair, she reached for the phone. Why was Michelle ringing her? Michelle Holmes was the presenter of the radio programme *Wildlife Ways*. She had made a programme about the hedgehog refuge that Mandy and her best friend James Hunter had helped to set up, and had even supplied them with radio tags for the young hedgehogs so they could keep track of them when they left the nest. Mandy hurriedly punched in the numbers. Michelle answered on the third ring.

'Michelle, it's Mandy Hope. Mum left a note to ring you urgently,' Mandy said.

'Oh, hi, Mandy. Thanks for getting back to me so quickly. I've got wonderful news. *Wildlife Ways* is being turned into a TV show! I wondered if you'd like to help at all . . .'

'Would I like to? I'd *love* to!' Mandy exclaimed.

Michelle laughed and went on, enthusiastically filling Mandy in on her plans. Mandy listened with mounting excitement. 'So, Mandy, I need to start as soon as possible. It will be great to have you and James to help,' she finished. 'Speak to your parents and, if it's OK, I'll see you later, at about six-thirty. Oh, just one more thing, Mandy . . .' Michelle hesitated, '. . . we need to start filming in a few days' time to make our deadline. So it's quite tight.'

'That's OK,' Mandy replied. 'We broke up for a week's holiday today. Wait till I tell James about this!' James Hunter was Mandy's best friend. He was a year younger than her, and almost as keen on animals as she was. 'Bye,

Michelle,' Mandy put down the phone. '*Yes!*' she said with a big grin on her face. She couldn't believe it!

Mandy dashed through the door connecting the old stone cottage where the Hopes lived to the modern vet's surgery at the back where Mandy's parents had their practice. She arrived in the waiting-room, still clutching her mum's note in her hand.

'Where's the fire?' Jean Knox the receptionist asked, removing her glasses and giving Mandy a startled look.

'Sorry,' Mandy gasped. 'It's just that I've got *such* exciting news and I can't *wait* to tell Mum and Dad.'

'Well, you'd better go through to the surgery,' Jean said, smiling. 'Your father's scrubbing up. He's got one more operation to do this afternoon and Simon's assisting him. I think your mum's in with them too.'

Mandy spun round and pushed through the surgery door. Jean followed her.

'Mum, Dad, guess what!' Mandy stood dramatically in the middle of the room, beaming broadly.

Adam Hope was leaning over the sink rinsing the soap bubbles from his hands. 'School's finished for the holidays?' he called over his shoulder.

'Much better than that!' Mandy was enjoying this. 'Fantastic, in fact!'

'Might it be anything to do with a telephone message?' asked Mandy's mum, who was sorting through some files.

Simon, the practice nurse, grinned at Mandy as he took a new pair of thin rubber gloves from the cupboard and began to unwrap them ready for Mr Hope to put on.

'You all know already!' Mandy said, pretending to be upset.

'*I* don't. Nobody tells me anything,' Adam Hope said, drying his hands. 'Simon mentioned to us that Michelle had an idea, and Mum spoke to her earlier, but *I'm* still in the dark.' He dropped the paper towels into the bin.

'Well,' Mandy began, trying to control her excitement, 'Michelle is making a *Wildlife Ways* TV programme and she wants to know if James and I want to get involved. She wants to make a film about foxes first, and we're going to help collect information about where they live and what they do.' The words all tumbled out at once. 'She wants to come here to tell us all about it after work tonight. Isn't that brilliant?'

'How exciting,' said Jean from the doorway. 'Our very own TV researcher!'

Mandy turned to face her, pretending to be haughty. 'One day, Jean, you might *beg* for my autograph.' Everyone laughed and then Mandy continued. 'Michelle is making three programmes to begin with. And if they're a success she gets to make a whole series! Isn't it great?'

Simon looked up from preparing the surgical instruments for the operation. 'I told Michelle a while ago that you found a vixen who'd given birth while caught in a trap.' He wheeled over the anaesthetic apparatus. 'She was very impressed that you'd rescued the newborn cub and his mother.'

Mandy felt a glow of satisfaction as she remembered how they had managed to free the vixen from the deadly trap and save her life. Mandy had named the cub Lucky, as he was the only one of four cubs to survive.

'Hey, wouldn't it be good if we spotted them? Lucky and his mum, I mean.' Mandy was delighted to think she might see the cub again. 'I wonder if they're still on their old territory. Do you think Lucky would remember me?'

'I'm sure he might, it wasn't *that* long ago, Mandy,' her mum replied. 'But you mustn't encourage him to make contact with you,' she reminded her, taking off her white coat and hanging it up. 'His best chance of survival is to stay wild.'

'When are you going to tell James the good news?' asked Mr Hope.

'Right now!' Mandy decided. 'Then I can be back in time to do all my jobs.'

'He's a member of the Welford Wildlife Watchers, isn't he?' her dad asked. 'That might come in handy.'

'Yep. James is really good at spotting tracks,' Mandy agreed. She would have liked to join the group herself but now she was twelve she had started helping out at Animal Ark and she didn't have the time.

'I'll do your jobs tonight,' Simon offered.

'Oh thanks, Simon,' Mandy said gratefully. She turned to her mum and dad. 'Is that OK?' Mandy asked them. She loved helping out in her parents' surgery but right now her head was full of foxes and she was dying to tell James the good news.

'Yes, go on love, we'll let you off this once,' Adam Hope agreed, holding out his arms as

Simon put an operating gown on him and tied it at the back.

'Thanks, Dad!' Mandy said, heading for the door.

Adam Hope called her back. 'I know you – you'll probably start looking for foxes before you've even met up with Michelle, but remember to ask permission if you want to search on people's land,' he warned her. 'Some farmers can be very particular about trespassers!'

Mandy grimaced. 'If you mean Sam Western, I don't think we'll be looking on *his* land. We all know he hates foxes.' Sam Western was a ruthless local farmer who wanted to start up a foxhunt and rid the area of foxes.

'See you later, everyone,' Mandy said, halfway out of the door.

'Don't forget to change your clothes first!' Emily Hope called after her.

Mandy was already on her way upstairs. She changed into a comfortable blue tracksuit and set off. As she cycled to James's house she racked her brains for a plan. They would have to check every woodland and spinney in the area and do some trekking on the moor as well. James was sure to come up with some good ideas.

Mrs Hunter was weeding the front garden when Mandy arrived. 'Hello, there. James is in the back garden with Blackie,' she said, smiling. 'He's mending his bike; he got a puncture turning into the drive this evening.'

Mandy walked around the house and looked out over the lawn. James had his bike upside-down by the beech tree and was just levering the tyre back on to its wheel. 'Hi,' he called. James's black Labrador spotted Mandy and bounded towards her.

'Whoa, Blackie! Down!' Mandy laughed, as the dog jumped up and tried to lick her face. 'I know you're always pleased to see me.' She kneeled down near James and rubbed Blackie's ears. He loved the attention and rolled over, thumping his tail on the ground.

'Listen, James, I've got some fantastic news!' Mandy sat back on her heels impatiently, waiting for his full attention.

Hearing the excitement in Mandy's voice, James stopped pumping up the tyre and looked at her.

'Are you ready for this?' Mandy asked. She took a deep breath. 'Michelle Holmes wants us to help with a television programme about foxes.'

For a while, James just stared at Mandy. Then,

as the news sank in, he leaped to his feet sending the pump flying. Blackie sprang up with an excited bark and made a grab for it. 'No you don't!' James got there first. 'That's fantastic! Us, helping with a TV programme! Wow! When do we start?'

'As soon as possible!' Mandy told him, jumping up. 'Let's go to The Riddings. We can ask the Spry sisters' permission to start our search on their land first thing in the morning,' she said excitedly.

James righted his bike and tested the tyre. 'I should take Blackie for a walk first, he's been waiting for it,' he said.

'We could take him with us,' Mandy suggested. James nodded, and fetched Blackie's lead.

Soon they were cycling slowly down the lane so that Blackie could trot beside them. There was a gentle breeze and the last of the blossom fluttered from the trees. The early summer sunshine was warm as they rode along.

'Walter Pickard showed me how to look for foxes once, when we were on a badger watch,' James called out to Mandy, who was riding in front. Walter Pickard was the secretary of the Welford Wildlife Watchers. 'We could ask him for some advice.'

'Can't hear you!' Mandy slowed down so James could catch up.

'I said, Walter must know more about the countryside than almost anybody,' James told her, keeping close to the side so Blackie could run along the grassy bank.

'That's a point,' Mandy said. She pushed a wayward strand of her fair hair behind her ears. 'You're right – he's the perfect person to ask.'

Mandy and James pedalled up the Walton road towards The Riddings, where the Spry sisters lived. From the crest of the hill they freewheeled down until they reached the bridge over the stream, where Mandy stopped so suddenly that James almost crashed into her.

'I wish you wouldn't do that,' James grumbled.

'Sorry,' Mandy said absent-mindedly. 'But just think, James, if we hadn't stopped here that day and heard the vixen's cries, Lucky and his mum would never have survived.' Mandy shuddered at the thought.

'But they did,' said James sensibly, 'and we might even see them again. Come on, let's get a move on!'

As soon as they turned into the drive that led up to the huge, old-fashioned house where the sisters lived, James put Blackie's lead on. The sweeping lawns at the front of the house were ready for the first cut of the year. Mandy and James leaned their bikes against the stone wall at the bottom of the steps.

'Now stay, Blackie, stay!' James said firmly. Blackie wagged his tail and sat down obediently beside the bicycles. 'See,' James said proudly, 'he *is* learning.' He hooked the lead over the handlebars of his bike and followed Mandy up the great stone steps.

Mandy knocked on the wooden front door. When it creaked open she saw that both the Spry sisters had come to the door. Miss Marjorie fiddled fussily with a row of pearls round her neck and clutched nervously at her cardigan. Miss Joan hovered in the background. They were twins, and as alike as two peas in a pod.

'Mandy, my dear!' exclaimed Miss Marjorie. 'How nice to see you.'

'And James,' finished Miss Joan. The elderly sisters lived alone in The Riddings but since Mandy and James had persuaded them to adopt Patch, one of their school cat's kittens, they had been gradually getting a little bit more involved with village life. Everyone admired the way they had stood up to Sam Western over the foxhunting issue in the village. Mandy had proved to the sisters that Sam Western was responsible for setting traps to kill foxes, and they had refused to support his hunting plans, banishing him from their land.

'Hello, Miss Marjorie, Miss Joan,' Mandy said warmly. 'Oh look, James, Patch has come to see us.' She bent down and ran her hand over the little cat's sleek fur.

'See how big he's grown,' Miss Joan said. 'Isn't he doing well?' Patch stretched out his front paws and yawned.

'What a good home you have here, Patch,' Mandy told him, rubbing him behind his ears and making him purr. The sisters blushed with pleasure as Mandy and James stroked their pet, who was their pride and joy.

'I'm sure you young people didn't come here just to see Patch,' Miss Marjorie said. 'What can we do for you?'

'We're going to be helping to make a programme about foxes,' Mandy said proudly, 'and we need to do some research. Could we look for foxes on your land, please?'

Miss Marjorie's face lit up with a smile. 'How exciting, Mandy,' she said. 'Will it be like *Wildlife Ways*? We always listen to that on our wireless.'

She stepped out of the doorway, her birdlike face pale in the sunshine.

'It *is Wildlife Ways*, but it will be on television,' Mandy told them.

'Television!' Miss Marjorie gasped, as if Mandy had said she was going to the moon.

'Television!' echoed her sister. 'Father didn't approve of new-fangled things like television.' Miss Joan frowned. 'He said it was a five-minute wonder that would never catch on. So we've stuck with the wireless.'

'But foxes, you say, Mandy?' Miss Marjorie had recovered from her shock. She came out further on to the top step and bent closer to Mandy and James. 'We see quite a lot of foxes up here.' She clenched her hands and looked around furtively, as if she expected Sam Western to pop up out of the flowerbed. 'Almost every evening we see them coming and going. *Last* evening there was one on the lawn.'

Mandy's heart leaped. She grinned at James who gave a little whistle. 'That *does* sound promising,' he said, nodding.

Not to be outdone, Miss Joan came out on to the step next to her sister. 'I've seen *lots* of foxes early in the mornings too. More than you!' she announced, pushing in front of her sister.

Suddenly there was a crash of bicycles hitting the ground. Blackie had 'stayed' long enough. He was heading for the steps, dragging James's bike behind him with his lead. As the bike caught on the bottom step, the lead slipped off the handlebars and freed Blackie. He bounded up the steps, eager to say hello to the Spry sisters. Mandy quickly jumped in front of the sisters so that Blackie didn't knock them down like skittles. Patch gave a screech and Miss Joan scooped him up in her arms.

The Labrador was almost at the top of the steps before James stopped him with an impressive flying tackle. They rolled back down, landing in a tangled heap at the bottom.

Nobody moved for a very long moment. The Spry sisters stared at the scene in astonishment. Patch now clung around Miss Joan's neck like an old-fashioned fur collar, with his tail up in the air.

Finally, holding tightly to Blackie's lead, James scrambled to his feet. He picked up his cap and pushed his glasses back up his nose, brushing off some of the dust now covering his clothes.

Blackie looked really pleased with himself. He

danced on the lead and looked eagerly up the steps as if expecting everyone's approval.

'Sorry about that,' James said, scarlet with embarrassment. 'He's um, well, not quite fully trained yet.'

Now that Mandy was over the initial shock of seeing it happen and realised that James and Blackie weren't hurt, it was all she could do not to burst out laughing.

'Um, perhaps we should think about getting back now.' James glanced pleadingly at Mandy. 'We don't want to miss Michelle this evening.'

'We'll come back early tomorrow morning,' Mandy promised the Spry sisters. 'That is, if that's all right with you?'

'Fine, fine. Help yourselves, go wherever you want,' Miss Marjorie replied.

Mandy said a hurried goodbye to Patch, who was just beginning to unwind himself from Miss Joan's neck.

'Good luck,' the Spry sisters called in unison, before hurrying inside and shutting the door firmly behind them.

'Are you OK?' Mandy asked when she got to the bottom of the steps.

'Yep. Fine,' James said shortly.

Mandy began to giggle. 'That dog is getting

worse, not better! You did look funny rolling down the steps.'

'I bet,' James said ruefully, bending down to pull out a bit of twig that was stuck in Blackie's collar. 'What am I going to do with you, Blackie?' he laughed, patting the dog's head.

'He just likes being with you, that's all,' Mandy said, picking up James's bike and wheeling it to him.

They cycled back down to the village and left Blackie at James's house, then made their way over to Animal Ark. They left their bikes and went into reception. It was empty; Jean had obviously gone home. But there was a light under the door of one of the examination rooms.

Mandy pushed the door open. Emily Hope was putting a jar of ointment into a cupboard while Adam Hope was pouring disinfectant into a spray bottle from a plastic drum.

'Hi, Mum, Hi, Dad. We went up to The Riddings. We can begin our search for foxes on the Spry sisters' land first thing tomorrow morning,' Mandy said, flopping into a chair. 'I bet Michelle will be pleased.'

James wedged his cap in his jacket pocket and perched on a stool. 'They've seen lots of foxes,' he told them. 'Even on the lawn. So let's hope it'll be easy for us.'

'Don't be disheartened if you *don't* find foxes instantly, you two,' Adam Hope said, crossing the room with a pile of patients' files in his arms. 'Remember the process of elimination.'

Mandy looked puzzled. 'What d' you mean?'

'Like detective work?' questioned James.

'Exactly,' Mandy's dad said, handing the files to Emily Hope. 'It's just as important to record where there *aren't* any signs of foxes. Then you can gradually build up an understanding of the kind of places foxes favour and you'll be able to make a map of the areas that they *do* use.'

'Oh, I see,' Mandy said slowly as she grasped the idea. 'So if we spent a whole morning and didn't see any signs it wouldn't be a waste of time?'

'That's it,' Mr Hope nodded. 'And speaking of wild animals, I'm going to check on the hedgehog I operated on this afternoon.' He raised his eyebrows at Mandy and James. 'Want to come?'

'You bet!' Mandy said with a firm nod. 'Is it going to be all right?'

'Fine,' her dad answered. 'You both know how

hardy hedgehogs are. Their ability to survive is quite amazing.'

Mandy and James followed Mr Hope through to the residential unit at the back of Animal Ark. This was where domestic animals recovering from operations or in for observation were kept overnight. An annexe had been set up for wild animals. Simon was just finishing up his rounds.

'Hi, you two,' he said, looking up from rolling a bandage. 'How's it going?'

'Great,' Mandy told him. Michelle's coming at half past six to tell us what she wants us to do for the *Wildlife Ways* programme.

'Look at this little fellow,' Adam Hope said, gently picking up the hedgehog. 'He's had a real bashing. The postman found him; he reckoned his head had been cut by a strimmer. His ear was hanging off when he arrived, so we had to remove it completely.' He pointed to the neat row of stitches where an ear should have been, and a big sore area behind with a scab on it.

'Will he be able to be released back into the wild?' Mandy asked, her voice full of concern.

'He should be right as rain,' her dad said. 'We'll just keep him in until the stitches come out and the scab comes off.' He put the hedgehog back. 'Now, I'm going to go and put my feet up, I'm whacked.' He put an arm round each of Mandy and James's shoulders and pretended to collapse on them.

'Da-ad! You're too heavy!' Mandy cried. She and James staggered along in fits of giggles, dragging him through to the kitchen, where they fell into chairs around the big, wooden kitchen table.

Mandy could hardly wait for Michelle to arrive, so she could tell them all about the programme. She wanted to start work on it right away.

Two

'Hi, everyone,' Michelle called. She had arrived just as Emily Hope was pouring out steaming mugs of hot chocolate.

'Hi, Michelle,' said Mandy. 'Come and have some chocolate.'

Michelle gratefully took the mug Mandy offered her and put her shoulder bag on the floor. She was a slim woman, not a lot taller than Mandy, with short, glossy brown hair. She was wearing khaki trousers that had lots of useful zipped pockets and a cream cotton shirt with the sleeves rolled up. Her dangly silver earrings tinkled when she turned her head.

'We've been so busy, I haven't stopped all

day,' Michelle told them as she took off her coat. She took a folder full of papers out of her bag and sat down at the table. 'So, how are my two helpers getting on? Any ideas on where we should start looking?' she asked Mandy and James. 'I am *so* excited about this project. I reckon we're going to make a really good film.'

'We went up to the Spry sisters' house this afternoon to ask permission to look on their land. We thought we could start searching for foxes tomorrow morning,' Mandy said. 'Miss Marjorie says the foxes sometimes come right up into their garden.'

'Foxes have large territories,' Michelle informed them. 'What I'd like you to look for is a breeding earth,' she carried on.

'How will we recognise it?' Mandy asked.

'Foxes usually have several earths on their territory but the vixen picks only one to breed in,' Michelle said, stopping to take a sip of her chocolate. 'Mmm, that's good! The cubs will stay in or around the breeding earth. The vixen will only move them before that if she's disturbed.'

'Do they drag leaves and stuff inside for a nest, like hedgehogs?' Mandy asked.

'Or collect fresh hay, like badgers?' James asked.

'It's interesting you should ask that. Foxes don't actually make a nest at all,' Michelle told them, warming to her subject. 'The vixen gives birth to the cubs straight on to the bare earth. For the first two weeks of life the cubs are too small to keep themselves warm so the vixen can't leave them at all.'

'How does she manage to eat?' James asked, picking up a biscuit from the plate in the middle of the table.

'Trust you to think of food, James!' Mandy said. James was *always* hungry.

'It's sensible question,' Emily Hope said, defending James as they all laughed. She sat down with them at the table. 'Foxes live in family groups, usually mum, dad and the cubs. But there are often other adult foxes in the group too, older brothers and sisters, and they will help to bring her food. Mostly it's the dog fox that brings most of the food.'

'So foxes aren't that different from us!' Mandy said, grinning at her mum.

Michelle nodded. 'Now, I'm not going to be able to start looking at sites until Monday evening. We've got to have the film ready to edit by the weekend, so if you two would like to make a start tomorrow, I'll give you some tips for fox-watching,' she said.

Mandy and James leaned forward.

'First of all, you have to stay as invisible as possible. A country fox is one of the hardest animals to get close to. Once you find an earth that's in use, position yourselves downwind of it. A fox's sense of smell is strong. Don't use insect repellent or take strong smelling food or drink with you. And don't forget that a fox's hearing is excellent – they can hear a mouse moving when it's nearly three metres away. So, you'll need to be even quieter than mice. For example, don't wear clothes that rustle. And you know not to wear brightly coloured clothes.'

Mandy nodded enthusiastically. 'So tomorrow morning should we start by looking for an earth?' she asked.

'Yes, please. If you can find a breeding earth, that would be great,' Michelle said. 'Foxes are amazingly clever, they will adapt anything suitable to use as an earth.'

'How will Mandy and James know if the earth is in use?' Emily Hope asked.

'There are a couple of giveaways,' Michelle told them. 'The cubs will be old enough to be playing outside now, so the grass will be flattened. You'll see lots of animal bones, feathers, remains of meals and other bits and pieces. I think you would certainly notice the mess! But you'll see most activity early in the morning and in the evenings.'

'You two will be out from dawn to dusk then,' Mrs Hope said to Mandy and James. She picked up the plate of biscuits and offered them to Michelle.

'I think we should start as early as possible,' Mandy decided. 'About five o'clock?'

James looked aghast at the thought of getting up so early on the first day of the holidays.

'The earlier the better, James,' Michelle advised, collecting her papers together and standing up. 'Let's hope it's not pouring with rain!'

'I think the forecast for tomorrow is fine,' Simon said, as he joined them in the kitchen.

'So that's all settled, then. See you Monday evening at five-thirty,' Michelle said, getting up to leave.

'Just a moment, Michelle,' Emily Hope said, as she collected all the mugs. 'I hate to be a spoilsport, Mandy, but what about your work at Animal Ark? Simon can't *keep* doing all your jobs for you,' she reminded her.

'I'll help,' offered James. Mandy shot him a grateful look.

'If James helps me, we could do any jobs in the residential unit before the dusk watch,' she said, looking pleadingly at her mother.

'I'm happy to do any extra jobs while this project is on, Mandy,' Simon said generously, 'but ...' There was a wicked glint in his eye. 'When it's over ...'

'I'll do anything you like,' Mandy begged with a grin. 'All the jobs you don't like doing, for as long as you want.'

'You're on!' Simon agreed. 'And I'll keep you to it.'

Mandy showed Michelle to the door. 'Bye, everyone,' she called over her shoulder as she went out. 'I'll see you on Monday!'

As soon as Mandy's alarm went off, she sprang out of bed. Within minutes she was dressed, downstairs and drinking a glass of milk from the fridge. Mandy closed the front door quietly behind her, so as not to wake her parents, and soon she was pedalling down the lane on her bike to meet James outside the post office, as they'd arranged.

They cycled towards The Riddings in silence, both deep in thought. Taking a short cut to the sisters' land, they left their bikes in the bushes and set off on foot.

At the bottom of the meadow an old path led through a wood of old, gnarled beech trees. A sprinkling of rain the previous night had made the earth damp. As they trod through the undergrowth of springy ferns, squirrels scrambled up tree trunks to peer down at them from a safe height.

Deep among the trees, Mandy and James came to a rickety plank bridge that crossed a narrow stream, marking the edge of the Spry sisters' land. They crossed it and headed up towards the open moors.

Suddenly James stopped and sniffed. 'Foxes!' he said softly. 'I think they've been here recently, marking their territory.'

Mandy could smell a strong scent in the air, something like a mixture of wood varnish, cheese and smelly socks. You could hardly miss it.

'Walter taught me to recognise that foxy smell,' James whispered to Mandy, as he studied the muddy track for telltale signs. Quickly he found what he was looking for. 'Mandy, look, here in the mud!'

Mandy peered to where he was pointing. She saw a clearly-defined set of prints crossing the path, narrower in shape than those made by a dog.

'These are fresh,' observed James, 'made since it rained, probably in the night or even this morning. And look, here are some more.'

Further on they found tufts of long fur caught on a bramble bush. With a surge of excitement, Mandy picked off some to take back and show her parents. She was sure the reddish fur belonged to a fox. She gazed at the great prickly mass of brambles that extended for several metres in all directions. 'This is exactly the sort of place Michelle said foxes would use,' Mandy breathed, getting down on all fours to peer underneath. There was no way that either she or James could crawl under the brambles to have a look. 'But there's nothing around to show it's an earth, is there?' Mandy noted. 'Have a look round the other side, James.'

James waded through the bracken surrounding the prickly bush. 'I can't see anything,' he said, after he'd walked right round. 'No feathers or bones. But I can't see right into the middle.' James looked thoughtful. 'You know, foxes can squeeze through a hole less than ten centimetres across.' He made a shape with his hands. 'Imagine a big dog fox getting through a gap not much bigger than a cricket ball.'

'There could easily be foxes in there, then,' Mandy said. 'It's a good safe place for them, isn't it?' She was feeling optimistic. 'Let's watch for a while. If we're really still and quiet they might come back.'

A short distance away, they found a fallen tree and sat down to watch the bramble patch. In silence they waited for nearly half an hour, but not a single fox passed by.

'Let's move on,' Mandy suggested, her enthusiasm ebbing. After they had discovered the footprints and the fur, she had felt sure there were foxes nearby.

Mandy and James worked their way through the woods, noting down any signs of foxes they saw along the way.

They walked out on to the moor and scanned the foreground. Suddenly, James tugged at her sleeve. Mandy looked to where he was pointing across the moor. A fox was crossing the rise above them!

Mandy hardly dared to breathe as she slowly raised her binoculars. She watched as it ran

along the crest, then stopped, head up, ears
twitching, sniffing the air. Then it was off again
across the moor where it disappeared into
Piper's Wood.

'Do you realise where that fox must have
come from?' James said softly, staring at Mandy
as he waited for realisation to dawn on her.

Mandy thought. Next to The Riddings' land
was . . . 'Oh no, James! It came from the
direction of Upper Welford Hall,' she said in a
faint voice.

James nodded. 'Sam Western's place,'
he groaned. 'We know how much *he* cares
about wildlife. He and Dennis Saville will

shoot anything that moves.'

Mandy nodded grimly. She and James had already had several run-ins with Sam Western and his gamekeeper Dennis Saville. The two men had poisoned one of Lydia Fawcett's goats and had been responsible for setting the traps that had nearly killed Lucky and his mother.

'If Sam Western found foxes on his land,' James voiced her thoughts, 'he'd be sure to want to start a foxhunt again.'

Mandy felt her heart jolt. 'And James! Remember what he did last year?' she said, gripping her handlebars so hard that her knuckles turned white.

'Yes,' James said, his mouth setting into a grim line. 'He organised the local farmers into a hunting party to get rid of the foxes.' He stared angrily in the direction of Upper Welford Hall.

'And they shot an innocent dog fox,' Mandy said grimly. She remembered how they had found the poor dead fox that Sam Western had shot for fear it would steal his pheasants. What if he found out that there were foxes on his land again? 'We'll have to make sure he doesn't find out about Michelle filming around here,' she told James. 'We can't put the foxes in danger.'

* * *

The sun was growing warm as Mandy and James cycled back and a cool breeze began to blow away unpleasant thoughts about Sam Western. Morning surgery was finished when Mandy and James arrived at Animal Ark. They got stuck into Mandy's daily tasks straight away. James swept the floor, while Mandy fetched fresh bedding for the patients in the residential unit.

'We saw a fox near Piper's Wood,' Mandy told her parents, as she and James worked. She remembered the fur she had brought home. 'And we found this,' she said, taking it out of her pocket and showing it to her dad.

'Yes, that's fox fur,' he confirmed. 'These long hairs are called the guard hairs. Foxes begin their moult about this time of year and they can look very ragged. Fascinating creatures, foxes. You two are going to enjoy this, aren't you?'

Mandy nodded happily. 'We plan to take Blackie for a walk this afternoon and then go straight back to Piper's Wood to look for an earth,' she told him as she finished tidying up.

After lunch, Mandy and James took Blackie

down to the river and let him off the lead. They sat on the warm sand, whilst Blackie raced along the riverbank.

'I've made a note of everything we've seen so far connected with foxes,' Mandy said, chewing the end of her pencil and squinting. 'When we go tonight,' she declared confidently, 'we can fill in exactly where we find the earth. Then Michelle can start filming right away on Monday.' She sprang to her feet, brushed the sand from her trousers and handed her notebook to James.

'*If* we find it!' James reminded her, looking through her notes. 'It's not a hundred per cent certain that we will.'

'We will, James,' Mandy smiled. 'I know we will.'

At that moment Blackie, who had decided to take a dip, came bounding out of the river towards them. 'Aaargh, look out, James!' Mandy warned, jumping out of range, but it was too late. Blackie shook himself vigorously, spraying James from head to toe with droplets of water.

'Oh, thanks, Blackie,' James laughed. 'I was feeling a bit warm.'

'Come on,' Mandy said, laughing. 'Let's take Blackie home and then we can start.'

* * *

The late afternoon sun was on their backs as they cycled up the lane to Piper's Wood. In the distance they could just make out the ivy-clad walls of Upper Welford Hall, Sam Western's house. Mandy stuck her arm out to signal to James and veered off down a track. She stopped beside a stile. 'Let's leave our bikes here,' she said.

They left their bikes against a wooden post. Then they searched through the rest of the woods, carefully checking out any possible places that a fox might use as an earth. They were so busy with their project that they hardly realised it had begun to get dark. Eventually, Mandy flopped down on an old tree trunk. 'OK,' she sighed. 'What have we got so far?'

'Not much, really,' James shrugged. 'Two disused earths and one possibly in use.'

'Just because you found an empty take-away box,' Mandy teased, 'doesn't mean it's possibly in use.'

'No, I know,' James blushed.

'We'll just have to keep searching,' Mandy said in a resigned voice. 'Nobody said it would be easy.'

'I didn't think it would be this hard though,' James acknowledged. 'They certainly know how to hide themselves.'

'We'd better start back soon,' Mandy said, looking around. 'It's beginning to get dark.'

James led the way as they hurried back to their bikes. 'There's the stile,' he said, climbing over to collect their bikes.

'Oh no, I forgot to get a new battery for my front light,' groaned Mandy, looking along the dark lane.

'I'll go in front, then you can take mine when we reach my house,' James offered.

All of a sudden, out of the darkness of the wood came a bloodcurdling scream. Then another, closer now.

'What's that?' Mandy cried. 'It sounds like someone's being murdered!' She was not easily spooked but it sent a cold shiver through her.

James face split in a grin from ear to ear. 'That's foxes!' he exclaimed. 'Mandy, they *are* here.'

Three

'Why did the foxes have to wait until it was time for us to go home?' Mandy said. She sat on her bike and looked longingly back at the wood. The eerie screams came again. 'Right James,' Mandy's eyes flashed. 'Tomorrow we're going to find them!'

When they reached James's house they arranged to meet the next morning. 'I'll come here for you, if you like,' Mandy called, as she sped off. 'That will give you five minutes more in bed!' Laughing, she set off for Animal Ark.

Mandy was just passing under the oak tree by the village pond when she spied Walter Pickard crossing the village green. She swerved and rode over to him.

'Hi, Mr Pickard,' Mandy called, as she drew near.

'Hello, young Mandy, what's bringing you this way?' Walter Pickard stopped and waited till Mandy reached him. 'Are you looking for your Grandad? It's bell-ringing practice tonight.'

'No, I'm just on my way home. James and I have been looking for foxes,' she explained, stopping to take a breath. 'Maybe you could help us? We've just been up at Piper's Wood.'

'Aye, but did you see 'em there?' Walter rocked on the heels of his shoes.

'Not yet,' Mandy said, shaking her head. 'We found old earths and heard some foxes scream but . . .' Then the words all spilled out and soon she had told him the whole story about the film and the urgent need to find a breeding earth. 'And we're looking again tomorrow morning,' Mandy finished. 'We haven't much time and we don't want to let Michelle down.'

Walter Pickard gazed down at Mandy with a long, thoughtful look. 'There's been foxes breeding in Piper's Wood since I was a lad,' he told her. 'But not many people knows where to look. That's what keeps 'em safe.'

'I bet *you* know where to look, Mr Pickard?' Mandy said, knowing full well he did, but trying to flatter him into helping them.

'Aye, happen I do,' Walter said, nodding slowly. He hesitated for a few more seconds then made his decision. 'You tell young James to look where I showed him the mushrooms that time,' Walter told her. 'But make sure nobody else knows.'

Mandy beamed. 'Thank you, Mr Pickard, you won't regret it.'

'Eh-up, here comes Ernie Bell, he'll expect me to have the church opened up by now,' Walter said, drawing himself up. 'Mind what I said, now, about keeping the information to yourselves.'

'I will,' Mandy nodded. 'And thanks.' She waved to Ernie Bell and set off down the lane towards home. Pedalling fast and furiously, Mandy almost collided with a camper van as it came slowly around the bend.

'Hello, Mandy love,' her grandad said, winding down the window. 'You're in a hurry. Are you late for something?'

Mandy laughed. 'No, but you are, Grandad! Walter Pickard and Ernie Bell are already at the church.'

'I thought they might be. I was watching the sunset with your gran. It's a real shepherd's sunset.' He gazed back the way he'd come. The sky was flame red with streaks of gold where the sun was slipping below the horizon.

'Red sky at night, shepherd's delight,' Mandy recited. 'That's good. James and I are off at dawn to search for foxes. Walter Pickard has told us where to look!' Mandy told him.

'Well if anybody knows, it'll be Walter.' A peal of bells rang out. 'Oops! I'd better get a move on,' Grandad said guiltily.

'Bye, Grandad,' Mandy called as he pulled away.

Mandy skidded to a halt on the drive outside Animal Ark, put her bike away and rushed up the steps to reception, eager to tell her parents the good news.

'Dad and I had an idea, too,' Emily Hope said, after Mandy had told them all about her afternoon. 'As you don't have much time, why don't you ask Mrs Ponsonby if the people involved with Fox Watch have seen any vixens with cubs?' She wiped the table down. 'I know that when she started Fox Watch Mrs Ponsonby had the wrong intentions. Driving the foxes out wasn't quite the right idea!' She gave Mandy a wry smile. 'But she did come good in the end.'

'Fox Watch!' Mandy's face lit up. 'That's a brilliant idea, Mum. Why didn't I think of that?'

'You just have incredibly brilliant parents,' Adam Hope joked. 'Don't forget it was me who convinced Mrs Ponsonby that saving foxes was saving part of our natural heritage.'

'Oh!' Mandy's face fell.

'What's wrong?' Mrs Hope asked, rinsing her hands.

'Well, Fox Watch is a great idea . . .' Mandy faltered.

'I sense a "but" coming now.' Adam Hope had a twinkle in his eye.

'It's just that Mrs Ponsonby, she's so . . . so . . .' Mandy floundered around for a polite word. 'Forceful! She takes over everything.'

'Now, Mandy, don't be unkind,' Emily Hope said. 'She may be forceful, as you say, but she certainly gets things done. And she's not afraid to stand up to people.'

Mandy looked to her dad for support but he was feeling generous too. 'She's not so bad, Mandy,' he agreed. 'She's all huff and puff but underneath it all, she means well.'

'Go on, Mandy,' Emily Hope said, putting all

the surgical instruments into the steriliser and turning it on. 'Go and call her now.'

Mandy waited while the phone rang at Bleakfell Hall, the huge Victorian mansion where Mrs Ponsonby lived.

'Hello, Bleakfell Hall, the Ponsonby residence,' a voice said. Mandy stifled a laugh. She could hear Pandora, Mrs Ponsonby's Pekinese, yapping noisily, and Toby, her mongrel, barking excitedly.

'Hello, Mrs Ponsonby, it's Mandy Hope here,' she said.

'Oh, Mandy dear!' exclaimed Mrs Ponsonby. 'Hold on a moment.'

Mandy waited as the yapping got louder and louder. Eventually it sounded as though the dogs were yapping straight down the phone.

'Pandora wants to say hello,' Mrs Ponsonby told her. Mandy moved the phone away from her head as Pandora yapped in her ear. 'Do say hello to her, then she'll be quiet.'

'Hello, Pandora,' Mandy said, pulling a face as she saw her mum and dad standing at the surgery door, grinning.

'Good. Now, what can I do for you, Mandy?' Mrs Ponsonby said, as if chatting to a dog on the phone was perfectly normal. However, Mrs

Ponsonby had been right – Pandora had
stopped yapping.

'Well, it's about Fox Watch.' Mandy proceeded
to tell Mrs Ponsonby all about the programme
and finding foxes. 'Dad wondered if you had
seen any cubs recently?'

'I'm sure we should be able to help, Mandy,'
Mrs Ponsonby said happily. 'We haven't been
meeting much lately, I have to say. Everybody
was so busy with the Easter celebrations,' she
continued. 'But I will get in touch with the rest
of the group and see if there's any news. How
would that be?'

'Fine,' Mandy answered, feeling a bit
disappointed that Mrs Ponsonby didn't have
anything to tell her now. 'Thank you very much,'
she added, remembering her manners.

'Mandy! Before you go,' Mrs Ponsonby called
down the telephone. 'I expect they will want to
interview *me* for the film – in my capacity as
head of Fox Watch, of course. Perhaps I should
come along to the filming? Meet the producer
and give them some tips? I do know quite a lot
about foxes now, dear.'

Mandy was horrified. 'I'll tell Michelle,' she
said in a strangled voice. 'It's up to her. Bye.'

Mandy replaced the receiver and turned to

her parents. 'She wants to be in the film!' she spluttered. Adam and Emily Hope were leaning against the door, laughing at Mandy's shocked expression.

'Don't worry, Michelle will sort Mrs Ponsonby out,' Adam Hope reassured her.

'I hope so,' Mandy gulped. 'Now I'd better ring James and tell him the good news.'

But when James came to the phone he was puzzled. 'Mushrooms? I don't remember any mushrooms. Didn't he say anything else?' he quizzed Mandy.

'No. James you'll have to think hard,' Mandy said in a pleading voice. 'This is our big chance. You *have* to remember!' They said goodbye and Mandy hung up. Her face was set into a frown.

'Give him time, love,' her dad said cheerfully. 'He'll probably remember by the morning.'

It was still dark when the alarm rang next morning. Mandy reached out and switched it off. She was still so tired by all the excitement of the day before that she promptly fell asleep again.

'Mandy, wake up, love.' Emily Hope shook her gently and switched on the bedside light.

Mandy sat up with a start. 'Oh Mum,' she said, rubbing her eyes. 'I've been gathering mushrooms in my sleep all night!'

Emily Hope gave her a broad, warm smile. 'Did you dream where the foxes were too?' Her green eyes crinkled with amusement.

Mandy grinned. 'I wish it was that easy,' she declared, jumping out of bed and throwing on her clothes. 'I told James I'd be extra early today.'

'Now take it easy, it's not five yet,' her mum replied. 'I'm going to grab another hour's sleep. Mind how you go.'

'Okay, thanks Mum.' Mandy flew downstairs, grabbed an apple from the fruit bowl on the way out and put on her cycling helmet.

Dawn was breaking as Mandy saw James coming towards her down the drive. They had arranged to meet at the front gate, so as not to disturb the rest of the Hunter household.

'Have you remembered anything?' she asked excitedly.

'Nope.' James shook his head dolefully. 'Zilch.'

'Perhaps it will come to you when we get there,' Mandy said positively, as they set off on their bikes towards Piper's Wood.

When they reached the stile, they left their bikes and stood at the edge of the wood. 'Which way?' Mandy asked.

'I don't know.' James looked gloomy. 'I mean, when they're out, the whole wood is full of mushrooms, they grow everywhere.'

Mandy looked around anxiously. James was right. 'Well, could it be a special mushroom, something unusual?' she asked.

James looked down at his shoes and scratched his head. 'That's it!' he suddenly exclaimed. 'Follow me.' He began to stride away into the wood.

Mandy could hardly keep up as James trekked through the wood up towards the moor. Suddenly he put up his arm in a halt position. 'It will be around here somewhere,' he said confidently.

'How do you know?' Mandy asked, puzzled.

'Trust me!' James answered. 'And start looking.'

Where the moor met the wood there was an area of scrubland that was covered with bramble and long, tufty grass. They began their search for evidence of foxes.

Eventually, James spotted what he was looking for and sighed happily. He looked across at

Mandy, who nodded. She'd spotted it too. Halfway up the sloping bank was a small burrow. The grass all around it was trodden down. There were bits of bone scattered around, and scraps of plastic bags and paper here and there. Now they just needed proof it was occupied.

'Please let's see a fox,' Mandy breathed, crossing her fingers.

Downwind of the earth they waited. And waited, and waited.

Mandy was just beginning to lose hope, when she noticed something moving a little way off. Coming down from a rise with a rabbit in its mouth she saw a fox, its golden red fur shimmering as it ran. Its tail was the same length as its body, and was tipped with white. They watched it reach the earth and look around suspiciously. Its amber eyes seemed to stare right at them before it disappeared down the burrow.

'It's not very big, but it looks mature,' James whispered in Mandy's ear. 'I think it's a vixen.'

'Good,' she whispered back. 'Then it's more than likely there'll be cubs.'

As they watched, the vixen came out again and settled herself on the grass beside a

bramble bush near to the earth. Mandy held
her breath as a movement at the mouth of the
burrow caught her eye. Still wobbly on its legs,
a tiny cub came out of the earth. It stumbled
and then tripped over a bramble, falling on its
snout and rolling over on to its back, mewing
sorrowfully.

'Is it hurt?' Mandy mouthed to James. James
shook his head.

Legs waving in the air, the cub threw itself
on to its side and staggered to its feet. Just then
another cub came out and chased after the first
one. The two cubs ran towards each other and
collided, tumbled over each other and landed

in a heap. Both cubs still had their chocolate-coloured first coat, but patches of bright reddish-orange fur just showed through where they'd begun to moult. One cub had an edge of white fur around the tip of its ear; the other had grey flecks on its right forefoot. The cubs sat up, blinked in the light and mewed for their mother. The vixen got up and immediately herded the cubs back down the burrow. In silence, Mandy and James crept away. It was only when they were out of earshot that they spoke.

Mandy was elated. 'We've done it, James, we've found a breeding earth! Weren't the cubs gorgeous?'

'Really sweet,' James agreed, smiling. 'It was funny when they bumped into each other.'

'How old do you think they are?' Mandy asked, as they reached the stile.

'A few weeks?' James suggested thoughtfully. 'Their eyes were amber, not blue any more. Remember how Lucky's eyes changed colour?'

Mandy vaulted the stile and stood grinning at him. 'You're brilliant! Now, what I want to know is what made you suddenly remember where to look?'

'Actually,' James said, turning pink with pleasure, 'it was when you said about a special mushroom. That's when I remembered. I was out with the Welford Wildlifers bird-watching. Walter called me over and showed me a place where all these mushrooms that looked like white tennis balls were growing. They're called puffballs. I remembered that they were by the edge of the wood and there was a big dead tree nearby.'

'Michelle is going to be so pleased,' Mandy said, her face full of excitement.

James grinned. 'I wonder if Michelle will start filming tonight?' he said.

'I hope so,' Mandy replied, sitting astride her bike. 'I can't wait!'

Four

'So Michelle's going to start the actual filming tonight, then?' Emily Hope said, as she whizzed round the kitchen preparing lunch for the family.

'I hope so,' Mandy nodded. 'We've found a breeding earth so we don't need to spend any more time looking. She and Janie, she's the camera operator, said they will collect James and me at about half-past five.' She was sitting at the big kitchen table cleaning her binoculars with a soft cloth. 'That will give them plenty of time to set up the camera and get everything ready before the vixen starts hunting for the night.' Mandy put her binoculars down on the kitchen table. 'You should have seen the cubs, Mum, they're *gorgeous*.'

Adam Hope came through the door that connected the surgery to the cottage. 'Simon said he might pop up and have a look sometime,' he said. 'That is if you'll still be up there when he finishes work?'

'Oh, I should think we will,' Mandy said, nodding her head vigorously. 'Michelle is hoping to film all night. By the way, is it all right if I stay out with her?'

Mandy's mum and dad exchanged looks and then Mr Hope nodded. 'But you'll be falling asleep on your feet,' her dad teased.

'Not me, Dad,' Mandy retorted, jumping up to lay the table. 'Not with foxes to watch, no way!'

Emily Hope put a big bowl of homemade vegetable soup on the table. 'There's bread in the oven, Mandy, could you fetch it for me please?' she said, gently stirring the soup with a ladle. 'Mind you don't burn yourself, it's hot!'

Mandy got a clean cloth and carefully took a crusty loaf of granary bread out of the hot oven. 'I'm starving!' she announced.

'I'm not surprised,' Mrs Hope laughed. 'I bet you didn't eat any breakfast.'

'I had an apple,' Mandy replied, putting the loaf on the breadboard and taking the butter from the fridge. 'James is coming over after lunch and we'll do all my chores before Michelle arrives.'

'The energy of the girl!' Adam Hope said, feigning exhaustion. 'Where does she get it all?'

Mandy grinned and tucked into her soup. Finding the foxes had filled her with excitement and she couldn't wait to start on the filming. She ate her lunch and took her bowl over to the sink. 'Right, I've got time to do my jobs in the residential unit before Simon gets back from lunch,' she announced. 'Any new patients?'

'One pet rabbit in with a broken leg. The ginger cat with the poisoned foot has been discharged,' Adam Hope told her. 'Lucky for you we're not run off our feet at the moment.'

'And for Simon!' Emily Hope added.

In the residential unit Mandy put on an apron. Her job was to check that every animal had a clean bed or litter tray and a bowl of fresh water to drink. She worked her way around the room, checking on the rabbit with the bandaged leg. It lay still and half asleep, its leg straight out in front of it. 'You're quite comfortable, I can see,' Mandy told it, gently stroking its ears.

James was late but Mandy didn't mind. She loved her work at Animal Ark and being busy made the time pass quickly.

'Sorry, Mandy,' James said sheepishly when he eventually arrived. 'I fell asleep and Mum thought I needed a rest, so she didn't wake me up!'

'That's OK. You're here now. I've nearly finished,' Mandy said. She was just taking off her apron when there was a 'toot' from the drive.

'That's them!' James said eagerly.

Grabbing their coats, they raced through reception and down the steps to Michelle's Jeep. Emily Hope came out of the cottage carrying Mandy's binoculars, a big Thermos flask of hot chocolate and hefty slices of Gran's fruitcake for them all.

'That should keep you going for a while,' she said. 'Good luck.'

'Thanks, Mum.' Mandy planted a kiss on her mum's cheek and jumped in the back beside James.

Michelle rolled down her window. 'I'll get them back safe and sound in the morning, after what I hope will be a good night's filming,' she said cheerfully. 'If you need to contact us, Simon knows where we'll be. And tell him I'll shoot him if he makes a noise and disturbs our foxes!' She laughed and started the engine.

The woman in the passenger seat turned to face Mandy and James and introduced herself. 'Hi, I'm Janie, the camera operator for this project.' Janie had cropped bleached hair and friendly brown eyes.

'Janie's a brilliant camera operator,' Michelle put in.

'What sort of camera do you use?' asked James, who was always interested in the technical details.

'It's an E.N.G. type camera with a sun-gun and image intensification,' Janie told him.

'That sounds complicated,' James said. 'What does E.N.G. stand for?'

'Electronic News Gathering, and it's not at all complicated. It's the same sort they use to make the outside broadcast TV news,' Janie went on eagerly. 'Hand-held, and with no extra wires or lights. It makes me a one-man band. It's brilliant.'

Michelle slowed down and pulled the Jeep off the road beside Piper's Wood.

'How far is it from here, Mandy?' she asked, looking at her watch.

'About five minutes,' Mandy said, leaning forward and peering through the windscreen. 'You see where the moor begins to rise from the forest, by that dead tree sticking up higher than the rest?'

'Uh huh.' Michelle nodded.

'It's just there,' James finished.

Mandy and James helped carry the big metal box that contained the camera equipment up to the wood.

When the fox's earth eventually came in sight, Michelle was delighted. 'This is perfect, you two,' she enthused. 'Well done! We can see all we need from here. And once they get used to us and realise we're not dangerous, the foxes won't take too much notice.' Michelle watched the earth through her binoculars for a few moments.

Janie soon set up her equipment and they settled down to wait.

It wasn't long before the vixen emerged from the entrance to the earth. She went to the same patch of grass that Mandy and James had seen her choose earlier that day and lay up in the last of the sunshine. Moments later, the first cub toddled out of the entrance, closely followed by the second.

Mandy had to resist the urge to gasp as a third, and then a fourth cub followed. It was even better than they had originally thought. Four cubs! She watched in delight as the cubs scampered around their mother and rolled about in the grass.

After a while, the light began to fade and Janie switched on the sun-gun. A filtered light washed over the earth like a ray of sunshine. The vixen immediately stood up and herded her cubs to the entrance of the earth.

Through their binoculars they could see her looking straight at them, fully aware of their presence. Behind her in the darkness of the entrance, four pairs of amber eyes stared unblinkingly at them and four pairs of ears stood straight up and alert. Except for the occasional twitch of a whisker and the trembling of a shiny nose, the four fox cubs stood motionless, watching and waiting for a cue from their mother.

Suddenly she gave a cough and, as if by magic, the cubs vanished down the earth.

Everyone stayed as still as possible. Mandy's heart was thumping. The low whirr of the camera sounded like an aeroplane engine. Surely the vixen must hear it. For several seconds, though it seemed like hours, the vixen watched them. Then she turned and went into the earth. Mandy tried hard to suppress a sigh of relief.

'I think she's accepted us,' Michelle whispered.

'How old are the cubs, Michelle?' Mandy asked quietly.

'I would say these cubs are about five weeks old,' Michelle replied. 'They're beginning to look foxy but their noses haven't turned black yet.'

They continued to watch the earth in silence and after a while the vixen and her cubs emerged above ground again. Mandy couldn't believe her eyes. She looked from Michelle to James. Both looked equally surprised. Now there were not four cubs, but six!

Racing around, they slammed into each other and rolled in the grass. Chasing through the brambles, they danced around the vixen, pulling at her mouth to see if she had any food, until she pushed them away with her snout.

'That means they're hungry,' Michelle said quietly. 'She'll go hunting soon.'

'Look,' breathed James. 'Near the earth, another fox!'

Sure enough, another fox was joining in the

play. It had specks of very dark brown fur round its eyes. Tails wagging and ears drawn flat, the cubs were clambering all over their mother and the new fox, squealing and making clicking noises. All her life Mandy had loved animals, almost more than anything else. But she had never seen such a beautiful sight as this fox family. Both the adult foxes had bright eyes and looked strong and healthy. The cubs were brimming with life, and even though they kept knocking each other over in their boisterous play, they were obviously enjoying it. Mandy and James looked at Michelle. 'Could that be the dog fox?' Mandy asked.

'No. Too small.' Michelle shook her head slowly. 'More likely it's the vixen's daughter from an earlier litter. Last year or even the year before.'

'So she's their big sister?' James suggested.

'Exactly. She's called a "helper",' Michelle told them. 'Foxes are very social creatures. The more foxes there are in a family group to hunt for food, the better the cubs' chances of survival.'

Now the two vixens were herding the cubs to the earth and shooing them inside. Janie switched off the camera and began to change the film.

'How do you think it's looking, Janie?' Mandy asked.

'Fantastic!' Janie grinned. 'We should get some great footage over the next few days.' She had just reset the camera when both vixens appeared at the entrance to the earth. Janie filmed them as they set off to hunt.

The two vixens spent most of the night hunting, bringing back food for the hungry cubs. Michelle had asked Mandy and James to make notes on how many times each vixen hunted and what sort of things they brought back.

By midnight Mandy was beginning to feel really cold from standing still. She zipped up her fleece and carefully moved her aching limbs, edging over to where James was leaning against a tree. 'James!' She nudged him gently.

'Huh!' James started awake and dropped his notebook. 'Phew, Mandy, I was almost asleep,' he confessed.

'I know,' Mandy agreed. 'I'm struggling to keep my eyes open. It's hard to stay awake when it's so quiet.' Mandy was tracking the mother while James noted the helper's movements.

'It's easier when the vixens come back, there's something to do then,' James said. 'Especially for you.'

Just before dawn, Michelle suggested they grab a quick break. 'Have you noticed,' she asked, as they drank the welcome hot chocolate and ate the delicious cake, 'how much more experienced the mother is at hunting?'

'I make it about twelve expeditions for the mother,' Mandy reckoned.

'And about six for the smaller vixen,' James said.

'And the smaller one doesn't bring back so much food, does she?' Mandy added, biting into a chunk of cake.

'She's been bringing back worms and beetles.' James said, 'but the mother seems to be bringing back larger things, like rats.'

'That's right. The younger vixen is still learning from her mum,' Michelle told them as she poured the last of the hot chocolate.

Suddenly, they were all startled by a loud noise. *BOOOM!* The noise rang out from far away on the moors.

'Oh blast!' Michelle smacked her fist into her hand. 'That's someone shooting on the moor!' She sounded really annoyed. 'That will upset our foxes.'

'Not guilty!' they heard a soft voice say behind them.

'It's Simon,' Mandy said, spinning round. 'Where've you been? We thought you'd come up last night.'

'I was too tired, with all that extra work.' He grinned at Mandy's worried expression. 'Only joking. I though I'd get up early this morning before work. How's it going?'

'It was going fine until just now. Did you hear that shot?' Michelle said crossly.

They waited anxiously for any more shots but none came. The young vixen came back with a mouse in her mouth.

'Good!' Michelle breathed softly. 'They obviously weren't bothered by the noise. It was probably just a farmer shooting on his own land.'

'Some poor animal, just getting on with life, but the *farmer* doesn't happen to want it there,' Mandy said angrily.

'So long as the hunters stay on their own land, Mandy,' Simon said, 'like it or not, there's nothing we can do.'

While the cubs squabbled over the mouse, the young vixen went off again.

'They have to work really hard to get enough food for the cubs, don't they?' James said. 'Look! There's the mother!' He pointed at the moor. High on a rise in the last of the moonlight the vixen stood silhouetted against an indigo sky.

Mandy stared at the sight until the vixen turned, and then she had to stifle her laughter. The vixen's head was almost obscured by a large fluffy object. She looked as if she could hardly see over the top of it. 'What on earth has she got this time?' Mandy giggled to James. 'It's enormous.'

James was also trying not to laugh. 'It looks like a pigeon or something.'

'Be quiet, you two!' Michelle pretended to be serious, but she and Janie were smothering their laughter too. 'Let's try and control ourselves, we don't want to frighten her away. It's bigger than a pigeon, anyway,' she added, setting Mandy and James off again.

The vixen began to trot down the moor towards them. She reached the edge of the wood and was melting in and out of the shadows when *BOOOM!* – the gunshot rang out again. But this time the noise was much louder and closer than before.

Mandy felt the blood pounding in her head as she frantically tried to spot the vixen through her binoculars. Then she saw the fox, struggling to move, her back leg spotted with blood. 'She's been hit!' she cried out.

Five

Mandy was horrified. 'She's been shot. Look! Look at her back legs.'

Using only her forelegs, the vixen was dragging herself back to the earth. Dropping her catch, she was struggling to reach her cubs. As she got closer, Mandy could see the pain in the animal's eyes. The vixen stopped and looked around her. She was panting hard, trying desperately to gather strength. With a huge effort, she started forward again, taking three wobbly paces before dropping to the ground where she lay motionless. Mandy wanted to scream but no words would come out.

'Come on!' Simon said. 'We've got to get her to Animal Ark.'

Mandy suddenly sprang into action. She ran towards the vixen, followed by Simon, James and Michelle. She dropped to her knees beside the wounded animal. Mandy felt for a pulse in her neck. She was still alive! But blood was beginning to ooze from shotgun pellets that were embedded in her back and legs and she was panting hard.

'Hold her head, Mandy,' Simon said, whipping off his jacket. 'James, help me put this under her so I can keep her flat.'

Michelle moved a few paces away, pulled off her coat and waved it above her head. 'HOLD YOUR FIRE!' she yelled loudly, looking around frantically for the gunman. 'THERE ARE PEOPLE HERE!'

Tears ran down Mandy's cheeks and dripped on to the vixen's glossy red fur. 'She looks so small,' she said, her voice catching. 'She seemed so big and majestic on the moor.'

Just then heard voices coming towards them. Michelle called out a warning again.

'Oh no,' James groaned. 'Look who it is.'

Sam Western and Dennis Saville were approaching, shotguns hanging in the crook of their arms, a German shepherd dog trotting behind them.

'Quick, Simon, let's go,' Mandy urged. Simon had the vixen in his arms now. 'Don't let them see her.' Mandy ran alongside him.

'You stay here,' Simon said, turning to Mandy. 'Keep them away from the cubs.'

Mandy hesitated, torn between going with the vixen and staying to protect the cubs.

'I can manage,' Simon said firmly. 'I parked my car at the end of the track, it's not far.' Holding the fox in a gentle embrace, he strode away.

When Mandy turned and saw the men laughing and grinning, she felt her anger boil over. Screaming like a banshee, she ran at full speed up the moor towards the startled men. James glanced back at a cub peeping out of the earth, terrified. Then he was off, racing after Mandy.

'You . . . shot . . . a fox,' Mandy said, her breath coming in gasps. She managed to stop herself pummelling her fists on Sam Western's chest by jamming them into her pockets. 'You're not . . .' she took a deep breath, '. . . allowed to.'

'It's out of season,' James added, joining her. 'And this is common ground.'

Sam Western snorted. 'We've been shooting hares on my land and there's no season for that. I can't help it if a fox got in the way.'

'Do you realise you could have caused a very nasty accident, firing at random like that?' Michelle said, reaching them, her face thunderous.

'I wasn't firing at random. I aimed at the fox and I hit it,' Dennis Saville said proudly, stepping forward. 'Foxes are vermin,' he sneered. 'And anyway, that fox had a chicken in its mouth. Stolen from Blackheath Farm, I'll wager.'

'If that fox got into the chicken house it

probably killed half of Masters's hens tonight,' Sam Western agreed. 'Everyone knows foxes kill for the fun of it.'

'That's not fair!' Mandy blurted out. It was typical of Sam Western to say something like that. Wild animals killed because it was their instinct. It wasn't fair to blame foxes for being wild.

Sam Western eyed them suspiciously. 'Anyway, what are you doing out in the woods?' he demanded.

Mandy glanced at James. She knew he was thinking the same thing. If these two men found out about the cubs they would certainly kill them.

'We're bird-watching,' James announced quickly.

'A project for school,' Mandy added. 'Michelle's helping us.'

'Humph,' Sam Western snorted. 'Well, we're going to see Mr Masters now. And we'll see just what damage that fox *has* done. He'll be angry, *very* angry. You mark my words, we'll have a hunt in Welford before you can blink an eye.'

'And not before time,' Dennis Saville spat out over his shoulder as they left.

'What do we do now?' Mandy asked Michelle.

'We wait. And cross our fingers that the "helper" comes back. Hopefully, she'll take over the care of the cubs,' Michelle told them.

'Suppose she's too frightened to come back?' Mandy asked, worried that all the commotion might have scared her off.

'She won't be. Foxes live on the edge of fear all the time,' Michelle sighed. 'Being a wild animal is a tough business.'

They waited for most of the morning growing increasingly worried, but the little vixen didn't return.

'The cubs need food,' Mandy said. 'We could bring some with us tonight.' She looked anxiously at Michelle.

'It's more than that, Mandy.' Michelle pursed her lips. 'Food is important, of course, but the cubs will need the vixen to teach them how to fend for themselves.'

'What about the chicken the mother had in her mouth?' James said, suddenly 'It must still be there. We could find it and give it to the cubs.'

'Good idea, James,' Michelle agreed. 'You two go and find it while we finish packing up.'

Mandy and James backtracked through the wood and up to the moor. The picture of the injured fox was so strong in Mandy's mind that she couldn't remember where they had seen the vixen drop her catch. They searched in silence.

James found the chicken. They stared down at its soft white feathers.

'I know Mr Masters has to protect his chickens,' Mandy said sadly, 'but to her it *is* food, and she's such a good mother.' Mandy bent down and carefully picked up the chicken. 'She must have been really pleased to find this for her cubs.'

'Well, at least now we can make sure they get it,' James said. 'No wonder she had a job carrying it, it's enormous.'

They walked back to the earth. Not long ago it had been full of life and activity. Now it seemed sombre and still.

'Let's put the chicken right down in the entrance so the cubs don't have to come out for it,' James suggested.

Mandy nodded. 'I couldn't bear the thought of Sam Western and Dennis Saville coming back and finding the cubs,' she said with a grimace.

As they drove back to Animal Ark, Mandy was worried. What if the helper vixen had raided the chicken farm too? Suppose Sam Western saw her and shot her as well? She glanced at the others. Michelle stared straight ahead in silence. Janie wore an anxious frown. Beside her, James's face was pale and worried. Mandy wondered what was happening at the surgery. What if the mother was so badly hurt that she couldn't be put back with her cubs for *days*? Mandy couldn't bear to think what might happen to the cubs then.

Almost before Michelle had stopped the Jeep, Mandy was out and running up the steps of Animal Ark. 'Please let her not be too badly hurt,' she begged silently. 'Please let her be all right.'

Six

'Mum! Dad! How's the . . . ?' The door to the consulting room was open but Mandy faltered in the doorway at the sombre looks on her parents' faces.

'Mandy,' Emily Hope said, her face full of dismay. She put her hands on Mandy's shoulders. 'You're going to have to be brave, Mandy.'

'Is she badly hurt? I'll look after her,' Mandy hurried on. 'I know the rules about keeping wild animals, but Dennis Saville shot her on purpose.'

Mandy looked pleadingly at her father. 'Please, Dad, let me look after her. Just this once,' she begged.

Adam Hope looked stricken. 'Mandy, you know I would do anything I could to save an animal,' he said gently. 'But this time there wasn't anything we could do. She went into shock and died. I'm so sorry.'

'Dead! No, she can't be. She's got six cubs to look after!' Mandy could hardly take the news in. Slowly she realised that the proud little vixen, who had trusted them enough to let them film her cubs would never return to her earth. Mandy's dad came over and took her in his arms. Gratefully she fell against him and wept sad, bitter tears.

Eventually, Mandy's tears dried up. Guiltily, she realised that, up until now, she hadn't spared a thought for the others. She looked up and saw that Michelle and Janie were dabbing at their eyes and James was studying the floor.

'We did all we could, Mandy,' Michelle said softly.

'They'll *have* to rely on the helper now, won't they?' Mandy asked, her voice cracking.

Michelle nodded. 'I wanted to ask you about that,' she said to the Hopes. 'The young vixen is quite small. And we know that between the two foxes they hunted more than twenty times last night. I'm worried that the helper won't be able to manage on her own. What's your opinion?'

'I should think she'd wear herself out after the first week,' Emily Hope said honestly.

'I'll tell you what,' Adam Hope said, 'when are you going up to Piper's Wood again? I could come with you and see what condition she's in if you like.'

'That would be great. I'd like to go back tonight,' Michelle suggested. 'Do you feel up to it, Mandy?'

'Yes, I'm all right now,' Mandy said, nodding her head. 'It was just such a shock, I suppose I wasn't expecting it somehow.' She felt the tears begin to well up again and blinked several times.

'Then I suggest we meet you there,' Adam Hope suggested to Michelle. 'Why don't you all get a rest and then I'll bring Mandy and James up about sixish?'

'That suits me.' Michelle grimaced. 'Let's hope we have a happier outcome tonight.'

'I'd better go home and take Blackie out,' James said with a watery grin. 'Or he'll forget who I am.'

'I'll drop you off, James,' Adam Hope said. 'I've got to call in at High Cross Farm.'

'There's nothing wrong with Lydia's goats, is there, Dad?' Mandy said, alarmed.

'No, not really. It's just Houdini's got a grass seed in his eye and Lydia can't shift it.' Adam Hope hung up his white coat and collected his bag. 'You know what Houdini's like if he doesn't want to do something!'

Mandy and James grinned at each other. 'That goat is the stubbornest goat in the whole world,' said Mandy.

'Are you OK?' Emily Hope asked, as the Land-rover pulled out of the drive. She put an arm round Mandy's shoulders.

'Mum, do you think you ever get used to it?' Mandy asked softly. 'When an animal dies, I mean?'

'To tell you the truth, Mandy, no, I don't think you do.' Emily Hope ran her hands through her red hair and twisted it into a knot. 'Each one you lose is an individual.'

'But what about wild animals?' Mandy quizzed her. 'They're not pets and you hardly know them at all. Do you think it's silly to get upset?'

'Oh love, of course it's not,' Emily Hope reassured her. 'Dad and I were both terribly upset that we couldn't save the vixen. Wild animals are so brave and they have such dignity.

It's right to be sad. But then you have to let it go, and get on with helping the others, like the cubs.' She put the kettle on to make some tea. 'You must do the best you can for them, now.' She turned round and put her hands on her hips. 'Within reason, I mean.' She smiled gently but firmly. Mandy knew her mum meant that wild animals should never be reared as pets, as it would always put them at a disadvantage when they were returned to the wild.

'I know, Mum,' Mandy said. 'I feel better now.'

'And don't even think about toughening up where animals are concerned, Mandy Hope,' her mum said. 'After all, where would the animal population of Welford be without you?'

That evening when Mandy and James arrived at Piper's Wood with Adam Hope, they were surprised to see that Janie hadn't bothered to set up her camera.

'I've got a funny feeling about this earth. It's cold and quiet this evening,' Michelle explained. 'We've been here a while and there's been no activity whatsoever.'

'Do you think it's empty?' Mandy asked. 'That the cubs have strayed?'

'Yes, and I'm hoping that the helper vixen

has moved them.' Michelle replied. 'But we have to be prepared for the possibility that she didn't come back and they've wandered off looking for their mum.'

'I think I should take a look in the earth,' Adam Hope suggested. 'I can't stay too long, though, I've got to be back for evening surgery.'

Mandy clenched her fists and waited as her dad walked up to the earth. When he reached it, he crouched down and peered into the darkness. After a minute or so he stood up and beckoned the others.

'They've gone, I'm afraid,' he said dismally. 'I'm sure of it. The earth is silent and I'd expect to hear them mewing for their mother by now.'

'OK,' Michelle said. 'The cubs are too small to have gone very far. How long could they go without food, Adam?'

'Three or four days,' he told her.

'Look,' Mandy said, 'they've eaten the chicken.'

'Or something has,' James observed. On the patch of grass where the vixen had sat in the sunshine, only the carcase and a few feathers remained.

'So, what we should do is have a search around to see if we can find any sign of them,'

Michelle decided. 'We'll meet back here in half an hour.'

'OK. I'll look on the moors,' Adam Hope said, 'Michelle, if you and Janie check the woods, then Mandy and James can search the immediate vicinity.' Looking at Mandy he added, 'And don't forget how inquisitive foxes are. Check out even the most impossible-looking places.'

They started their search. Mandy got down on the ground and looked under the bramble bushes, James peered in holes in trees. Adam Hope searched on the moors and Michelle and Janie scoured the woods. Mandy grew more and more worried as the appointed time to meet up grew closer. As they made their way back to the earth, still looking desperately for the cubs, Mandy's head was buzzing with anxious thoughts.

'James, we *must* find them,' she burst out. 'They'll never survive on their own!'

'I don't know what else we can do,' James said miserably. 'Perhaps the others will have some news,' he added, trying to sound hopeful.

But Mandy felt that the chances of them finding the cubs were lessening.

'Nothing,' Michelle and Janie said when they arrived back.

'I'm afraid I didn't find anything either.' Adam Hope shrugged as he told them his news.

'Well, I think this means the young vixen must have come back and moved them.' Michelle sounded confident. 'She may have carried them one by one in her mouth to another earth.'

'So what are you planning to do now?' Adam Hope asked.

'Nothing, I'm afraid,' Michelle said glumly. 'We have to start again, I suppose, and find some more foxes. But what you could do, Mandy and James, is come up here some time tomorrow and see if there's any sign that the foxes have been back. I doubt they will have, but you never know.'

Mandy nodded vigorously. 'We'll do anything if it helps the cubs,' she told Michelle.

'Don't be too optimistic, Mandy,' Michelle said, seriously. 'Sometimes we never find out what happens to the animals we're watching.'

'Why don't we pop in at Bleakfell Hall on the way home?' Adam Hope suggested. 'You could ask Fox Watch to keep a special eye out for the cubs.'

'Thanks, Dad,' Mandy sighed. 'I've got to know what's happened to them.'

Mrs Ponsonby opened the door of Bleakfell Hall. 'Come in, do come in,' she said, her arms full of Pandora whilst Toby, dancing round her feet, did his best to trip her over.

'We can't stop, I'm afraid. I'm already late for surgery,' Mr Hope said in a purposeful voice. 'But we wondered if the Fox Watch volunteers could look out for a family of orphaned cubs? Six in all.'

'How utterly dreadful!' Mrs Ponsonby said, after Mandy had blurted out the full story. 'This is outrageous. Sam Western behaves as if all the countryside around here belongs to him.' Mrs Ponsonby popped Pandora on the floor and wrung her hands together. 'I'll phone everyone immediately. And, Mandy dear, I hope this doesn't mean the end of the film. I'm looking forward to helping with that.'

'Er, um . . .' Mandy was speechless.

'We'll let you know,' Adam Hope said, ushering Mandy and James back towards the Land-rover.

'That's all we need!' James muttered as they drove off.

* * *

Mandy and James had agreed to meet after breakfast the next day. Mandy had forced herself to eat a banana but she just wasn't hungry. Nothing could cheer her up. Although she had promised Michelle they would go and look at the earth, in her heart Mandy knew it would still be empty.

Now they were standing beside the deserted earth, Mandy scuffing the grass with the toe of her shoe. 'See that thin stick, over the entrance?' James asked.

Mandy looked. 'Yes, what about it? It's just a stick, isn't it?' she said irritably.

'Yes,' James said patiently, 'but I put it there last night. So we would know for sure if anything had visited the earth. It looks as if nothing has been near this place since we left,' he added with conviction.

· 'Oh, well done, James.' Mandy smiled briefly. She didn't tell him she didn't need a stick to know the earth was empty. She felt it, somehow.

'What should we do now?' James asked carefully.

'There's nothing much *to* do,' Mandy answered glumly.

James pushed his glasses up and down, then

shoved his hands deep in his pockets. 'We ought to start looking for another earth. We could go and ask Walter Pickard,' James suggested.

'Aah!' Mandy sucked in her breath. 'James, what shall we tell him? We promised to keep the earth a secret.'

'But it wasn't our fault,' James reminded her. 'We didn't lead Sam Western and Dennis Saville to the foxes. They were out shooting anyway.'

'James, let's leave Mr Pickard for the time being,' Mandy said. 'Why don't we go and see Mr Masters at Blackheath Farm and find out how many chickens he lost? The young vixen might have raided his farm too.' Mandy's mood had begun to lift now that she had something constructive to do. 'And we could go and see Libby.' Libby Masters was a few years younger than Mandy and James but they had become friends when her pet hen, Ronda, hatched out chicks.

'Race you up to the moor.' James shouted, as he scrambled on to his bike.

They were neck and neck when they reached the farm track that led to the Masters's farm, but James touched the gate first. 'I win!' he said jubilantly. 'Phew, it's windy up here.'

Mandy looked up. Puffs of white cloud sped across the sky.

The Masters's farm was high on the moor and they could see Welford village neatly laid out below them. Avoiding the potholes, Mandy and James rode down the farm track and into the farmyard. Mr Masters was at the door of the farmhouse, scraping mud off his wellington boots.

'Hello, Mandy, James. How are you both? Have you come to see Libby?' he asked. 'Her mum's taken her and Ryan into Walton.' Ryan was Libby's three-year-old brother.

'Actually, it was more you we wanted to speak to, Mr Masters,' Mandy said cautiously. 'About Sam Western.'

'And foxes,' James added nervously.

'Ah! Well you'd better come into the house,' Mr Masters said grimly.

Mr Masters took off his boots and went into the kitchen in his socks. Mandy and James wiped their feet on the mat and followed.

'Put the kettle on, Mandy, would you?' Mr Masters said. 'I'll just fetch my slippers. I'll have coffee but there's milk or juice in the fridge. Help yourselves.'

Mandy couldn't tell from Mr Masters's face what his reaction to them bringing up the subject of foxes was. He was just his usual, calm self.

It seemed an age to Mandy until they were sitting round the table with their drinks and a tin of shortbread. Eventually, Mr Masters sat down, took a breath and began talking. 'Sam Western and Dennis Saville did come to see me the other night,' he began, 'and they reckon most of the folk around here are itching to start a foxhunt.' Mandy tried to swallow the shortbread she was chewing but it wouldn't go down. Mr Masters continued. 'Western seems

to think that as I'm the only chicken farmer around here my agreement would swing it for him.'

'Oh, Mr Masters, won't you change your mind?' Mandy pleaded miserably. 'The vixen that Dennis Saville shot last night had six cubs, and she worked so hard to feed them. I know she stole a chicken but they had to eat.'

'Change my mind about what, Mandy?' Mr Masters said, looking bewildered.

'About agreeing to a foxhunt,' Mandy said, puzzled.

'I didn't agree, Mandy!' Mr Masters laughed. 'In fact, I sent him off with a flea in his ear.'

'You did?' James said, surprised. 'You don't mind foxes?'

'I like foxes, James.' Mr Masters bit on a piece of shortbread. 'A lot of chicken farmers do.'

'But how many chickens did she get from the hen-house?' Mandy rushed on. She was still puzzled by Mr Masters's attitude, but wanted to hear the whole story.

'None!' he replied mysteriously, grinning at their blank expressions. 'Let me tell you what happened.' He leaned back and took a few sips of tea. 'I was just shutting the hen-house yesterday evening when I got distracted by a hot-air balloon going over. Ryan, it seems, managed to open the door when I wasn't looking. Don't ask me how!' He threw up his hands. 'And *all* the hens got out. It was chaos.' He grinned at the memory. 'Anyway, eventually, I thought we'd caught them all, but obviously we must have missed one. *That's* the one the fox got.'

'So she didn't get into the hen-house at all?' Mandy smiled with relief.

'Nope,' said Mr Masters, smiling.

'We were worried that you might have lost loads of chickens.' James said.

'It does happen, James,' Mr Masters told them. 'If a fox gets into a hen-house it thinks, 'Wow, lots of easy food.' Its instinct is to kill more than it needs so it can bury some.'

'Isn't that called *caching*?' James asked. 'I've read about that.'

'That's right, James,' Mr Masters went on. 'It means that on a night when food is short, the fox can dig up the cached food.'

'But doesn't it go all mouldy?' Mandy screwed up her nose.

'Foxes aren't fussy about maggots, Mandy,' Mr Masters laughed. 'It's all food as far as they're concerned.'

'Yuck!' Mandy exclaimed.

'My problem is not with foxes at all. I pride myself on keeping my hen-house properly secure so that foxes *can't* get in.' Mr Masters immediately touched the wooden table and whistled. Mandy and James smiled at the old superstition. 'Foxes can break through chicken wire, so I've put weld-mesh wire on all my runs now, and at all my windows in the hen-houses. It's much stronger,' Mr Masters finished proudly.

'So that's why you're not bothered by foxes,' Mandy said.

Mr Masters nodded, then his face clouded over. 'My problem is rats. There seem to be so many at the moment and they *can* get in. They steal the eggs *and* kill the chicks. To tell the truth, I'd be happy if we had some foxes about the farm, to keep the numbers down. Most chicken farmers would.' He smiled. 'Very useful creatures, foxes.'

Mandy and James grinned in appreciation. It was all beginning to make sense.

'That's the other thing, Mr Masters.' Mandy suddenly remembered her worries. 'The six cubs have disappeared from the earth.'

Mr Masters ran a hand through his hair. 'If

the vixen didn't return they would probably have gone looking for her,' he said.

'But, well, there was another, younger vixen, a "helper", and we're hoping she's taken over the cubs. But, well, we just don't know where any of them are now.' Mandy's voice was full of anxiety as she thought of the cubs. 'If you see any foxes, will you let us know?'

'Of course I will,' Mr Masters said, getting up as the phone out in the hall began to ring. 'I'll keep my eyes peeled. But if they're not big enough to hunt for themselves,' he said, 'I wouldn't hold out too much hope for them, I'm afraid,' he finished quietly.

Seven

That night, Mandy lay in bed going over and over all the different things that might have happened. She couldn't get what Mr Masters had said out of her mind. Even as she drifted off to sleep, she could hear his words, 'If they're not big enough to hunt for themselves, I wouldn't hold out too much hope for them.'

What seemed like only minutes later, Mandy was jolted awake by the phone ringing. She tumbled out of bed and flew down the stairs. She glanced at the clock in the hall. It was seven o'clock already!

'Welford 703267, Animal Ark,' she answered politely.

'Mandy? Is that you, Mandy?' a quiet voice said on the other end. 'It's Libby Masters here.'

'Hi, Libby,' Mandy replied. 'Yes, it's me. Is something wrong with the chickens?'

'No!' Libby laughed. 'Nothing like that. It's just that Dad said that you would want to know straightaway, you know, about the foxes.'

Mandy's heart did a little nervous flip. 'Oh, Libby,' she swallowed hard. 'They haven't caused trouble, have they?'

'No, Mandy, it's *nice* news. I was woken up really early this morning by a strange noise, and when I looked out of my bedroom window there was a little fox, hunting about near the barn,' Libby told her happily. 'So I watched where it went and then when I took Ryan out for our daily farm walk before breakfast, I went to have a look.'

'Libby,' Mandy said in a trembling voice. 'Tell me, please, what did you find?'

'Some baby foxes!' Libby said excitedly.

Mandy was over the moon. 'Libby, you're a star!' she shouted. 'That's wonderful news. I'm on my way. Thanks.' Mandy hung up the receiver.

'What's wonderful news?' Adam Hope said, coming down the stairs in his dressing-gown.

'Libby's found the fox cubs, Dad!' Mandy did a little dance around him. 'Isn't that great?'

'Hold on a minute. How do you know they're *your* cubs?' her dad queried as he began making the tea. 'They could belong to another vixen.'

Mandy's doubt lasted for only a fraction of a second. 'They *are* my cubs,' she said emphatically. 'I just know it.'

'Far be it from me to question you.' Adam Hope gave her a lopsided grin. 'You seem to have a sixth sense where animals are concerned.'

'I'm going up there right away,' Mandy gabbled. 'I've just got to get dressed and phone Michelle and James . . . will you tell Mum the good news?'

When Mandy arrived at Blackheath Farm, Michelle and James were already in the farmyard, talking to Libby. 'I'm just telling Libby how grateful we are that she found the cubs for us,' Michelle told her, as she clambered off her bike and caught her breath.

Libby beamed. She was a friendly girl with pink cheeks and dark brown curly hair. 'I'll show you where the cubs are,' she offered.

Libby led them past the hen houses, round

the barn and across a field, to a spinney on the edge of the farmland. There she pointed past the trees to a small, derelict shed that had collapsed against a drystone wall. 'They're somewhere around there,' she announced.

'Let's wait quietly for them to come out,' Michelle said.

They settled under an oak tree on the edge of the spinney to wait. Mandy didn't take her eyes off the shed. James was just showing Libby his binoculars when the vixen came back, with two rats in her mouth.

Mandy felt a rush of excitement. 'It *is* the young vixen,' she breathed. 'You can't mistake her. Look at the dark fur round her eyes.'

The vixen slid through a gap and disappeared under the shed. Seconds later she emerged without the food and, finding a comfortable spot, curled up in the early morning sunshine.

'Look,' James whispered. 'Here come the cubs.' One by one the cubs emerged, their tummies fat and full of food.

'She's doing a good job, then,' Michelle observed.

Mandy was busy counting the cubs. She checked again. 'There's only five! One's missing,' she said, trying to keep the alarm out of her voice. 'You know, the one with the white ear tip.'

'Perhaps it's still down in the earth,' James suggested.

They waited and watched but the missing cub didn't surface.

'Mandy's right, I think,' Michelle said. 'It must be missing. There's no reason for one to stay behind in the earth. This *does* happen, you know. It's rare for *all* the cubs in a litter to survive.'

For a few moments they all stood silently watching the family of foxes. The vixen was trying to round up all the cubs but they wanted to play. As fast as she got one to the entrance of the earth the others chased off in the opposite direction. Eventually, she shepherded them all back under the shed. Then she gave a last look around and followed them down.

'She'll probably sleep all day now,' Michelle said softly. 'Listen, I've got to go to work but I suggest we come back and film for a couple of hours tonight. Is that all right with you two? I could pick you up at five.'

'We'll be ready,' Mandy and James promised.

'Now they've all gone into the earth, James and I could have a look for the lost cub,' Mandy offered.

Michelle looked doubtful. 'Well, OK, but

don't spend too long, Mandy. If the cub was anywhere near either this earth or the old one, the vixen would have found it.' She shrugged. 'But by all means have a look – you've nothing to lose.'

Mandy and James hunted through the spinney, then they walked all around the farmland but they didn't find the missing cub. Mandy knew she had to accept that the cub might have died. They cycled home, Mandy to help Simon with the lunch-time chores and James to take Blackie for a long-awaited walk.

'It's a shame,' Michelle said, when she came to pick them up later. 'But we've got five cubs and a vixen, which is a lot more than we had yesterday.' She grinned. 'I'd say this is turning into a success story.'

Once they had reached the farm and Janie was setting up the equipment, Michelle suggested that Mandy, James and Libby noted all the play items around the earth while they waited for the vixen to emerge.

'There's my yellow tennis ball!' Libby exclaimed softly, peering through Mandy's binoculars. 'I wondered where that had gone.'

'And that looks like a gardening glove,' James

noticed. 'The vixen *must* have been out today, they weren't there this morning.'

'You're right, James,' Michelle agreed.

'Look, here she comes,' Mandy said, tugging Michelle's sleeve.

Slowly the vixen came out from under the shed. She stretched and then trotted off on the first hunt of the night. Only minutes later, she returned with two rats in her mouth.

'She's so fast!' Mandy said, full of admiration for the little vixen.

'That will please your dad,' James whispered to Libby.

When the vixen took the food down to the cubs, she was welcomed by excited squeaking. But the next time she popped out from under the shed, the cubs tried to follow her. This became a routine – the fox cubs would eat inside the earth and follow the vixen out. No matter how much she shooed them down to safety, each time she set off they popped out again. It was perfect for the fox-watchers.

Libby put her hand over her mouth to stifle a giggle as three of the cubs had a tug of war with the gardening glove. The two other cubs barged into the threesome and they all tumbled over each other. A bit later, one found an old shoe and tried to drag it away before the others saw it.

'Too late,' Mandy said softly, as the other four charged after it, sinking their sharp, pointed teeth into the soft canvas. She was absolutely entranced. Within minutes the play became serious as each cub instinctively fought to possess the shoe. Soon, the spitting and snarling cubs had ripped it apart.

'They're very fierce for such little things, aren't they?' James said.

'It's only play-fighting,' Michelle said. 'But it's how they will learn to claim their portion of a vole or a rabbit.'

Mandy spotted the vixen coming through the trees. 'I wonder what she's got this time?'

Running to greet her, the cubs were wagging their tails and whimpering. The vixen dropped two items and the cubs pounced.

'That looks like a vole,' James said.

'But what's the other thing?' Michelle murmured.

As they watched, one of the cubs tossed the object into the air and the others pounced on it.

'Let me see,' said Libby. James let her look through the binoculars. 'Oh no,' she said in a worried voice.

'What's the matter?' Mandy asked.

Everyone looked at Libby. 'I know what that is,' she said, with a tremor in her voice. 'That's Ryan's favourite teddy bear. He lost it this morning.' Everyone looked back at the cubs. 'He won't go to sleep without it!'

'I'm afraid he'll have to,' Mandy said. 'Just look at it as Ryan's contribution to the cubs' education!' Everyone burst out laughing.

Mandy looked back at the vixen with her adopted cubs. This really was a perfect way to spend an evening.

'Thanks for the lift,' Mandy said, as Michelle dropped her home. She yawned as she walked up the drive. This was the third night she'd been up late watching the foxes at Blackheath Farm.

'And *I* say it most definitely was.' Mrs Ponsonby's voice rang out from Animal Ark's reception even though the door was closed.

Mandy looked at her watch. Evening surgery should have been over ages ago. What was Mrs Ponsonby doing here? Mandy pushed the door and her mouth dropped open. The reception was full of people. Her dad was standing behind the desk looking concerned as Mrs Ponsonby was lecturing the entire room.

'Everyone knows dogs like *that* chase and kill anything that moves,' she announced, glaring at the offending dogs. Her eyes flashed behind the pink glasses, and the brim of her hat wobbled furiously as she shook her head.

'I can assure you, madam,' said a tall thin man with long hair in a ponytail, and a gold earring in one ear, 'my dogs would never hurt anybody or anything. They are far too well-trained.'

The man was holding something wrapped in a shawl in his arms. The two 'dangerous' dogs sat perfectly still and well-behaved behind their master. Beside him stood two scruffy-looking children and a woman with short, spiky, maroon-coloured hair. Mandy was delighted to see them all. Jude Somers and his wife Rowan were travellers who helped out occasionally at the Spry sisters' place.

'Hi, everyone,' Mandy said from the doorway, just managing to make herself heard during a pause in the argument. Everyone turned to face her. She squatted down in the doorway and the two children ran over and threw their arms round her neck.

'Mandy, Mandy, we're back!' they squealed happily, as Mandy hugged them tight.

SURGERY HOURS
M _ 9 - 10·30   4 - 6
TU _ 0 - 10·30   4 - 6
W _ 9 - 10·40   4 - 6
TH _ 0 - 10·30
F _ 9 - 10·30   4 - 6
S _ 9 - 10
AFTERNOONS
BY APPOINTMENT

'So I can see,' Mandy grinned, holding them at arm's length. 'Skye, you've grown so tall!'

'And me, and me,' Jason said, standing on tiptoes and pushing his sister away. 'I'm tall too.'

Mandy stood up, Jason and Skye each holding one of her hands. 'What's happening here?' she asked, looking at her dad.

'I'll tell you, Mandy,' said Mrs Ponsonby, striding across the room. 'I found these . . . these . . . *people*, coming down the lane carrying a dead fox cub.' She paused and gestured at the bundle in Jude's arms. Mandy felt her face draining of blood. Mrs Ponsonby peered over her glasses at her. 'I thought you'd be shocked. Those wretched dogs are to blame.'

Jude and Rowan were silent. Each wore a look that said 'We've heard all this before.'

'Humph,' Mrs Ponsonby snorted. 'Wild, completely wild. The poor fox cub didn't stand a chance against those vicious animals.' She took out a hanky and blew her nose. 'No!' she declared solemnly. 'Fox cubs will never be safe with those dogs back in Welford.'

'Dad?' Mandy raised her eyebrows at her father.

'May I see the cub please, Jude?' he asked, coming out from behind the desk.

'Of course,' Jude replied. 'We were bringing it here when we were' – he gave a little cough – 'interrupted.'

Adam Hope took the bundle from Jude and looked at the cub. 'Well,' he said seriously, 'there's no question about it . . .'

Mrs Ponsonby smiled smugly to herself.

'Neither of those two dogs could possibly have killed this cub.' Mr Hope announced.

'WHAT?' Mrs Ponsonby demanded. 'What did you say? That can't possibly be right.'

'I said, neither of those dogs could have done it,' Mr Hope repeated. 'It's as simple as that.'

'But, but how?' Mrs Ponsonby spluttered. 'How do you know?'

'Although small dogs *can* be responsible for killing cubs, in this case, I can tell by the teeth marks that a much larger animal has taken this cub in its jaws and killed it,' Adam Hope explained. 'It must have been a big dog with a wide snout, at least as big as a German shepherd or a Labrador. Those dogs' snouts,' he nodded towards Spider and Joey, 'are far too narrow.' Mandy winced, thinking of Dennis Saville's dog. 'Also, Mrs Ponsonby, I happen to agree with Jude that his dogs are very well-trained.' Adam

Hope smiled kindly at Jude and Rowan. 'Did the dogs track the body down?'

Jude nodded.

Mrs Ponsonby visibly deflated. 'I don't know what to say,' she admitted, turning to face Jude and Rowan. 'I've made a dreadful mistake. How can you ever forgive me? Well, of course you can't!' She had made up her mind. 'What a fool I have made of myself.'

'Forget it!' Jude said graciously. 'It happens. We're used to it.'

'Forget it?' Mrs Ponsonby declared. 'I couldn't possibly forget it. I jumped to all the wrong conclusions and didn't stop to listen. I am very sorry.' Mrs Ponsonby was becoming agitated. She sat down heavily on a chair and began fanning herself with a folded-up handkerchief. Mandy looked pleadingly at Jude.

'Madam,' he said, 'please, it's no big deal. You said you're sorry, and we accept. Now let's just forget it.'

Mrs Ponsonby looked gratefully at Jude. She stood up and held out her hand. Jude gave a little bow and shook it.

'Sir,' Mrs Ponsonby declared, 'you are a true gentleman.'

Mandy crossed to the desk where Adam Hope

was holding the cub. 'Dad,' she asked softly, 'can I see?'

'Are you sure you want to, love?' her dad asked.

Mandy nodded and moved the shawl aside. She turned the little head and her heart sank. The tip of the ear was white. Mandy caught her breath. 'It's the cub that went missing,' she said.

Eight

Mandy quietly told the Somers family about the fox family, stroking the cub's ears as she spoke. 'Will you bury it with its mum, please, Dad?' she asked quietly.

'Of course, love,' her dad agreed. 'We'll do it tonight.'

Mrs Ponsonby wiped the corner of her eye with her hankie. 'Mandy, we *must* do something,' she insisted. 'This fox issue has to be sorted out once and for all. We can't have fox cubs being orphaned all over the place because of Sam Western.' She took a deep breath and stuck out her chest. 'A petition is what's needed,' she declared. 'Yes, and *everyone* will sign it, or I shall want to know why. You and James can take it around.'

'Yes, but . . .' Mandy began to explain that she and James were too busy, but Mrs Ponsonby interrupted.

'No buts, Mandy dear,' Mrs Ponsonby said. 'We'll clear this matter up and be done with it.' She put her hankie back in her handbag and shut it with a firm snap. 'I shall expect to see you at Bleakfell Hall first thing in the morning. Goodnight, everyone.'

By early the next morning Mandy had decided on a plan of action. 'James and I will go up to check on the cubs and the vixen as we arranged with Michelle,' she told her parents over breakfast. 'Then we'll call in on Mrs Ponsonby, get the petition and take it around the village. When we've done that, we'll come back and do my chores here and then . . .' Mandy paused to take a bite of toast.

'And when are you planning to breathe, Mandy?' Adam Hope asked, raising his eyebrows.

'After we've met up with Michelle this evening to do the filming.' Mandy finished, laughing.

Michelle was right, Mandy thought to herself as she cycled to meet James. It *was* turning into a success story. The vixen and the cubs were safe. She was glad she knew the fate of the lost cub and, although she felt sad about it, it was almost a relief to know it wasn't wandering around about to starve to death. At least Sam Western couldn't shoot the foxes on Mr Masters's land.

James was waiting outside his gate. 'Your dad just rang. Michelle and Janie have gone up to the farm already,' he said. 'Oh, and Michelle said that Mr Masters has seen the vixen going hunting during the day as well as at night.'

'Gosh, she won't be able to manage that for long,' Mandy said with a frown. 'She's got to get *some* sleep.'

The vixen was outside the earth when Mandy and James arrived, curled up asleep in a patch of sunlight. Her usually glossy coat was beginning to look dull and they could see the outline of her ribs.

'She's getting run down,' Mandy said, anxiously.

'Oh look, the cubs are coming out,' James observed. The little fox cubs trotted over to the vixen and began worrying her. Nibbling at her ears and chewing on her tail, they forced the vixen to wake up. She stood up to move away but the cubs followed her.

'They're hungry,' Michelle said. 'Although she's hunting almost constantly it's not providing enough food for them.'

The vixen began grooming the cubs, licking their ears and nuzzling at their feet. She herded them back to the earth and turned to set off hunting but as she turned her back they were out again, running after her. The vixen suddenly whirled around, causing the cubs to skid to a halt in a heap. Thumping the ground with their tails they lay on their sides with their ears flat against their heads.

'That's the submissive posture,' Michelle told them. 'It shows they know who's boss.'

The vixen led the cubs back to the earth again and this time they stayed put. She trotted off and was gone a long time, returning with a small rabbit in her jaws. The cubs rushed at her all at once, leaping on the kill, each one trying to claim it for itself. Off went the vixen again.

'At this rate she's going to wear herself out,' Michelle said, a note of concern in her voice.

'What can we do?' Mandy said, frowning. 'She's only been feeding them on her own for a few days. What will happen to her after a week?'

'We'll have to wait and see, Mandy,' Michelle said, thoughtfully. 'We'll come back again tonight.'

As they walked back to the farmyard, Mandy told Michelle and Janie about the cub Jude's dogs had found. She had already filled James in on the bike ride over. 'Anyway,' Mandy told them, 'now Mrs Ponsonby is going to start a petition.'

'That would be excellent, Mandy,' Michelle said. 'You can count on my name for a start.' She climbed into her Jeep.

'And me,' Janie added, going round to the passenger seat. 'See you later.'

When Mandy and James arrived at Bleakfell Hall, Mrs Ponsonby's car was just pulling up outside the house. 'Goodness me,' she puffed. Her face was as red as the poppies on her hat. 'I *have* been busy this morning. I went into Walton to the library to get the petition photocopied. Hold this for me please, James.' She lifted a box out of her car.

James nearly sank to his knees when he took

the weight of it. He gave Mandy a panicky
look.

'Come along, darlings!' Mrs Ponsonby said,
opening the back of the car. Toby jumped out
on to the drive, and Mrs Ponsonby lifted
Pandora down beside him. 'Come along,
children, inside.' The dogs rushed up to Mandy
and James, yapping round their feet.

Mandy grinned at James. 'Does she mean us
or the dogs?' she whispered.

James struggled with the heavy box. 'If this is
the petition, there are enough copies for the
whole village to have one each,' he said.

'Put the box on the table, please, James. It's

full of dog food,' Mrs Ponsonby ordered, taking off her coat, then putting on a vast apron and tying it behind her back. 'There, my precious,' she said to Pandora, who was trying to climb on to Mandy's lap. 'I'll get you a drinky in a moment.' She bustled around in the kitchen. 'Thank you, James. Now, rosehip tea or lemonade?'

'Are you asking us?' Mandy said with a smile.

'Of course, Mandy,' Mrs Ponsonby replied starchily. 'The dogs prefer water!'

'Lemonade, please,' Mandy and James said together.

'Now,' Mrs Ponsonby said, when they were seated at the table. 'Here's the petition.' She reached into a folder, pulled out a sheaf of papers and handed them a copy each. Mandy stared at the piece of paper. FOX WATCH FIGHTS FOR FOXES it said in big capital letters. There was a terrible picture of a pack of hounds killing a fox underneath, with *Don't Let This Happen In Welford!* emblazoned across it. Underneath were columns for people's names, addresses and signatures.

'What do you think?' Mrs Ponsonby asked eagerly, her eyes shining behind her glasses with their pink frames.

'It's very ... hard-hitting,' James said, struggling for words.

'All the more reason for people to sign then, isn't there?' Mrs Ponsonby said. 'You only get one chance with petitions.'

'You don't think it'll put people off?' Mandy asked carefully.

'No! Petitions have to get straight to the point,' Mrs Ponsonby retorted. 'Now, here are some for you to take back down to Welford with you.' She handed James a dozen copies and gave the same to Mandy. 'I've made some posters to go up in the shops, you two do the houses.'

Mandy and James sped off to petition the whole village house by house. By late afternoon Mrs Ponsonby had made sure that the village was covered with posters. They were posted on the windows of the Fox and Goose, with a note saying *Come in and sign*. Mrs McFarlane from the post office put up three on her notice-board, and had the petition on the counter. The oak tree had posters in plastic folders telling people where they could go to sign. There were two stuck up next to the village hall, and one by the church. Mandy and James arrived back at Animal Ark, tired but elated, their petitions covered with signatures.

'It's the picture that does it,' Mandy told her mum and dad. 'As soon as people saw the picture and realised how cruel hunting really is, they couldn't wait to sign.'

'And some kept the petition, so that members of their family who were at work could sign later,' James said. 'They promised to deliver them to the post office.'

'Can I put one on the notice-board, please?' Mandy asked her mum.

'Yes, of course,' Emily Hope said, signing her name on the bottom of James's form. 'Are you going back up to watch the foxes tonight?'

'Yep,' Mandy said, looking at her watch. 'And we should be going soon.'

'I've made you a plate of sandwiches to eat before you go,' Emily Hope said. 'And don't worry about your chores, good old Simon has already done them.'

'Brilliant, Mum, thanks,' Mandy said, giving her mum a hug.

'Thanks, Mrs Hope,' James called over his shoulder, as he followed Mandy through to the kitchen.

'Wow,' Mandy said. 'I didn't realise how hungry I was.' They'd finished the sandwiches and were

smearing jam on some of Gran's scones which
Emily Hope had left out for them.

'I hope you've saved one of those for me.'
Adam Hope said, coming into the kitchen and
taking a seat at the table. 'How's the film going?'

'There's a couple left in the tin,' Mandy said,
'and the film's going well. But I meant to ask
you about the vixen. She isn't getting any rest.
She spends all her time hunting.'

'She's really worn out,' James added, picking
up the last crumb off his plate.

'Could we take her some food?' Mandy said.
'What do you think, Dad?'

'It would certainly help, but you'd need to be
careful what you gave her,' Adam Hope said.
'People often leave out a bowl of dog or cat
food, but in this situation you would need to
leave food she can carry back to the cubs.'

'Like a chicken carcase?' James asked.

'Normally, I would say yes, James,' Mr Hope
said, smiling, 'but I shouldn't think Mr Masters
wants the foxes to get a taste for chicken. What
does Michelle want to do?'

'Michelle wants the film to be as natural as
possible,' James said. 'We're supposed to be
observing and not interfering.'

'But man has already interfered by shooting

the mother vixen,' Mr Hope pointed out. 'In a way you're just redressing the balance. Michelle will know what to do.'

When they arrived at Blackheath Farm that night, Michelle was already waiting for them. 'Good, I'm glad you're here, we've got a problem,' she told them. 'Janie and I arrived quite early and we've been watching the cubs. And I'm certain another one has gone missing.'

Mandy fought to keep the panic from rising inside her. 'Quick, let's look for it before it gets dark!' she said, urgently.

'Where shall we start? It could be anywhere,' James said. 'Still, at least Mr Masters's dog is too well-trained to have taken it.'

'James! That's it!' Mandy exclaimed. She looked at Michelle. 'James has just given me an idea. Why don't we ask Jude to bring Joey and Spider? They'll find it easily enough.'

'Can we get hold of him?' Michelle asked, taking her mobile phone out of her bag. 'Has he got a phone?'

'We can ask the Sprys to give him a message,' Mandy said, thinking on her feet. 'The camper van is parked up there. He could get over here really quickly.'

'OK, Mandy, you call the Sprys.' Michelle

handed her the phone. 'I'll just go and tell Mr Masters what we're doing.'

Mandy dialled the number but the Sprys' phone just rang and rang.

'They don't always answer it, you know,' James told her.

'Well, they'll have to. I'm not giving up,' Mandy hissed between her teeth.

Miss Marjorie answered eventually on the twelfth ring. Mandy poured out their request.

'I'll go right away, Mandy,' Miss Marjorie said, hanging up.

Mandy and James found Michelle in the farmyard and told her they'd got through, then walked up the track to wait for Jude. Tense with worry, Mandy paced up and down, as minutes seemed to take hours to pass.

'Here he comes!' James exclaimed, peering through his binoculars across the fields to the road. 'I didn't recognise the van, he's painted it in some sort of pattern.'

The battered old red van that the family lived in came chugging up the track.

'It's the fox posters,' James said, as it drew closer. 'Jude's covered the van with our posters.'

The van pulled into the farmyard and the back door opened. Rowan and the children got out. Spider and Joey sat in the back, waiting.

'Right,' Jude said, getting out of the driver's seat. 'First I'd like to look at the earth and decide where I think it's best to start.' Calling the dogs he set off with Mandy and James, while Michelle talked to Rowan and the children.

'As likely as not, the cub's in that spinney,' Jude pointed. 'We'll start on the far side and work our way toward the earth.'

Dusk was just beginning to fall and shadowy shapes in the wood began to merge. Jude worked the dogs in ever decreasing circles. Several times they surprised rabbits, but there was no sign of the fox cub.

Mandy was beginning to lose hope. It wasn't looking good. But then, suddenly, Spider veered away to the right, his nose on the ground, sniffing as he went. Soon Joey joined him and Jude loped along behind them. Mandy followed, with James hot on her heels, fear shooting through her at the thought of what the dogs might find.

They were at the other side of the wood now, following the drystone wall that marked the boundary of Mr Masters's land. Joey and Spider stopped at a place where the wall had collapsed. They looked expectantly up at Jude, their tails wagging. Mandy and James were out of breath as they caught up. Jude put a finger to his lips and then cupped his hand behind his ear to listen.

Mandy concentrated hard, but all she could hear was her heart pounding and the blood rushing in her head.

Then she heard it, a faint mewing. It was coming from underneath the pile of heavy stones where the wall had fallen down. 'The wall's fallen on it!' she cried in alarm.

Nine

'We've got to get it out,' Mandy said, collapsing on her knees in front of the wall.

Jude and James hurried to join her. With their bare hands they began digging frantically at the loose stones. Mandy worked hard, not wanting to think about the injuries the cub might have sustained, buried under all this rubble.

Suddenly, Jude stopped digging and stood up.

'What is it?' Mandy asked.

Jude grinned. 'I think if we move this big flat stone, we'll find the cub,' he said, 'I'm beginning to think it crawled in underneath here,' he pointed to an opening, 'and dislodged a stone that trapped it inside. I don't think the wall fell on it at all.'

'Oh, I hope you're right, Jude,' Mandy said, crossing her fingers while he pulled away the stone. Sure enough, as they watched, the cub wriggled out. Mandy was itching to help it, but Jude put a hand out to stop her.

'Don't touch it!' he said. 'You'll transfer your smell to it. Now it's free, the vixen will find it soon enough.'

When Mandy and James reached the farmyard, Michelle was just coming back with Rowan and the children. 'We saw the foxes, we saw the foxes,' Skye sang to Mandy and James.

'They were having their dinner,' Jason told them.

Michelle didn't need to ask Mandy if they had been successful, she could tell by their smiling faces. 'Oh, well done, dogs,' she said, bending down to stroke their brindled coats.

'We'd never have found the cub without them,' Mandy told her proudly. Then she asked, 'How's the vixen?'

'She's very tired, but just about coping, I think,' Michelle said. 'She hasn't been back since the cub went missing, though.' Jude said he had to go, so they all waved him and his family off as they drove back down the track, then they returned to watch the foxes.

Mandy and James had just crept back to their watching place near the earth, when the vixen returned. She dropped a vole by the waiting cubs, then ran inside the earth. Almost immediately she shot out and gave a warning cough. Instantly, the cubs dived for the safety of the earth.

'Do you think she knows the cub's missing?' James asked.

'Course she does!' Mandy said. 'She knows how many cubs she's looking after.'

With a loud bark the vixen made off into the spinney.

'I bet she comes back with the cub,' James said.

'Dad said it wouldn't hurt to give the vixen some food,' Mandy told Michelle as they waited. 'If you don't mind, that is.'

'I've been thinking the same thing, Mandy,' Michelle said thoughtfully. 'I don't want to interfere, but . . .'

'We've got action, guys!' Janie announced.

Mandy looked through her binoculars, hardly daring to hope that James had been right. Relief flooded through her as she saw the vixen trotting back, with the runaway cub held gently by the scruff of its neck in her mouth. 'She's found it,' she breathed.

'You'll have to help Mrs Ponsonby, Mandy,' Emily Hope said next morning as she put the breakfast things on the table. 'She's gone to such a lot of trouble. All you have to do is collect up the petitions from the various notice-boards in the village.'

'James and I had planned to spend all day watching the foxes.' Mandy groaned, flopping in a chair. 'We wanted to make a note of how many times the vixen hunts during the day. It's important.'

'And so is Mrs Ponsonby's petition,' her mum said. 'This might be your best chance to stop Sam Western in his tracks. I've heard she's got a huge convoy of people coming to lend support.'

'I know you're right,' Mandy said, wrinkling her nose. 'It's just that I love watching the cubs. What time is she coming?'

'At one o'clock,' Emily Hope said, glancing at the clock. 'That should give you enough time.'

'Right,' Mandy agreed. 'I'll call James and tell him.'

Mandy walked down to the village. She had arranged to meet James outside the post office without their bikes, to give Blackie a walk. Her mum was right as usual. It would be brilliant if the petition stopped Sam Western's hunt plans.

Mandy and James quickly collected up all the petitions. They were astonished at the number of names that had been signed.

In the post office, Mrs McFarlane, the postmistress, took the petitions from the board while Mandy and James were choosing crisps. 'Here we are,' she said. 'And best of luck!'

'Let's sit on the bench outside the Fox and Goose and look at these while we're eating our crisps,' James suggested.

'I didn't think there *were* so many people in Welford,' Mandy said, slipping her foot out of her shoe and tickling Blackie's tummy with her toes. 'Look, James,' she said passing him a petition form. 'Lydia Fawcett's signed, and look!' Mandy's mouth fell open. She could hardly believe it. 'Mr Parker-Smythe has as well.'

'Wow,' James said, opening his crisps. 'And he lives right next door to Sam Western!'

'Let's see if the Gills have signed.' Mandy flicked through some petitions. 'Their place is nearby, too,' she said, crunching on a cheese and onion crisp. 'Nope, can't find them.'

'Never mind, what we've got is very impressive,' James said. 'Sam Western can't ignore this, especially if your mum's right and lots of people turn up as well.'

'They're all meeting up at Animal Ark at one o'clock,' Mandy said checking her watch.

James nodded, reading another form. 'Here's Walter Pickard's name.'

'Someone talking about me?' a familiar voice said behind them.

'Hello, Mr Pickard,' Mandy said. 'We just found your name on the petition.'

'Aye, it's there all right,' Walter said. 'Along wi' all the others.' He shook his head and sucked his teeth. 'That were a bad do up at Piper's Wood.' He looked from Mandy to James. 'Make sure that Sam Western knows we don't want any more foxes *mistaken* for hares!'

'We will,' Mandy promised. 'But aren't you coming?' she asked, disappointment in her voice. Walter Pickard would be a good person to have along when they faced Sam Western, because of all his special knowledge of the countryside.

'I had planned to, young Mandy, but my grandson Tommy is feeling a bit peaky.' He bent and scratched Blackie between the ears. 'I promised I'd go and stay with him while his mum goes out.'

'That's a shame,' Mandy said. 'I hope Tommy feels better soon. Tell him all about the fox cubs, won't you?'

'I will that,' Walter promised. 'Welford Cubs were right proud when they had Lucky as a mascot. Tommy's always interested to hear about foxes.' Walter put his cap on and walked away.

'I was thinking,' Emily Hope said. 'Why don't you get Mrs Ponsonby to drop you at Blackheath Farm on the way back from delivering the petition?' Mandy and James had gone back to Animal Ark for lunch and were tucking into cheese-on-toast.

'Good idea,' Mandy said. 'At least we'd have the afternoon to watch the foxes that way.'

'And Michelle's doing the last bit of filming tonight,' James said, cleaning his plate.

'Seconds, James?' Mrs Hope asked. 'You'll need to keep your strength up today.' She grinned.

'Please.' James pushed his plate forward. 'It's delicious.'

At a quarter to one Mrs Ponsonby arrived in

her car. She was wearing a pale-green flowered dress and her freshly curled hair was covered by a straw hat weighed down with mauve and pink artificial busy Lizzies.

Mandy had to bite her cheek to stop herself from laughing.

'She looks like she's going ballroom dancing,' Adam Hope muttered behind them. 'Not leading a protest.'

'Adam!' Emily Hope nudged him with her elbow.

'Nobody here yet?' Mrs Ponsonby said, looking around her. 'I do hope we'll have enough cars to carry everyone.'

Just then, Jean came out from reception with a message. 'I'm afraid your regulars from Fox Watch won't be here,' she said to Mrs Ponsonby. 'They were coming together in one car and they've just phoned to say they've broken down.'

'Oh dear, that's too, too bad,' Mrs Ponsonby said with a sigh. 'Ernie Bell stopped me in the village. He's got an appointment at the opticians in Walton, so he won't be joining us either.'

'And we met Walter Pickard this morning,' Mandy remembered. 'He's got to look after his grandson.'

'Where *is* everybody else?' Mrs Ponsonby

looked at her watch. 'It's nearly one o'clock.'

'Who else are you expecting?' Adam Hope asked.

'Well,' Mrs Ponsonby floundered a bit. '*Everyone* who signed my petition promised they'd come.' She looked at the Hopes. 'Will we have *your* support?'

Adam Hope coughed. 'Much as I'd like to come . . .' he said. Mandy looked up at him. '. . . duty calls in the form of an Afghan hound in Walton with kidney failure.'

'And I've got afternoon surgery,' Emily Hope smiled apologetically.

'Michelle said she and Janie wanted to come, but they've got too much editing to do,' Mandy said. 'The programme's important too.'

'Well, Mandy and James,' Mrs Ponsonby decreed. 'It looks like saving the foxes of Welford is completely down to us three. Come along.' She opened the car doors and waited for them to get in. 'Let battle commence!'

Mandy and James exchanged glances. *Some protest this is going to be*, Mandy thought nervously to herself.

'I bet Sam Western won't take a bit of notice of us,' James whispered to Mandy behind his hand.

'Wait and see, James,' Mrs Ponsonby said, overhearing. 'It is quality, not quantity that counts. We can be just as forceful as a big deputation.' She adjusted her hat in the rear-view mirror and then set off. 'After all, we feel *very* strongly about this. We just have to put that across to Mr Western.'

When they reached the entrance to Upper Welford Hall, James jumped out to open the gate.

'I have to admit I admire his gardens,' Mrs Ponsonby said, looking around as she drove up the drive. 'It's a gardener's paradise. Every plant behaves itself perfectly. These roses wouldn't *dare* grow suckers.' She leaned back and said conspiratorially. 'I *have* heard that they even vacuum the paths.'

Mandy and James stifled giggles. Mrs Ponsonby was always inclined to believe gossip, however unlikely it seemed.

'I prefer your gardens, Mrs Ponsonby,' Mandy reassured her. 'At least they look more, more . . .' She looked to James for help.

'More *natural*,' James said. 'More lived in.'

'Thank you, dears. With two dogs like mine what else can they be?' She parked the car opposite the house and they all got out. The

Hall had an old-fashioned bell-pull and Mrs Ponsonby gave it such a hard tug they could hear it jangling through the house.

Dennis Saville came from round the side of the house and stood at the bottom of the steps watching them.

'This concerns you too,' Mrs Ponsonby called down to him. 'Come along.'

Reluctantly Dennis Saville climbed the steps. 'I'm a busy man,' he said, glaring from Mandy and James to Mrs Ponsonby.

Mrs Ponsonby pulled the bell-pull again. Moments later, the door flew open and Sam Western stood there. 'What on earth is going on?' he shouted angrily. 'They must have heard that in Walton.'

'Don't be silly, Mr Western,' Mrs Ponsonby said lightly. She drew herself up and declared in a loud voice, 'We, from Welford Fox Watch, summon you to take notice of this petition.' She turned to Mandy and James and urged them forward with a nod of her head. They both entered into the spirit of things by solemnly holding out their armfuls of paper. 'Duly signed by virtually every person in this village and its outlying districts,' Mrs Ponsonby continued.

'Huh!' Sam Western snorted. 'So where *are* they all, these *concerned* people, then?'

Mandy had had a horrible feeling he was going to ask that. She looked at James and he gave a little grimace.

'MR WESTERN,' Mrs Ponsonby's voice was as cold and hard as steel. 'The three of us, and a few other people, *know* what happened up at Piper's Wood the other morning.' She paused to let the message sink in.

'I didn't do anything wrong,' Sam Western said. 'I was shooting hares, *that's* legal.'

But Mandy thought he looked a bit nervous now.

'We know that a fox *was* shot, *on* common land *and* out of season.' Mrs Ponsonby was in full swing now. 'Mandy, James and I chose, yes chose, out of the goodness of our hearts to come alone. We chose not to embarrass you in front of all your business associates, and indeed, the whole of Welford.'

'And its outlying districts,' Mandy added. *Good old Mrs Ponsonby!* she thought. James nodded vigorously.

Mrs Ponsonby delivered her ultimatum. 'Now, either you give up this idea of a foxhunt or I shall take this whole matter one step further.'

'And you've got to promise not to shoot any more foxes,' Mandy said, warming to the subject.

Sam Western looked at the pile of petition sheets. Then he looked at Mrs Ponsonby. Lastly he looked at Mandy and James. He sighed. 'You're nothing but trouble, you two kids,' he said in a resigned voice.

Dennis Saville's face was beetroot red. Mandy felt a shiver down her back as he glared at her and James. 'Take no notice of these two, Boss . . . ' he began, stepping forward.

But Mrs Ponsonby interrupted him. 'Make up your mind, Mr Western!'

Mandy's heart was beating rapidly. She had to stay calm. She clutched the petition with an iron grip to stop her hands from shaking.

Sam Western gave another loud sigh. 'All right. I'll stop my plans for a hunt. But for this season only.' He narrowed his eyes at them. 'And if I find that foxes have bred in vast numbers and are causing trouble then I'll have to think again.'

'What about shooting foxes?' Mandy asked. It was no good stopping the hunt if he and Dennis Saville were still going to shoot them. 'You have to agree to stop that too.'

Mr Western looked weary. 'That too.'

'What about him?' James indicated Dennis Saville who was standing by with a look of open-mouthed disbelief on his face.

'He works for me. *I* give the orders round here,' Sam Western said sternly.

Mrs Ponsonby was satisfied. She looked at Mandy and James. They nodded. 'Then we'll just need your word on it, Mr Western,' she said sweetly.

'Good Lord, what are you on about, woman? Don't you trust me?' Sam Western spluttered furiously.

'Don't you "woman" me, Sam Western.' Mrs Ponsonby glared at him. 'And the answer to your question is no, I don't!'

'I give you my word. Are you happy now?' Sam Western said through clenched teeth.

'Not quite,' Mrs Ponsonby said, tapping her chin with a finger. 'I will expect confirmation of your resolve in writing, please.'

'Bah, you drive a hard bargain, woman,' Sam Western said, his face flushing. 'You'll have a letter from me in the next couple of days. *Now* are you happy?'

'Perfectly happy now, Mr Western.' Mrs Ponsonby gave him a smile. 'Perfectly.' She turned to Mandy and James. 'That's that then,' she said, giving them a broad wink. 'Goodbye, Mr Western, and don't forget now, or I will have to visit you again.'

Mrs Ponsonby ushered them down the steps towards the car.

James did a small running jump and punched the air. 'Yes!' Mandy exclaimed. 'We really did it!'

Ten

'Mrs Ponsonby,' Mandy said, with a note of awe in her voice. 'You were fantastic!'

'Well, thank you, my dear,' Mrs Ponsonby replied. Mandy saw her satisfied smile. 'I must admit I *am* feeling rather pleased with myself,' she said, slowing down behind a tractor. 'I will *not* be bullied, nor will I let the people of Welford be bullied!'

James elbowed Mandy in the ribs. But Mandy didn't care how over-the-top Mrs Ponsonby was today. 'Or the foxes of Welford,' she added happily.

'I didn't think just the three of us could convince Mr Western,' James said, joining in.

'Sam Western knows when he's beaten,' Mrs Ponsonby replied, nodding sagely. 'But I couldn't have done it without you two to support me.' She glanced at them quickly over her shoulder. 'You know, most of the local farmers signed our petition.'

'It's *so* brilliant that foxes will be safe around Welford now,' Mandy burst out.

'But we mustn't let up!' Mrs Ponsonby said. 'You heard what Sam Western said. It's only for this season.' She slowed down as she neared Blackheath Farm. 'We've got to keep the support up and do everything we can to keep the farmers on our side.'

'Mr Masters is already on our side,' Mandy told her.

'And Lydia Fawcett,' James added.

'If you could drop us here, that would be great,' Mandy said, as they approached the gate to Blackheath Farm.

'Right,' Mrs Ponsonby said, looking at her watch. 'I really must get back to the dogs. They'll wonder where I am. Shall I ring your parents and tell them the good news?'

'Yes, please,' Mandy said gratefully, getting out of the car.

She and James waved as Mrs Ponsonby drove

away. 'She *was* pretty impressive, wasn't she?' James said, setting off down the track.

Mandy nodded. 'It's like Mum and Dad said, there's a lot of huff and puff but she *does* get things done.' She laughed out loud. 'Did you see Dennis Saville's face?'

James grinned. 'I thought he was going to explode.'

'Now, we just want the little vixen to be coping,' Mandy said, as they crossed the field to the spinney, 'and everything will be great.'

When they reached the earth there wasn't a fox to be seen. 'She could be out hunting,' Mandy suggested. 'Or perhaps the cubs are letting her sleep more now. Let's sit under that oak tree and wait,' she said.

Mandy and James watched and waited. By late afternoon they were both feeling worried. The little vixen hadn't been out once.

'James, what do you think has happened?' Mandy said anxiously. 'Yesterday she was in and out all day.'

James nodded glumly. 'I know.' He thought for a few moments. 'But there could be lots of reasons.'

'Such as?' Mandy asked, her eyes bright with concern.

'Well,' he began, then paused.

'Tell me, James, I have to know,' Mandy said, sensing that he didn't want to upset her.

'Sometimes,' James began, 'vixens go away from their cubs to rest up somewhere else, to get a bit of peace and quiet. They just come back to feed them and play with them.'

'I don't think our little vixen would do that,' Mandy said. 'She's been too good a mother so far. And wouldn't the cubs be out calling for her?' She wasn't convinced.

'That's true,' James agreed. 'You know, she could have gone out and . . .' he looked at Mandy, '. . . not come back for a reason.'

Mandy thought about this for a moment. It would be too dreadful if something had happened to the little vixen. 'But surely the cubs would be out, wouldn't they, if she hadn't come back?' Mandy said. 'Maybe she's moved them again?'

James frowned. 'Or maybe she's in the earth and is just too exhausted to hunt any more!' he said.

'It's awful not knowing,' Mandy said in a small voice. 'I don't think I could bear it if we lost them now.'

'Perhaps Michelle will have some ideas,'

James said, trying to cheer her up. 'She and Janie should be here soon.'

But when they did arrive, Michelle seemed just as concerned as Mandy and James. 'I have to admit, I have been concerned about her wearing herself out,' she said. 'It's a terrific amount of work for a single vixen. Five hungry cubs.'

'Wait!' Janie said. 'She's coming out.'

Through her binoculars Mandy saw the little vixen coming out of the earth. Ears flicking she sniffed the wind, then trotted jauntily off to hunt. She didn't seem tired at all. She seemed positively perky.

'What *is* going on?' Michelle said softly. 'There's obviously nothing wrong with her at all. She must have got some rest.'

'But if she hasn't been hunting all day, why aren't the cubs hungry?' Mandy asked, feeling mystified.

'Look!' James said, under his breath. 'Another fox.'

Mandy felt a fizz of excitement go through the group as they saw an unfamiliar fox appear at the scene. As the fox drew nearer to the earth they could see it had a rabbit in its mouth.

'She's getting help from another vixen,'

Michelle said, with rising excitement in her voice. '*That*'s the answer.'

The fox took the rabbit into the earth and stayed down. After a few minutes she came out with the cubs following behind her. She picked up the gardening glove that was lying nearby and tossed it into the air. They all pounced on it, embarking on an energetic playfight.

But Mandy was only half watching the cubs' antics. She'd noticed something else.

'What is it, Mandy?' said Michelle. Mandy's eyes were wide and she was holding her binoculars with trembling hands. 'What's wrong?'

'Nothing's wrong!' Mandy said. 'But look at the cubs.' She waited while they looked. 'There's *six* cubs now and one is quite a bit bigger than the rest. You wait, when they stop jumping about you'll see.'

'Good gracious!' Michelle declared. 'You're right Mandy. I hadn't counted.'

Mandy was so excited now she could hardly keep still. 'Look, James, look at the new cub,' she blurted it out. 'Don't you recognise it?'

'It can't be, can it? It is! It's Lucky, I'm sure of it.' James was grinning widely.

'Mandy, look through the camera,' Janie said,

bending to be shoulder height to her. 'The foxes will be much clearer.'

Mandy looked through the viewfinder. For a few seconds she couldn't work out what she was seeing. Then slowly the scene came into focus. There was the bigger cub and as she watched, he turned and looked right at her. It was definitely Lucky. She recognised the way he put his head on one side when his ears pricked up.

Janie took over the camera to carry on filming, obviously delighted by the new, surprising twist in their film.

'But how has this happened?' Mandy asked Michelle, once she'd got over the surprise.

Keeping her voice as low as possible Michelle explained, 'I think that this vixen is the little vixen's grandmother.'

'So would the vixen that Sam Western shot have been Lucky's mum's daughter?' Mandy asked, catching on.

'That's right,' Michelle agreed. 'She would have been born three years ago, and Lucky's mum obviously let her daughter take over half her territory. The daughter had the young vixen last year, and she stayed to help with these cubs this year. That's often what happens in fox families.' She tapped her chin with her finger and smiled. 'I see now, this also solves another problem I had.'

'What was that?' James asked, keeping his eyes on the cubs.

'Well, I really didn't think we'd see Lucky and his mother around here.' Michelle explained. 'Normally, if you remove a fox from its territory, as you did with Lucky's mum when she was injured, within about four days another will have taken it over, and then the first fox will be driven off. So although you let Lucky and his mum loose on their original territory, I very much doubted we'd see them again.'

'But because Lucky's mum shares the territory with her daughter, there wasn't any problem,' Mandy guessed.

'Right,' Michelle agreed. 'What has happened here – and I'd stake my reputation on it – is that Lucky's mum came across the little vixen and the cubs, realised that she couldn't cope and decided to pool the litters and rear them together.'

'With two vixens hunting there shouldn't be a problem, should there?' James asked.

'No, there shouldn't. Lucky's mum will also be much more experienced at hunting and she'll know this territory like the back of her hand,' she said. 'Or should I say paw!'

Mandy and James laughed. Janie was too absorbed in her filming to hear.

'What would have happened if, say, Lucky's mum wasn't related to the little vixen?' Mandy wondered. 'And she found the cubs on her territory then?'

'She'd probably have killed them and driven the young vixen away,' Michelle said seriously. 'She's the dominant vixen on this territory and she wouldn't let an intruder in.'

'The young vixen is coming back,' Janie said, turning her head slightly, but keeping the camera on her shoulder perfectly still.

They all watched in silence as the young vixen took her catch down into the earth. The cubs followed her down immediately. Lucky's mum herded the last one in and then followed them down.

'Isn't it amazing to see the co-operation?' Michelle said. 'This is an excellent result. We couldn't possibly have wished for anything better.'

Mandy grinned. She couldn't agree more whole-heartedly.

A short time later in the fading light of dusk, both vixens came out of the earth with the cubs.

The two adults groomed the young foxes one after another. Mandy could see how much more foxy Lucky's face was now than the smaller, younger cubs whose faces were just beginning to lose their puppy look. She sighed happily.

'I think we have enough footage now, if you two can prise yourselves away,' Michelle said, interrupting Mandy's thoughts. 'I'd like to go back to Animal Ark and do a couple of pieces to camera, including a little piece about how you found Lucky.'

'Then we can get back to the studio and finish off the editing,' Janie said, turning off the camera.

Mandy and James took one last long look at the foxes.

'The cubs seem really safe now, don't they, James?' She looked at her friend who had a huge grin on his face.

They trooped back to the farmhouse and told everybody there the good news.

'I've already noticed a difference,' said Mr Masters, beaming at them. 'I haven't lost nearly so many eggs recently. Let's hope they keep up the good work. By the way, how did the petition go?'

Mandy and James looked at each other. They

could hardly believe it. In all the excitement with the foxes, they had both completely forgotten the petition.

'It's brilliant news,' Mandy told them. 'Sam Western promised *not* to start up a hunt and *not* to shoot any more foxes.'

'I'd say you two have had a pretty successful day,' Michelle said. 'And I think the fox population of Welford has a lot to thank you for!'

Eleven

Janie set the camera up in the garden at Animal Ark, while Michelle gave Mandy some pointers. James had insisted that Mandy should be interviewed alone, as he got embarrassed easily.

'Just look at the camera and speak naturally,' Michelle was saying. 'Talk about how you found Lucky in that dreadful trap, and then how you set him and his mother free after you had hand-reared him.'

Adam and Emily Hope were on the patio listening, and Jean and Simon stood at the back door of the surgery. On the third attempt all Mandy's nerves disappeared and she told the story perfectly without any hesitations.

'Mrs Ponsonby rang and told us all about the petition,' Mandy's dad said later, when they were sitting at the table eating supper. Michelle and Janie had dashed off to work on the film but James had stayed. 'We're very proud of you both. Mum and I think you've done a terrific job, both with the petition and with the film.'

'Michelle says it will be on early next week.' Mandy said. 'It's a shame the Spry sisters and Jude and Rowan won't be able to watch it.'

'We plan to record it anyway, but why don't we invite them here to see it?' Emily Hope said. 'It will be a bit of a squash but I should think they'd enjoy it nevertheless.'

'Mum, that's a great idea.' Mandy jumped up and gave her mum a hug. 'James and I will go over in the morning and ask them.' She looked at James.

'Fine,' James said. 'But please, Mandy, not *too* early.'

It was late when Mandy woke up the next morning. She went downstairs in her dressing-gown and phoned James. 'I'll meet you in about

half an hour at the post office and we can go
over to the Sprys'.'

'OK,' James answered. 'I'll bring Blackie. He's
very cross that we've been out so much without
him.'

'Tell him we'll make it up to him today,'
Mandy said, laughing. 'Let's take him up on the
moor for a really long run.'

Mandy got dressed and popped into Animal
Ark to tell her parents her plans.

'So, have you come back to work at last,
Mandy?' Simon teased, as he was cutting a
guinea-pig's claws.

'Tomorrow!' Mandy said. 'Definitely
tomorrow. I just want to go up and spend one
last day with the foxes. Is that OK?

Simon nodded. 'Of course, you deserve it
after your hard work.'

Jude was mowing the lawn in front of the house
when Mandy and James arrived at the Riddings.
He turned off the mower and came over to see
them. 'How are the foxes?' he asked, jumping
down from the little wall on to the drive. 'All
present and correct?'

'Better than that,' Mandy said, going on to
tell him all about the pooling of the litters.

Jude walked up to the house with them. Rowan, who had waved to them through the window, opened the door with a duster in her hand.

'Hi,' she greeted them with a grin. She led them into the sitting-room.

Mandy noticed that everywhere was sparklingly clean and smelled pleasantly of lemon-scented polish. Miss Marjorie sat on the sofa with Skye on one side and Jason on the other. She was reading them a story. Miss Joan stood behind her looking over her shoulder.

'We've come to invite you all to Animal Ark on Tuesday to watch the first *Wildlife Ways* TV programme,' Mandy declared. 'You will come, won't you?'

Miss Joan put her hand to her mouth. 'Oh, we don't usually go out, *especially* in the dark!'

'Then perhaps it's time we did,' Miss Marjorie suggested. 'I should love to come, Mandy.'

'We'll take you in the van,' Rowan informed them, dusting the china cabinet. 'If you don't mind a bit of a squeeze.'

'Please come, Miss Joan,' Mandy said. 'There's something in the programme I know you'd love to see.' She winked at James.

'That's true,' James said, joining in. 'You'd be really sorry to miss out.'

'What's up, love?' said Adam Hope, putting an arm round Mandy who was standing outside the back door. She spun around and flung her arms round his waist.

'Oh Dad, I'm *so* nervous,' Mandy said in a shaky voice. 'I've been so excited for the last few days, dying to see the film, and now all of a sudden it's hit me.'

'I'm not surprised, Mandy. After all, it's not every day you're on television,' Adam Hope said. He gently prised her away. 'Come on, you'll be fine. Now if we don't go back in we'll miss it completely.'

Mandy went back into the sitting-room which was crammed with familiar faces. Mandy and James had ended up inviting a *few* more people than Emily Hope had expected, but she'd been great about it and had even laid on refreshments.

Mandy hurried over to her seat as the announcer said, 'And now, *Wildlife Ways*.'

Mandy watched in a trance as Michelle gave her introduction and a picture of the cubs came on. When she saw the cubs' real mother, playing with her cubs and the younger vixen, she couldn't help feeling a lump in her throat. She looked over at James who looked equally upset.

Michelle began her voice-over as the vixen was shown returning with the chicken. She explained how the death of this fox had brought almost the whole of one village together and that because of it, for the meantime, there would be no more foxhunting in the area. When the film cut to the helper vixen hunting and playing with her surrogate cubs, Michelle told the viewers how worried they had all been about her. Then, as the scene changed to the family plus Lucky and his mum, Michelle explained how in the nick of time help had arrived in the form of the young vixen's grandmother. Suddenly, with a jolt, Mandy realised her face was filling the screen and it was her own voice talking. Eventually the camera pulled back and the picture showed Lucky and his mother nuzzling each other and playing with the cubs. There were a few shorter articles and announcements, and then the music started and the credits began to roll.

When the words *Chief Researchers: Mandy Hope and James Hunter* appeared, Mandy's heart skipped a beat. Everyone had stood up and was cheering. She looked over at James, who was blushing, and then around the room. Old Ernie Bell, who had helped them look after Lucky, was beaming, his eyes shining. The Spry sisters were dabbing at their eyes with lace-edged handkerchiefs. And Jason and Skye were talking excitedly, nineteen to the dozen.

'We shall have to get a television, Joan,' Miss Marjorie was saying. 'I insist.'

'Oh, I agree,' Miss Joan said. 'We must certainly purchase one. But how does one go about it?'

'I'm sure Jude and Rowan will help you,' Emily Hope said.

'First thing tomorrow,' Jude agreed.

'You did a grand job there, young Mandy,' Walter Pickard said, coming over to stand beside Mandy. 'And you, young James. And I'm pleased to say you couldn't tell nowt about where it were filmed. So no one's going to go meddling with them foxes.'

Suddenly the phone rang. Simon was nearest and picked it up. 'Mandy, it's for you,' he yelled over the hubbub of chatter and laughter.

Mandy squeezed her way through the crush. 'Hello?' She could hardly hear over the noise.

'Oh, Michelle,' Mandy said into the phone. 'Yes, everybody *loved* it.' She listened for a moment. 'What? Say that again,' she shouted down the phone.

Adam Hope was watching from the other side of the room and he clapped his hands for silence.

'The producers loved the programme,' Mandy relayed to the room, 'and they want Michelle to do a weekly series.' Everybody cheered. She paused, listening and then went on. 'And she says how do we feel about helping with some more research?' Mandy grinned at James who was nodding his head vigorously.

'Great, Michelle,' Mandy said into the phone.
'We'd absolutely love to!'

Badgers
– by the –
Bridge

One

'Is this all for me?' asked Mandy Hope's father, Adam, as he eyed the large bowl of trifle in front of him.

'No, it is not!' laughed Mandy. 'You're supposed to serve it out to everybody.' She nodded round the kitchen table where her family and friends were gathered for Saturday lunch at Animal Ark.

Mandy had been looking forward to this special lunch with friends and family all together. Adam and Emily Hope, Mandy's parents, had finished morning surgery, and Simon, their assistant, had stayed to lunch along with Grandma and Grandad Hope, Mandy's best friend James Hunter, and their special guest, Michelle Holmes. Michelle was the presenter of the popular radio series, *Wildlife Ways*, which had recently been made into a television programme too.

'Trifle for you, Michelle?' Adam Hope asked, picking up a serving spoon. 'Made by Mandy's own fair hand, you know!'

'Dad!' said Mandy. 'Michelle will think I never cook anything!'

'Yes, please,' Michelle grinned. 'It looks wonderful, Mandy.'

'It looks almost too good to eat,' declared her father, spoon poised over the trifle. 'Here goes . . .' But before he could plunge the spoon into the creamy top the door-bell rang.

'Who can that be at two o'clock on a Saturday afternoon?' Adam Hope groaned.

'Go and see, will you, Mandy?' said Mandy's mum.

'And tell them we're busy,' commanded her father, laughing.

Mandy jumped up from her seat and opened the back door to find Walter Pickard standing there.

'Hi, Mr Pickard. Can I help?' asked Mandy.

'Hello, young Mandy. I wanted a quick word

with your dad,' the elderly man replied.

Mandy hesitated. 'Ah, well, you see we've got guests . . .'

'Oh, I am sorry,' Mr Pickard said, looking embarrassed. 'I didn't mean to interrupt . . . It's just that I've found summat a bit odd . . .'

'Well, you'd better come in.' Mandy held open the door. 'It's Mr Pickard,' she called to the others. 'He's got something to tell you, Dad.' Everyone looked up and smiled a welcome at the elderly man.

'Hello, Walter,' said Adam Hope. 'Come on in.'

But Walter stood near the door, still uncomfortable at the sight of them all sitting down to lunch. 'I'm sorry to disturb you, Mr Hope,' he began.

'Not at all, Walter,' said Mandy's mum. 'Come and sit down. Get that spare chair from the corner for him, Mandy.'

'Yes, come and sit by me,' said Mandy's grandad. 'You look as if you could do with a bit of a rest.'

'Aye, well, I've just been up in Piper's Wood,' Walter explained, pulling up a chair. 'You know the place where Landmere Lane runs between the wood and that old quarry?'

Mandy nodded. 'So what was this odd thing you saw?' she prompted him.

'It weren't so much a *thing* as an *animal*.' Walter looked over at Adam Hope. 'See, first off I thought it were all right ...' His voice faltered.

'What was it?' Adam Hope prompted.

'Badger. Big young male, he was, in a right mess, an' all ...' Walter sat down heavily, and frowned, as if trying to puzzle something out.

'Oh, poor thing!' said Mandy.

'What was the trouble with it?' asked her dad.

Walter Pickard shook his head. 'I reckon he were dead,' he said.

'Dead?' Mandy echoed, horrified. 'But how?'

Walter shrugged. 'Looked like summat had had a go at him,' he said. A murmur went round the table.

'Any idea what did it, Walter?' asked Grandad Hope.

He shook his head.

'Perhaps some really fierce animal,' James suggested. He and Mandy both knew that most wild animals would fight an enemy to the death.

Walter shook his head. 'There's not many animals 'ud tackle a full-grown badger,' he observed.

Adam Hope nodded. 'I can't think of anything big or brave enough up in the woods around here,' he said. 'Can you, Michelle?'

Michelle thought for a moment. 'Not unless he got in a fight with a really fierce dog,' she suggested. Mandy shivered, remembering the time she and James had rescued an abandoned badger cub from a dug-out sett – in Piper's Wood, too!

'I'd better ring Ted Forrester,' Adam Hope said. Ted was the wildlife inspector at the local RSPCA unit and would want to know about the death of a protected animal.

'He'll need to go up there and collect the body anyway,' Simon observed.

Adam glanced round at the table, where everyone was now busy discussing the news. 'It'll be quieter in the office,' he smiled, and went off to phone Ted.

Mandy's mum sighed. 'We'd better wait and see what's happening before we start on the trifle,' she said. 'You know what Adam's like once he's on a case.'

Mandy smiled at her mother, knowing what she meant: her father was fascinated by wild creatures. If Ted Forrester needed any help investigating the dead badger, Dad would be off to Piper's Wood – guests or no guests!

'See, I wouldn't even touch the poor creature,' Walter was explaining to Grandma Hope, 'in case it were carrying a nasty disease. I've got my three cats to think of.'

Dorothy Hope nodded sympathetically. 'I know how you feel,' she said. 'I wouldn't want to risk my Smoky catching anything either.'

'So that's why I just covered that badger up with leaves and left it there. I knew Mr Hope 'ud know what to do about it,' Walter told her.

Mandy wished with all her heart that Ted Forrester would find the badger still alive. Even if it was badly wounded her father might be able to help it.

Just then, her father came back into the room. 'I'm meeting Ted Forrester in Piper's Wood in about quarter of an hour,' he announced. There was a cry of dismay from the rest of the party.

'I'll come with you,' said Michelle.

Simon nodded. 'Me too!' he said.

'But what about the trifle?' Grandma Hope protested. 'Mandy spent so much time making it . . .'

'We'll have some when we get back,' Adam told her. 'You carry on – we shouldn't be long.

Now, Walter, can you tell me exactly where you left the badger?'

Walter did so, at great length, while Simon got his emergency bag and Michelle fetched her jacket.

Mandy looked across at James, who nodded slightly. 'Take James and me with you, Dad, *please*,' she begged.

Mr Hope thought for a moment and then nodded. 'But we've got to get off right away – no messing about!' he warned.

Mandy and James were already rushing out to the Land-rover.

'We'll stay and clear this lot up,' said Grandma Hope, looking at the remains of the lunch party. 'We can have the trifle with tea when you all get back. You'll stay too, won't you, Walter?' she asked kindly.

Walter Pickard beamed. 'So long as you let me help you with all this clearing up. I'm a good little washer-upper!'

The others piled into the Land-rover and were soon off down the lane and through the village. They didn't say much; the party spirit had quite evaporated with the news of the dead badger.

'At least we got out of the washing-up,' Mr Hope said, trying to jolly them along a bit. But

Mandy couldn't laugh. She was wondering just what they would find when they arrived at the other end of Piper's Wood.

Mr Hope drove up to Landmere Lane, round the far side of the woods. When he turned off the lane they scraped and bumped their way up the rough forestry track until it became so narrow even the Land-rover could go no further.

'Everybody out!' he announced, pulling up.

They all piled out and stood looking into the wood.

'No sign of Ted Forrester yet,' observed Simon.

'He'll be along soon,' said Adam Hope, coming round to join them. 'Meanwhile, we can be looking for a silver-birch copse – that's where Walter said he'd seen the dead badger. Ted will find us when he gets here.'

The others all piled out and looked around. Piper's Wood was an old, mixed forest, with oaks and elms and beeches interspersed with younger silver birches. Adam led the way, pushing through the brambles which almost covered the path, and Mandy followed close behind.

'How on earth did Mr Pickard get through this lot?' James muttered.

'He didn't,' said Mandy. 'He was walking down from the top of the woods, remember. There's a bridle-path over there.'

Soon they pushed their way into a clearing in the birch woods, just as Walter had described, and the others caught up with them.

'Now, all we need to do is find the place Walter hid the badger!' said Mr Hope, surveying the scene.

Mandy followed his gaze anxiously. She was still half hoping they'd find the badger alive. If they found it in time maybe her dad could save it.

'Go carefully, just in case the animal isn't dead,' Simon warned, as they began their search.

Mandy's spirits rose. Just hearing Simon admit there was a chance of helping the poor badger made her feel better. She set off, determined to be the one who found him. They walked slowly and cautiously through the grasses and bracken, heads bent, eyes on the ground.

It was Michelle who called out, 'I think I've found him!' She prodded a heap of leaves with the toe of her boot.

They ran across to help her and soon they

were standing looking down at the sleek, grey-black body of a large, full-grown male badger. At first glimpse he appeared to be streaked with dirt and mud, but as Mandy looked more closely she saw it was blood that was staining his brindled grey coat. 'Oh, the poor, poor thing!' she whispered.

Simon crouched down beside Adam Hope and asked him something in a low voice. Mandy saw her father shake his head, sadly. 'There's no pulse,' he said simply.

The badger was dead all right. Mandy turned and blinked away the tears. Michelle came over and put an arm around her and gave her a little hug.

'I know it's hard, Mandy,' she said, softly. 'Working with wild animals always is, you know that.' Mandy nodded and sniffed hard.

'And it doesn't get any easier, either,' Michelle said. 'I'll always hate facing up to seeing a dead animal.'

'What do you think happened to him, Dad?' Mandy asked, brushing away a tear.

Her father pulled on a pair of rubber gloves and, kneeling by the body, began to examine it carefully. 'I can see the cuts and scratches now,' he said. 'And some deep bites round his neck.'

'So do you think he could have been fighting?' asked Michelle.

Mandy shuddered. 'Fighting with dogs, you mean?'

Michelle nodded. They all knew that badger-baiting was a 'sport' that had come to Welford once before. Perhaps it was all happening again!

'Not necessarily,' her father replied. Then he sighed. 'But it *is* a possibility.'

They stood there in silence, watching Simon clear the rest of the leaves off the badger. Mandy looked over at James and saw he was frowning.

'Are you thinking what I'm thinking?' he said.

'Bonser?' Mandy murmured. James nodded unhappily. Mr Bonser had been prosecuted for organising badger-baiting in Welford once before – mainly on evidence that Mandy and James had collected.

'Don't go jumping to conclusions!' Mandy's dad warned. 'Badgers have other enemies besides men and their dogs.'

'Bonser left the district after he was prosecuted, didn't he?' said James.

Mandy sighed, thinking about Mr Bonser. What if he had come back? What if this dead badger had something to do with him? Mandy felt herself going cold all over.

Suddenly they heard the sound of a car lurching up the track. A door slammed, and someone moved cautiously through the under-growth and worked their way along the bridle-path on the other side of the clearing. Mandy stiffened and looked across the clearing, hardly daring to breathe. Was this one of the badger baiters, she wondered, come back to bury the evidence? Could it be Mr Bonser himself?

Two

It was Ted Forrester who emerged from the opposite side of the clearing. Mandy gave a sigh of relief.

'Sorry I'm late,' Ted called, as he strode across to them. 'Right then – what have we got here?'

Adam shifted aside to let Ted take a look at the dead animal.

Ted whistled softly to himself as he examined the dead badger. 'Been in a bit of a scrap, he has,' he observed. 'Broken jaw and a nasty bite on his neck . . .'

'But the artery's not severed,' Adam Hope told him. Ted frowned. 'There's a couple of ribs broken,' Adam Hope continued. 'He could have punctured a lung.' He stood back and watched as Ted felt round the animal's body. 'Check the head carefully, Ted – found something interesting there just as you arrived.'

Ted gently felt all round the badger's narrow skull. 'Ahhh!' he breathed. 'Here it is.' He looked up at Adam. 'There's a fracture here.'

'That's right,' said Adam Hope. 'But there's no wound on the scalp – not even any teeth marks up there.'

'No,' agreed Ted. 'It wouldn't have happened during the fight.'

'So how did it happen?' asked Mandy, puzzled.

'I think he was hit,' Ted Forrester said softly.

'By a car, you mean?' James asked.

Ted Forrester stood up. 'By a tree, I suspect,' he said. He pointed across the clearing, back to the way he'd come. 'I think somebody must have chucked him into the undergrowth from over there and he hit this tree.'

'Threw him?' Mandy was outraged.

'I should think they threw him from a car or van,' Ted said. 'They probably drove into the woods along the track over there.' He gestured to the path. 'He was half dead anyway and they wanted to be rid of him.'

Mandy stared at Ted, absolutely horrified. Of course, she knew there were people who hated badgers. Some farmers believed they spread diseases among their cattle, but surely they would never get rid of them in such a brutal way. No, the only people who'd do that were . . .

'I'm afraid you may be right, Mandy,' sighed Mr Hope. 'It looks as if we're dealing with badger-baiting again.'

'What do you mean – again?' asked Michelle.

Swallowing hard, Mandy told her all about Mr Bonser's earlier activities, and the little cub, Humbug, whom they'd rescued from a dug-out sett. 'I never thought it would happen in Welford again,' she finished tearfully.

'Hang on, Mandy, we don't know for certain it has, yet,' said Ted, taking a black plastic bag from his pocket. 'I'll take this chap up to the lab on Monday, and have them run some tests. Give us a hand, will you, Simon?' he asked.

They gently placed the dead badger into the bag. Mandy watched, fighting back more tears. Beside her, she heard James swallow hard and sniff several times.

Ted sighed. 'I'll get some photographs and an official report. If this is a case of badger-baiting, we'll need all the evidence we can get.'

'Do you think you'll catch anyone?' asked James.

'We'll certainly be trying,' Ted said. 'I'll get the wildlife police officer on to it. But they're a crafty lot, these badger-baiters. Move off as soon as they see anybody official, like.'

'So it's best if somebody *unofficial* keeps an eye on them?' suggested Michelle.

'Well, perhaps,' Ted agreed, cautiously. 'Trouble is, if they don't know what they're doing they ruin the evidence and warn the blighters off.'

'Surely a video would count as evidence?' asked Michelle.

Mandy stared at her. 'You mean you're going to help?'

'Well, don't you think an item on *Wildlife Ways* would be useful publicity?' Michelle asked.

'Oh, yes!' cried Mandy. 'That's a great idea!'

'Hang about!' Ted interrupted. 'If those men see anything on TV they'll move off somewhere else and we'll never catch them.'

'We won't even mention Welford,' Michelle promised. 'Just a brief report on how to spot signs of badger-digging.'

Mandy felt a pang of disappointment: she'd been expecting Michelle to come up with something more useful than a few tips on badger-watching.

'We might pick up some useful information as we're filming,' Michelle explained. 'And if we can get a few shots of a dug-out sett – well, there's your evidence! I'm sure Mandy and James here will let me know if they spot anything worth filming.' She turned to smile at them.

'That would certainly be useful,' Ted agreed. 'But just remember these are dangerous men. Don't go doing anything daft all on your own, now.'

'Oh, I won't do anything all on my own,' Michelle assured him. 'Janie, my camera operator and sound technician will be with me.'

Ted Forrester nodded. 'A couple of badger-baiters were arrested down in Derbyshire a few weeks ago, tough as old boots they were, but not too bright. Said they were digging out foxes and got away with a fine!'

'So do you think they could have moved on up here?' Mr Hope suggested.

'Aye, they could have.' Ted nodded. 'Now I'd best be moving off down to Walton with this poor chap.' He bent over the body of the dead badger.

'Here, let me help you,' Simon said. 'He's quite a heavy load.'

Mandy watched as they lifted the bag between them and walked slowly across the clearing. *Just as if the badger is asleep and they don't want to disturb him*, Mandy thought. She sniffed loudly and wiped her hand across her face.

'Come on, Mandy,' said her father, gently. 'There's nothing more we can do here.'

A few days later there was still no news of the badger-baiters. Mandy and James took Blackie for a long walk each day in Piper's Wood, but they found no signs of digging out. When they cycled around Welford they kept a look-out for any strangers but they never saw any.

'How can we stop any more badgers getting hurt, if we don't know who's doing it?' Mandy asked her mum.

'All we can do is to watch and wait.' Mrs Hope smiled, her green eyes sparkling knowingly. 'And that's something you're not very good at, Mandy Hope!'

Mandy knew her mum was right, but with every day that passed she became more and more worried. Nobody seemed to be doing anything to stop the badger-baiters. Michelle was busy working on *Wildlife Ways* and Simon was off on a training course, which meant that Mandy's parents were extra busy with the surgery and home calls. Nobody had time to share her worries – except James.

'It's as if we'd never found that dead badger,' Mandy complained to James, as they cycled back from Walton one afternoon. 'I thought it would be all systems go, like the time we found Humbug.'

'It was Humbug who was all systems go,' James reminded her. 'Remember when he escaped in your grandma's basement?'

Mandy smiled as she thought about the little cub they'd rescued. 'Yes, he certainly kept us on our toes, didn't he?'

'At least there are no abandoned cubs to worry about now,' James said.

'I almost wish we *had* found an abandoned cub again,' Mandy complained. 'At least it'd give us something useful to do.'

'All we can do is await developments,' said James, in a serious voice.

'That's just the trouble.' Mandy shifted down a gear and pedalled furiously up the hill. 'There don't seem to *be* any developments!'

When they skidded up the drive at Animal

Ark, they saw Mr Hope packing a dog-cage into the Land-rover.

'Hi, you two,' he said. 'I'm just off out. Apparently there's a bit of an emergency over at Bleakfell Hall.'

'Oh – is it Pandora again?' asked Mandy. Mrs Ponsonby tended to be rather over-protective of her much-loved prize Pekinese.

'No, it's Toby this time,' Mandy's father said. 'He's had an accident.'

'Can we come with you?' asked Mandy.

'We can keep Mrs Ponsonby calm while you see to Toby,' suggested James.

Adam Hope looked at them thoughtfully. 'Well, we'll have to be quick. Mandy, you go and get some bedding for the cage. And James, could you ask Jean for a couple of towels, please?'

As they drove up to Bleakfell Hall, Mr Hope told them that Toby had been knocked down on the drive. 'Mrs Ponsonby's there with him,' he said. 'I told her not to move him.'

'Do you think we'll need to bring him back to the surgery?' Mandy asked, concerned. She knew that Mrs Ponsonby tended to exaggerate about any problems with her dogs, but this could be serious.

'Mrs Ponsonby thinks he's lost a bit of blood,' Mr Hope told them. 'We may have to take him back for a transfusion.'

'I hope not!' exclaimed Mandy in alarm. 'Mr Dewhurst's away, so you can't use Tilly as a donor.' Tilly, a border collie, was registered as a blood donor at Animal Ark.

'We've always got a couple of other donors we can go to in emergencies,' her dad reassured her.

'But don't you need to have some for every blood group so you can match the injured dog's blood?' asked James, who had just been learning about blood groups in science.

'It's easier with dogs than with humans, James,' Adam explained. 'We don't have to match the blood group for the first transfusion.'

'You mean you could use *any* dog's blood?' asked James.

'Yes – it's very useful in an emergency.' Mr Hope smiled. 'Mind you, I suspect Mrs Ponsonby might need treatment more than poor Toby!'

Mandy felt sorry for Mrs Ponsonby; she knew she'd be frantic, watching and worrying over her poor injured Toby. Mrs Ponsonby might be the bossiest woman in the district, but she adored her dogs.

'There she is!' cried Mandy, as they reached Mrs Ponsonby's driveway.

Mrs Ponsonby was sitting on a grassy bank by the wrought-iron gates of Bleakfell Hall. Even in this emergency she was her usual immaculate self, dressed in a flowered dress, broad-brimmed straw hat and bright pink gardening gloves.

'Thank goodness you've come, Mr Hope,' Mrs Ponsonby said, without taking her eyes off the little mongrel. 'I did just as you said – I haven't moved him.'

'Quite right, too,' Adam Hope told her. 'Now, let's have a look at him.'

Mandy and James stood behind Mrs Ponsonby while Mr Hope pulled back the blood-stained towel with which the little dog was covered. Mandy waited anxiously to hear her father's verdict on Toby's injuries.

'He's had a bad knock on the side of his face.' Mr Hope lifted up the dog's lip and examined his mouth. 'He's probably bitten his tongue, but there's no teeth damaged, no bones broken.' He stood up. 'We'll get Toby into the Land-rover and drive him up to the house,' he said. 'I don't think we need take him to the surgery.'

Once Toby was cleaned up, thoroughly

checked over, and given a sedative injection, he curled up in his basket and fell fast asleep. Mrs Ponsonby insisted on making tea for everyone. 'But we'll have it the kitchen so that I can keep an eye on Toby,' she said.

'Did you see the accident happen?' asked Mandy, stroking Toby's rough head to soothe him.

'I was on the terrace, dead-heading my roses, when I heard the screech of brakes and then Toby started yelping. Oh, it was pitiful! I ran down the drive . . .' She paused for a moment, dabbing at her eyes with a lacy handkerchief. 'I saw this dirty white van,' she continued, as she handed round the teacups. 'They must have been turning round in my driveway. People often do, I'm afraid.'

'Didn't they stop when they heard Toby yelping?' asked Mandy angrily.

Mrs Ponsonby shook her head. 'I called to them but they just shot off down the lane,' she said, 'leaving poor Toby . . .' Her voice faded as she gazed across at the little sleeping dog.

'Well, he's going to be all right,' Mr Hope told her soothingly. 'Just keep him quiet for a day or two. No long walks, and a soft diet until his poor mouth heals.' He sipped his tea. 'Bring him into the surgery for a check-up next week. And it's about time you had him microchipped, you know, Mrs Ponsonby. He's always wandering off.'

Mrs Ponsonby sighed. 'I know,' she said. 'I did get Pandora done when she was a pup. But then, she's such a valuable dog . . .'

'And so is Toby,' said Mandy, rather indignantly. Pandora was a prize Pekinese, but Mandy preferred the little mongrel. 'I mean,' she added hastily, 'all dogs are valuable to their owners.'

'And to dog-thieves,' added James, trying to be diplomatic.

Mrs Ponsonby nodded. 'Quite right, James,' she said, approvingly. 'I couldn't bear to lose him. Yes, Toby shall be microchipped next week.'

Mandy was sorry to have to leave Toby, but relieved that he wasn't badly hurt. She gazed out of the car window, waiting for the jolt of the narrow, hump-backed bridge ahead.

But, just as they got to the bridge, a white van appeared from the opposite direction, bouncing and lurching at top speed. The driver was sounding the horn and Mandy could see his passenger gesturing at them to get out of the way.

Mr Hope veered over on to the grass verge just as the van raced past, narrowly missing the Land-rover's wing-mirror. Mandy turned to glare at the driver and noticed that he was a surly-looking man with a ponytail hanging out of his baseball cap. The van sped up the lane, gravel spattering under its wheels.

'Well!' exclaimed Mr Hope. 'That was a nice exhibition of bad driving.'

'I wonder where they're going in such a hurry?' said Mandy, still peering through her window.

'Did you notice it was a dirty white van like the one Mrs Ponsonby said knocked Toby down?' James asked.

'Oh, there are lots of white vans on the road,' said Mr Hope, as he pulled out ready to cross the bridge. 'It may not be the same one.'

'The same kind of bad driver, though,' said Mandy thoughtfully, still peering out of her window. 'Wait!' she suddenly commanded. 'Stop the Land-rover!'

'I can't stop here, Mandy,' said her father. 'I'm blocking the bridge.'

'But Dad – I saw something moving in the grass down by the riverbank.'

'Probably a water vole or something,' he suggested.

'No! I could see something white or grey like . . .' Mandy's voice shook with excitement. 'Please, Dad, we've got to stop and look!'

Mr Hope was already driving slowly and carefully over the bridge. 'All right,' he sighed. 'I'll pull in on the other side. But for heaven's sake be quick – I haven't got long before evening surgery.'

'It wasn't a vole,' Mandy told James as they ran back over the bridge. 'It was something much bigger.'

'Like what?' James asked.

'Let's see.' They were slithering down the grassy bank now. 'It's down there, at the bottom,' whispered Mandy. 'Come on!'

They made their way cautiously down to the river and stood for a moment, peering into the long grass. 'I can't see anything,' James muttered.

But as he spoke, the grass seemed to ripple, shift, and then part. A narrow little head poked up and a pair of darting eyes examined them. James looked down in amazement as the grey coat and white stripe of a young badger appeared.

'I was right,' breathed Mandy.

'It's a badger!' exclaimed James.

'No, it's not, it's two,' Mandy observed quietly. 'Look!'

They watched as another head popped up, and another pair of eyes regarded them. Neither badger seemed worried by their presence, or in any hurry to run off.

'This is odd,' murmured James, who was a member of the local wildlife watchers' group. 'These two must have strayed down from the woods.'

'Look – that one's got a cut on its leg. We ought to take them back to Animal Ark,' said Mandy, decidedly.

James nodded his head thoughtfully. 'Something must have happened to disturb the sett if they've come all this way . . .' They were both silent for a moment.

'Do you think someone could have been – digging?' asked Mandy. 'And they've taken the mother away?'

James nodded. 'Maybe that's why the driver of that van was in such a hurry,' he said. 'We should have got its number.'

Mandy gazed at the badgers. It was too late to do anything about the men in the van, the main thing now was to take care of the young animals.

'We'll take them back to Animal Ark,' said Mandy again.

James hesitated. 'They're not tiny cubs like Humbug was,' he pointed out. 'Their claws will be sharper and they're much stronger. I doubt if we could catch them, never mind carry them back to the car on our own.'

Even Mandy had to agree with that. 'You go back and tell Dad,' she said. 'I'll keep watch here.'

'What will you do if they make a run for it?' asked James.

Mandy grinned. 'Run after them, of course. Go on!'

* * *

While James was gone, Mandy sat down in the grass close by the two young badgers, who had settled down to sleep again already, curled round each other like little grey commas.

There was definitely no sign of any adult badger to look after them, Mandy thought to herself. She sat watching over them, hardly daring to breathe, until James came back with Mr Hope – and a couple of towels from the back of the Land-rover.

'Take hold of a towel each and be ready to pounce when I give the signal!' Mr Hope ordered.

Mandy and James held their towels out in front of them and stealthily advanced on the badgers. As they closed in on the two little grey humps in the grass, Mr Hope stamped his feet hard. Startled, the two badgers leaped up and James and Mandy threw the towels over them. The animals squealed and wriggled and scratched and struggled, but they didn't manage to get free.

'Hold on tight!' called Mr Hope. 'I'll tie the ends of the towels up and make a sling.'

He pulled the corners of each of the towels together and tied them up so that each badger was trapped in its own little hammock.

'I'll bring the Land-rover back over the bridge,' said Mr Hope. 'Can you manage to meet me up there?'

Mandy and James nodded breathlessly. They hauled the struggling bundles up the bank and stood waiting until Mr Hope arrived. He opened up the back of the Land-rover and unlatched the dog-cage they'd brought for Toby. Mandy and James put the badgers in, still wrapped up in the towels, squeaking and scrabbling blindly.

'I'm sorry we frightened you,' Mandy told them. 'Don't worry now, you'll be safe with us.'

'Now Mandy, you know they can't stay with us,' warned her father, as he drove them all back to Animal Ark. 'We have quite enough animals to look after as it is.'

'Well, maybe Gran . . .'

'I don't think so. Remember what she said last time, after Humbug?' James reminded her.

'Yes,' Mandy sighed. 'No badger is ever going to set so much as a paw in my house ever again.'

'Well, then, there you are,' said her dad.

'They're probably old enough to be set free,' said James, glancing back at the cage.

'Free for what?' asked Mandy indignantly. 'For

the badger-baiters to catch once they've grown?'

'I'll ring Ted Forrester,' Mr Hope told them. 'He'll know where to release them, once we're sure they're fit enough.'

Three

When they got back to Animal Ark, they opened up the back of the Land-rover to see if the badgers were all right.

'I'd better give them a thorough check-up – I don't like the look of that cut,' said Adam Hope. 'But I don't want to take them into the surgery.'

'What about the garden bench?' suggested Mandy. 'We could put the dog-cage down there.'

'Good idea,' her father agreed. 'Can you and James give me a hand to lift it?'

They carried the cage into the garden and put it on the bench. Mr Hope took each badger out in turn and checked them over to see if they had any other injuries or disease. Mandy and James sat with him, watching out in case the wriggling little animals got loose.

'Well, they're a bit scrawny and underfed,' Adam Hope said eventually, placing the second one back in the dog-cage. 'But they're basically healthy. I've cleaned up that wound and there's no infection. I'll ring Ted Forrester and ask what he thinks we should do about releasing them.'

'You mean they can be released right away?' asked Mandy.

'Well, yes, they're about six months old – big enough to look after themselves, now we know they're OK.' Mr Hope went off to phone Ted. Mandy sat by the cage watching the badgers gloomily.

'They do have to go back into the wild as soon as possible, Mandy,' James reminded her.

'I know,' she agreed. 'But where will they live if their sett has been dug out?'

James grinned at the young badgers, now rolling and tumbling around the dog-cage. 'They'll soon find a new sett – the woods are full of them.'

'But they won't find a new mother,' Mandy

retorted. 'What if she was taken by the badger-baiters?'

They sat in silence for a moment, both remembering what had happened to that poor, battered animal up in Piper's Wood. Mandy looked up anxiously as her father came back. Mr Hope was shaking his head. 'I can't get hold of Ted Forrester until tomorrow,' he said. 'He's gone off to Derbyshire.'

'I bet he's gone to check up on those badger-baiters he told us about,' said James.

'So does that mean we can look after these two badgers?' asked Mandy hopefully.

Her father smiled at her. 'Just for tonight,' he said. 'Until Ted gets back.'

James and Mandy put the cubs into a spare rabbit hutch out on the patio, and gave them some puppy-food and water to drink. The badgers ate all the puppy-food, then curled round each other and settled down to sleep.

'Oh, aren't they lovely?' said Mandy. 'I hope Mr Forrester stays away for a few days so that we can go on looking after them.'

But the next afternoon she came in from cleaning the outdoor kennels to find Ted

Forrester in the kitchen drinking tea with her father.

'Oh,' said Mandy, trying to hide her disappointment. 'You're back then, Mr Forrester.'

'I am that,' he agreed, smiling. 'I've come to collect those young badgers you've been taking such good care of.'

Mandy's heart sank. 'Where are you going to take them?' she asked.

'Well, they're a healthy young pair, thanks to you,' Mr Forrester told her. 'But they really ought to be set free up in the woods.'

'They'll be free but not safe,' said Mandy sadly. 'What about the badger-baiters?'

'Now, Mandy, don't go making wild assumptions,' said her father. 'We don't know that there are any badger-baiters in Welford.'

'I'm afraid we do now, Adam,' Ted Forrester told him. 'I've had a report from the lab and it was just as we suspected: the badger's wounds were made by a dog, although they weren't bad enough to have killed him.'

'So he was still alive when they threw him out in the woods?' asked Mandy.

'Only just. That lung was punctured – he'd lost a lot of blood.' Ted sighed.

'And the fractured skull?' asked Adam Hope.

Ted nodded. 'Yes, that's what finished him off,' he said. 'Hitting that tree when they threw him out.'

'Ugh!' Mandy shuddered. 'Anybody who could do that deserves to be shot!'

'You don't mean that,' said her father.

'Well, somebody's got to do something,' said Mandy stubbornly. 'They've got to be stopped.'

'I know how you feel, Mandy, but we don't know who killed the badger,' her father pointed out. 'They might well be miles away by now.'

'I think they're still around here somewhere,' Ted Forrester said. 'I've found signs of digging up in Piper's Wood. That's probably where the two youngsters came from.'

Adam Hope nodded. 'There were two men driving off in a white van close to where we found them,' he said. 'They could have been up in the woods earlier.'

'So you definitely can't take them back up there,' Mandy said indignantly. 'Piper's Wood isn't safe.' She was determined that these badgers were not going to fall victim to the baiters.

'As a matter of fact, it's probably the safest place,' Ted reassured her. 'The badger-diggers have done all they can up there. If they haven't found what they want they'll try somewhere else.'

'And if they *have* got what they want?' asked Mandy anxiously.

'In that case, there might well be rumours of a fight any time now!' Ted replied grimly. 'So keep your eyes open and your ears to the ground, and let me know of anything suspicious.'

Next day, Mandy was distracted by rumours of another kind. She had just finished mopping the surgery floor when Mrs Ponsonby brought Toby in for his check-up, and to have his microchip inserted. She stood in the doorway, looking down at the damp tiles. 'Is it quite safe, Mandy?' she asked doubtfully.

'Oh, yes, Mrs Ponsonby,' Mandy grinned. 'They're non-slip tiles.'

'No, I mean are you sure there are no germs?' Mrs Ponsonby looked pointedly at Mandy's mop. 'Presumably some animal has been sick – or – er – something?'

'It was just a little puddle,' Mandy explained. 'Nervous kitten,' she added, smiling.

'I think I'll carry him, just in case,' said Mrs

Ponsonby, sweeping Toby up in her arms, stepping daintily across the floor and settling herself and Toby down on the nearest chair. Toby was obviously feeling much better. He strained at his lead, trying to get down from Mrs Ponsonby's lap.

Mandy went over to greet him. 'Hello, Toby,' she said, gently scratching his ears. 'Are you feeling better, then?' Toby wagged his tail and looked up at her.

'Oh, he's much better now,' said Mrs Ponsonby. 'Although I think his little mouth is still sore. I'm feeding him on baby-food and ice cream – he loves it!'

'I'll bet he does,' Mandy smiled. 'But I think Dad will probably tell you it's time to put him back on his normal diet.'

'Oh, yes, of course. Once your father has checked him over it'll be back to liver and biscuits, won't it, my pet?' Mrs Ponsonby beamed and shook her floral hat at Toby, who twisted round and tried to lick her powdery nose, his tail wagging.

'Mrs Ponsonby?' Jean Knox, the receptionist, called. 'Mr Hope's ready for Toby in the surgery.'

Mrs Ponsonby started to get to her feet but

Toby beat her to it – he jumped off her lap and scuttled across the floor.

'Naughty Toby! Come back here!' called his mistress. But Toby bounded all over the waiting-room, keeping well out of Mrs Ponsonby's reach.

'I'll take him in,' Mandy offered, catching hold of the dog's lead and giving it a little tug. Toby trotted obediently into the surgery after her, with Mrs Ponsonby following behind. Mandy picked the little dog up and stood him on the examination table in front of her father.

'Hello, Toby,' Mr Hope greeted him, gently feeling him all over. 'Better today, are we?'

It didn't take Mr Hope long to establish that Toby was quite recovered. 'He has a beautifully clean mouth now, Mrs Ponsonby,' he announced. 'So, Toby, are you ready for your identification chip?'

'I'm so glad you suggested it,' said Mrs Ponsonby. 'It will be such a relief to know he's safe.'

'Yes, it's important with a dog who's given to wandering off,' said Mr Hope, feeling round Toby's neck for a loose fold of skin.

'Especially just now,' said Mrs Ponsonby, the

flowers on her hat shaking as she nodded gravely.

'Why just now?' Mr Hope looked puzzled.

'Haven't you heard about all those dogs going missing?' Mrs Ponsonby asked eagerly.

'Whose dogs?' asked Mr Hope, turning to look at her.

Mandy waited anxiously for Mrs Ponsonby's reply. She couldn't bear to think of anyone losing their dog.

'Well . . . er . . . nobody I know – but they do say dogs are going missing in the area,' Mrs Ponsonby replied, rather sheepishly.

Mandy breathed a sigh of relief. This was only one of Mrs Ponsonby's bits of gossip.

'I think you'll find those rumours are exaggerated, Mrs Ponsonby. I've only heard of one missing farm dog. I expect he went off rabbiting on his own . . .' Mr Hope was ready to put the chip in Toby's neck now. 'Can you pass me the tagging gun, please, Mandy?'

Mandy took the instrument out of its box and handed it to her father. He skilfully pressed it into the skin between Toby's shoulders and clicked the trigger. Toby yelped, then wagged his tail happily and turned to lick Mr Hope's hand as the vet stroked him reassuringly.

'There now, that wasn't really painful, was it?' He patted the little dog and turned to Mrs Ponsonby. 'Jean will fill in the records and give you his card, Mrs Ponsonby. Keep it in a safe place!'

'Oh, I will,' Mrs Ponsonby assured him. 'I'll tuck it into Pandora's file.'

Mandy had to smile at the thought of the little Pekinese having her own special file. Toby, being a mere mongrel, obviously didn't qualify for one! She lifted him down off the table and led him back to reception. 'Now we'll be able to find you, no matter where you wander off to,' she told him.

'Well, I hope he never meets that dreadful driver again,' said Mrs Ponsonby, following her to Jean's desk.

'Do you think he's still around?' asked Mandy, with interest.

'I'm certain,' said Mrs Ponsonby. 'The vicar himself was telling me he had an unfortunate meeting with a shabby white van and a very rude driver, just the other day.'

'Where?' Mandy's curiosity was really aroused now.

'That very narrow bend on Landmere Lane,' Mrs Ponsonby said. 'He was quite shocked at the man's driving.'

'Did the vicar get a good look at the driver?' asked Mandy.

'I should think he was far too busy keeping on the road,' said Mrs Ponsonby. She turned to Jean. 'Do you know, they wouldn't even move over. They took the wing-mirror off his car as they drove past!'

Jean tut-tutted sympathetically and prepared the bill on the computer. Mandy gave Toby's lead to Mrs Ponsonby and went off to put the mop and bucket away. When she came back into reception, James had arrived with Blackie, his black Labrador, following behind.

'Any news of the badgers?' he asked.

Mrs Ponsonby looked across at him sharply. 'What badgers?' she demanded.

Mandy shook her head at him. She didn't want to add to Mrs Ponsonby's store of gossip.

'Oh – just some information I need for the Welford Wildlife Watchers,' he said, quickly.

'Come on, Blackie,' called Mandy. 'You ought to be outside.'

They left before Mrs Ponsonby could question them further.

'What was all that about?' asked James, once they were outside.

'That white van – it's been seen around Welford again,' Mandy told him.

'So?' he asked.

'So it could mean the badger-baiters are still hanging around,' said Mandy excitedly.

'If the white van really has anything to do with them,' James reminded her.

'Well, I don't want Mrs Ponsonby to hear anything important,' said Mandy. 'You know how she gossips.'

James nodded. 'So what are we going to do this afternoon?' he asked. 'It's a bit too hot for a long walk.'

'Not for a short one, though,' said Mandy. 'I want to talk to Walter Pickard.' James looked at her curiously. 'Ted Forrester says that if the baiters have found another badger, there's bound to be rumours of a fight in the area,' she told him. 'Walter's sure to have heard if there are any.'

James looked at his watch. 'Walter's usually outside the Fox and Goose about this time, having a pint with Ernie Bell.'

'Right, we can walk Blackie down there,' said Mandy, crouching down to pat the Labrador. 'There's something else I want to tell you.'

As they walked down to the village green,

Mandy told James about Mrs Ponsonby and the rumours about the dog thieves. 'She seemed to think that dogs were going missing all over Welford,' Mandy said in a worried voice. 'You know, you ought to have Blackie microchipped.'

'Oh, come on, who'd pinch old Blackie?' James laughed. 'And anyway, he never goes anywhere without me.'

'You never know,' said Mandy seriously. 'Why don't you have it done? It'd be for his own safety.'

James sighed. 'It's a good idea,' he said, pushing his glasses back up his nose. 'But I think it would cost too much.'

They plodded along, both of them watching Blackie scuffling happily along the hedgerow.

'Well, I could find out from Mum and Dad,' said Mandy.

'Would you?' asked James.

'I'll ask them when we get back,' Mandy promised.

'Thanks,' he said gratefully. They were close to the Fox and Goose now and Blackie went bounding on ahead. 'Greedy guts! He's off to beg crisps from Walter and Ernie,' laughed James.

But it was not Blackie's lucky day: the men at

the table where Walter and Ernie usually sat were strangers, and not very friendly strangers either.

'Get aaht of it!' A man wearing a baseball cap kicked a thick, heavy boot out at Blackie, just missing his head.

Mandy saw that the man had a little ponytail hanging over the back strap of his baseball cap. She thought he looked familiar, but before she could say anything to James, the other man started on Blackie.

'Gerroff, you stupid animal!' he said, aiming a beer-mat right into the dog's face. Blackie backed off, tail between his legs, puzzled by such rough treatment.

'Did you see that, Mandy?' said James, indignantly. 'They can't get away with that!'

'No – wait!' Mandy whistled Blackie over and, for once, Blackie obeyed. 'Come on!' Mandy took James by the arm and led him towards the back of the pub.

'Where are you going?' James protested. 'We won't find Walter and Ernie out here.'

'I've got something to tell you – quick!' Mandy almost dragged him round the corner and into the car park. 'Listen, those two men back there, didn't you recognise them?'

James thought for a moment. 'I thought I'd seen the one in the baseball cap before, but I can't think where,' he said.

'I think you saw him driving the white van on the bridge last weekend,' Mandy told him.

'You mean he was that terrible driver?' James's eyes sparkled behind his glasses. 'Are you certain?'

'No,' she admitted. 'Not absolutely certain, but they look familiar, and the driver did have a ponytail sticking out of a baseball cap . . .' Her voice tailed off as she gazed around the car park. Suddenly she gripped James's arm. 'Look – over there!' She pointed to a dusty, battered white van, parked by the wall. 'I'm sure it's the same van!' she breathed. 'Mrs Ponsonby said it had been seen around the village.'

'That's probably the same white van that knocked poor Toby over,' said James.

'And almost crashed into us on the bridge,' Mandy added. 'Now I'm *sure* they're the same men.'

'Yes, but what can we do?' asked James. 'We can't just go up to them and accuse them of dangerous driving. You saw what they did to poor Blackie.'

Before Mandy could reply, Blackie raced across the car park, head down, tail up, sniffing hard as if he was on the trail of a rabbit. He stopped at the old white van, sniffing at the back doors. Watching him, Mandy remembered how they had helped catch Bonser, the badger-baiter, before. James had made a plaster cast of a tyre print they'd found by a dug-out sett, and matched it up with a bald tyre on Bonser's van.

'Wait here a moment, James, keep an eye on those men,' she said, glancing back to the table where the men were still sipping beer and talking.

Mandy followed Blackie to the van and crouched down to take a good look at the tyres. But Blackie kept getting in her way, jumping about excitedly, sniffing and yelping by the back door of the van.

'Stop it, Blackie!' hissed Mandy. 'You'll knock me over!'

As Blackie quietened down, Mandy became aware of strange sounds coming from the back of the van. She heard scratching and scrabbling, and the doleful whine of an animal.

'James!' she called excitedly, forgetting about the men at the table for a moment. 'Come over here.'

'What's the matter?' asked James, running to join her.

'There's a dog shut up in here,' she said. 'And no windows open! We've got to get those men to let it out before the poor creature suffocates!'

But before she could even stand up the two men came rushing into the car park. 'Hey you, get away from that van!' yelled one of them, gesturing to Mandy and James.

'And get that flippin' dog out of 'ere,' snarled the other. He aimed a passing kick at Blackie, shoved Mandy out of the way and clambered into the driver's seat. His companion jumped into the other side and then, revving the engine fast and loud, the driver swung the van round, looking neither right nor left and narrowly missing James.

Mandy ran over to join him and together they watched the lurching van disappear down the road.

'They've done it again!' Mandy was outraged. 'It's time somebody reported them for their bad driving, and for cruelty to animals! Just think of that poor dog in the back there – he's almost cooking!'

'Well, we *can* report them now,' said James.

He pulled a ballpoint out of his jeans pocket and began to scribble on the back of his hand. 'I've got their number – and you can give a good description of them both.'

Mandy beamed at him. 'Well done, James!' she said. 'What would we do without him, eh, Blackie?'

'Where is Blackie?' James said, spinning round.

'Gone to make some more friends,' smiled Mandy, pointing back to the pub door. Someone was just coming out of the pub and Blackie was running up to them, tail wagging madly.

'It's Mr Forrester,' said James, squinting into the sun.

James and Mandy ran back to the pub entrance.

'Did you see those men in the white van?' asked Mandy excitedly, not even stopping to say hello.

Ted shook his head. 'I've been inside this past half-hour, talking to Julian Hardy,' he said.

'The two men in the white van,' Mandy hurried on. 'They've just been here . . .' She gulped and caught her breath. 'You must do something, Mr Forrester, they've got a dog in the back and no windows open and . . .'

'Hey, calm down, Mandy,' said Ted Forrester. 'Now, come and sit here and tell me all about it.' He led them to the bench where the two men had been sitting a few minutes earlier. 'You look all hot and flustered,' he said. 'I'll get us all a drink.' He looked down at Blackie. 'And some water for Blackie,' he added thoughtfully.

So, as they sipped their cola, James and Mandy told Ted what they'd just seen. James gave Ted the number of the van and Mandy gave him a vivid description of the men, right from the baseball caps down to their dirty boots.

'And the one who kicked Blackie has a straggly ponytail and a London accent,' Mandy ended.

'Well done, you two!' said Ted Forrester. 'Now maybe we're beginning to get somewhere with this badger business.'

'You mean those two men are definitely involved?' asked Mandy.

'Well, they sound suspiciously like the men who were prosecuted in Derbyshire,' Mr Forrester said. 'I checked up on them when I was down there. If it's the same pair, they were pretty disorganised, so we may be in with a chance of catching them out.'

'So are you going to call the police?' asked James, examining the number on the back of his hand.

'And then they can pick them up,' Mandy suggested eagerly.

But Ted Forrester shook his head. 'What for?' he asked. 'A bit of careless driving? Leaving a dog in an unattended vehicle for ten minutes?'

Even Mandy agreed there was no point in that. If the two men thought they were being watched by the police, they'd leave the district and carry on with their badger-baiting somewhere else.

'So what should we do next?' she asked, keen to be doing something.

Ted Forrester took a deep breath. 'I'm just off to a meeting with Michelle Holmes,' he said. 'She's going to include the badger item on the next *Wildlife Ways*; we might get some response from that.'

'Yes, but what shall we do right now?' asked Mandy, although she knew what the answer would be.

Ted Forrester shrugged. 'We'll just have to wait for their next move,' he said, draining his glass.

'But what if they manage to catch another badger?' Mandy slumped dejectedly on to the table.

Ted Forrester picked up their glasses and stood up. 'You keep a good look-out,' he said, 'and we'll try to stop it happening.' He went to the pub door, waved his free hand to them, and disappeared.

'Come on, Blackie,' said James. 'Time to go home.'

Mandy sighed and got up to follow them. Watching and waiting was all very well, she thought, but it might take months to collect any evidence. And all the time those two beautiful young badgers would be growing bigger, more useful in a fight with dogs . . . She shuddered. They had to do something to stop the badger-baiters – and they had to do it soon!

Four

By the weekend there was no more news of the white van and Mandy had begun to think the two men had moved out of the district altogether.

'Well, at least they're not causing any trouble around here,' Mandy's dad said at breakfast on Saturday morning.

'That's not the point,' said Mandy indignantly. 'They'll be causing trouble for some poor animal *wherever* they are.'

'Yes, love, but you can't protect all the badgers in the entire country!' Her mother smiled, knowing that was exactly what Mandy would do, given half a chance.

'We could drive around looking for clues,' said Mandy, looking up from her cereal hopefully.

'Oh no we couldn't,' said Adam Hope, getting up from the table. 'I've got more important things to do than scour the countryside for stray badger cubs.'

'But Mum's taking surgery and it's just the day for a drive in the countryside.' Mandy gave him her most winning smile.

'No it's not,' he said, ruffling her hair. 'I'm off to attend a fascinating conference on bovine TB. So you'll just have to keep yourself busy, Mandy. And stop worrying about those badgers – Ted Forrester's got it all under control.'

So Mandy wandered off to the residential unit, where the animal patients stayed while they recovered. She cleaned out the cages, filled up the water bowls, and gave all the sick creatures a bit of her own special care, to help them get better. It was a job she usually enjoyed more than anything else in the world, but today all she could think of was the badgers up in the woods, with no one to protect them. If only there was something she could do to help them!

Mandy spent the whole morning in the unit. At

least it kept her busy, even if it didn't stop her worrying. At midday, she locked up the last empty kennel and went off to start making the sandwiches for lunch.

'Why don't we eat in the garden?' suggested her mother, coming in from morning surgery. 'Then I'm going to prune that holly bush that's spoiling the line of the hedge – you could give me a hand.'

'Good idea,' said Mandy, giving her mother a grateful look. She would be glad to have her company. She took the sandwiches outside while her mother brought a jug of fruit juice and two glasses.

'You know, I'm sure Ted Forrester's got everything under control, Mandy,' Mrs Hope said, as they settled down to eat. 'It's just that he can't prosecute until he's got some evidence.'

'Well, we won't get any evidence just by sitting around waiting,' Mandy pointed out. 'Somebody's got to do something.'

Her mother sighed. 'Michelle Holmes is coming round for tea later, maybe she'll have some news.'

'Good,' said Mandy, brightening. 'If anyone's going to get things moving, it'll be Michelle.'

*   *   *

It was idyllically peaceful in the garden at Animal
Ark. Mandy settled down on the grass with her
wildlife magazine, while her mother, perched
precariously up a ladder, clipped at the branches
of the overgrown holly bush. The afternoon was
filled with the sounds of the countryside: the
soft ripple of woodpigeons in the trees, the low
grumbling of Sam Western's cows coming in off
the meadows for milking . . . And the burr-burr
of Mrs Hope's mobile phone.

'Oh, help!' cried Mrs Hope. 'I've put it down
somewhere. Quick, Mandy, find it!'

The sound was coming from near the rockery
where Mandy's mum had dropped her old
denim jacket – with the phone in its pocket.
Mandy ran quickly across the lawn and picked
it up.

'If it's for me, take the message carefully,'
called her mother from the topmost rung of
her ladder. 'I'm on emergency call until Dad
gets back.'

'You'll be an emergency call yourself, if you
don't take care!' Mandy said. She extracted the
mobile phone from her mother's jacket pocket
and pressed the answer button.

'Animal Ark – can I help you?' she asked, in
her most official voice.

'Mandy – is that you?' James sounded breathless.

'Yes, of course it's me,' said Mandy, rather cross to find she'd wasted her best professional manner on her oldest friend.

'Thank goodness,' replied James. 'I've been ringing the house but nobody answered.'

He sounded so upset that Mandy forgot to be annoyed. 'Why, what's the matter?' she asked. 'Is it an emergency?'

'No, yes, well, sort of . . .' James's voice trailed off in confusion.

'Sort of? What do you mean?' asked Mandy. 'Come on, James, just tell me what's happened.'

'It's Blackie,' he blurted out.

'Blackie?' she repeated. 'Is he ill?' She looked anxiously across the garden at her mother, who was still clipping away at the hedge.

'No, he's not ill, he's missing,' said James.

'Missing? You mean he's run away?' Mandy was surprised. Blackie wasn't the most obedient of dogs, but he wasn't a wanderer either. He loved his home and his food too much to stray far.

'I don't know.' Mandy heard James's voice wobble as he swallowed hard. 'He was sniffing about by our gate, waiting for his morning run, and by the time I'd told Mum we were going and fetched the lead he'd disappeared.'

'He won't have gone far, not Blackie,' said Mandy, consolingly. 'Do you want me to come and help look for him?'

'Well, I've already been out calling him – but I'm sure between the two of us . . .'

Mandy sensed a hint of relief in James's voice. 'I'll be right over!' she said. She switched the phone off and took it across to her mother. 'I'm going over to James's,' she said, 'so you'll need to keep the phone where you can reach it.'

'Just shove it in the pocket of my jeans,' said Mrs Hope. She clambered down a couple of rungs and Mandy pushed the phone into her mum's back pocket, quickly explaining about Blackie's disappearance.

'I'm going up there to help James look for him,' she said.

'Don't forget Michelle's coming over for tea,' her mother called, as Mandy headed for the gate. 'Bring James back with you, if you like, and Blackie, when you find him.'

Mandy decided to walk up to James's house so that she could look for Blackie on the way. There was just a chance that he might have taken himself off down to Animal Ark. She checked both sides of the lane, calling and whistling, but Blackie didn't come to her. She was just about to give up the search and run straight on to the Hunters' house when a car pulled up behind her. Mandy turned and saw Mrs Ponsonby waving at her from the car window.

'What do you think you're doing, Amanda Hope, wandering all over the road like that?' she called. 'You must keep to the right and face the traffic on these narrow lanes, you know.'

Mandy flushed. 'Sorry, Mrs Ponsonby,' she said. 'I was looking for Blackie.'

'The Hunters' dog?' replied Mrs Ponsonby, with interest. 'Has he gone missing, too?'

'What do you mean, *too*?' asked Mandy.

'Well, I was telling your father in the surgery the other day about all the other dogs that have gone missing around here. Only your father didn't seem to believe me . . .'

'Oh, I'm sure he did,' said Mandy. She felt a heavy knot gathering in her stomach. What if Mrs Ponsonby's stories were true? What if Blackie . . .

'Could you give me a lift?' she asked, suddenly. 'I'm on my way up to James's house now.'

'Well, I suppose you'll be safer in the car than

wandering all over the lanes,' Mrs Ponsonby told her severely.

Minutes later, Mrs Ponsonby dropped her at James's house. Mandy waved her off and turned to find James hanging miserably on to his gate.

'I've been all round the lanes,' he told her, 'and he's not here. We really need our bikes to go further afield.'

'I haven't got my bike,' said Mandy. 'I walked part of the way to see if I could find Blackie, then Mrs Ponsonby gave me a lift.'

'And Dad's got our car in town so Mum can't drive us up to the woods . . .' James looked so

close to tears that Mandy's heart went out to him.

'We're better off on foot,' she told him. 'We can search more thoroughly that way.'

James sighed. 'Mum's rung all round,' he said. 'And everyone's checked their outhouses and everything . . .' His voice faded and he looked away, kicking absently at the gatepost. 'After all you told me about those dogs going missing,' he muttered, 'I should have got Blackie microchipped straight away . . .' He sniffed loudly and Mandy could tell he was near to tears. She wondered whether he too was thinking of that poor, frantic dog in the overheated white van in the pub car park. Was that a stolen dog they had in there?

'Look,' she said hastily. 'Why don't we go back to Animal Ark? He might have gone down the old bridle-path and maybe I missed him.' She knew there wasn't much chance of that, but she felt she had to do something. 'Come on, James, it's worth trying.'

James looked doubtful. 'But if you were calling him he'd have come out on the road,' he said.

'Well, he might have.' Mandy smiled, remembering all the times Blackie had ignored their calls. 'But then again, he might not.'

After James had popped back to tell his mum where they were going, he and Mandy were soon jogging down the old bridle-path back to Animal Ark, whistling and calling Blackie's name all the way. But it was no use, Blackie was nowhere to be seen.

When they eventually arrived back at Animal Ark, James's face was white with worry.

'Look, as soon as Dad's back, I'm sure Mum will drive us up to look in the woods,' Mandy said, desperately trying to cheer him up.

But when they went into the kitchen they found Michelle making herself a cup of tea.

'Hi, you two!' she said cheerfully. 'Mrs Hope's just gone out on a call – she said to expect you back any time. Get yourselves a mug and come and tell me all the news.'

Mandy hesitated; she knew how James was feeling. He'd want to be out looking for Blackie, not sitting at the kitchen table drinking tea. On the other hand, Michelle was a visitor and Mandy felt she should stay with her. And, she suddenly realised, Michelle did have her Jeep with her . . . Quickly, she told Michelle all about Blackie's disappearance.

'So we wondered whether you could drive us

up to the woods to look for him,' Mandy ended, smiling up at Michelle.

But, to her surprise, Michelle was looking quite grim.

'I saw a couple of rough-looking men with a dog this morning,' she said, slowly. 'In fact, they were by that copse just above your house, James.'

James looked up. 'In a white van?' he asked.

Michelle nodded. 'And I saw them bundling a dog into the back of it.'

Mandy's eyes widened. 'A dog?' she said breathlessly.

'Was it . . .' James couldn't go on.

'Was it a black Labrador?' Mandy helped him out.

Michelle thought for a moment. 'Well, it was about that size,' she said. 'But they'd just about got it into the van before I drove past so I didn't see the colour. I thought they were just coming back from a walk, so I didn't look too closely.'

Mandy thought of the way those men had treated Blackie that morning outside the Fox and Goose. Her heart was thumping and she felt sick to the pit of her stomach. 'We don't know it was those two men,' she said, trying to convince herself as well as James. 'We don't even know it was Blackie they had with them.'

James turned to her, his face white and strained. 'But we don't know where Blackie is either,' he pointed out.

'Before we jump to any conclusions, we'd better do a bit of checking up,' said Michelle briskly. She looked around the kitchen. 'May I use the phone, Mandy? My mobile's in the car.'

Mandy nodded. 'Of course,' she said, glad to have Michelle's help.

Michelle rang the RSPCA and asked for Ted Forrester. Mandy and James sat looking at one another, listening intently as Michelle told Ted about Blackie's disappearance.

'Yes, right, thanks,' said Michelle eventually. 'I'll tell them that.' She put the phone down and turned back to the table, looking even more serious.

'Ted says he'll contact the police about Blackie.' She looked at James very seriously. 'I'm afraid they've had several reports of local dogs going missing.'

'So Mrs Ponsonby was right,' murmured Mandy. 'But *why* are they going missing?'

Michelle sighed and reached out to touch James's shoulder. 'Ted Forrester thinks the two men I saw earlier may be part of a badger-baiting ring,' she said, gently. 'Apparently when they were prosecuted in Derbyshire there were rumours of untrained domestic dogs being put in the ring.' She frowned. 'Of course, fighting dogs are usually terriers. I can't believe that anyone would be stupid enough to think that a Labrador . . .'

Mandy felt her stomach lurch. 'You mean they might have taken Blackie off to . . . to . . .'

'To fight a badger?' said James, in a quiet, anguished voice.

Michelle sighed. 'We just don't know,' she said.

Five

James took a long, shuddering breath. 'We've got to find Blackie,' he said in a small voice. 'Before anything happens to him.'

'Yes, but we don't know where he is,' Mandy pointed out. 'If only we knew where to start looking.'

'He's with those men in the white van, I know he is.' James turned to look at Michelle. 'We've just got to find them,' he said. 'You'll help us, won't you?'

Michelle hesitated and Mandy knew she was trying to let James down lightly. 'There's no point in our racing around the countryside,' Michelle said. 'We could be looking in entirely the wrong area.'

'But we must do *something*,' pleaded James. 'We can't just sit here waiting for . . . for . . .' He sniffed loudly and turned away.

Mandy knew just how awful he must feel. She couldn't bear to think of Blackie being badly treated, perhaps even being set up to fight a big, strong badger – and all she and James could do was wait. Her eyes filled with tears and she put out a hand towards James, desperately trying to think of something to say.

But before she could speak, the phone rang. Mandy raced across the kitchen and picked up the receiver. 'Animal Ark,' she said efficiently. 'Can I help you?'

'Aye, perhaps you can, Mandy,' said Ted Forrester's voice. 'You see, that old white van has been spotted parked by the quarry on Landmere Lane . . .'

'Oh, that's great! Are you going over there now?' asked Mandy excitedly.

'I can't, I've got an emergency call about ten miles away.' Ted told her. 'But I'll check the quarry out after that.'

'What about the police?' Mandy asked. 'Surely they can do something if the men have got stolen dogs . . .'

'They could prosecute them for stealing dogs, that's all,' Ted told her. 'We still need to catch them badger-baiting.'

'But think of those poor, frightened dogs,' Mandy protested.

'I know how you feel, Mandy,' said Ted Forrester. 'But now there's a chance we can stop this nasty business for good. Then we'll have no more frightened animals – dogs or badgers.'

Mandy sighed. 'Well, I suppose the police will sort it out,' she said.

'That's the trouble, there's a big football match down in Walton today,' Ted Forrester told her. 'The police won't be able to send anyone in till that's over.'

'You mean there's nobody to keep an eye on the van?' gasped Mandy, horrified.

'Well, that's what I want to ask Michelle about,' Ted Forrester said. 'And I thought maybe if Simon or your dad was around . . .'

'Michelle's here,' said Mandy, quickly handing over the phone.

Mandy and James waited while Michelle talked to Ted Forrester.

'Yes, I think I can do that . . .' she said. 'See you later!' She went on to ring Simon, quickly telling him all that had happened. She arranged to meet up with him in the woods above the quarry. '. . . and I'll ring Janie – will you pick her up with all the gear? We might get some good footage from this,' she ended. She put down the phone and turned to Mandy and James. 'You don't need to worry about Ted or the police keeping an eye on those men – I'll be there in minutes.'

'But what about us?' asked Mandy. 'You can't expect us to sit here waiting patiently.'

'Not while Blackie's missing,' added James.

Michelle hesitated. 'Those men are very dangerous, violent people,' she said. 'Ted Forrester warned me not to go anywhere near them.'

'So if you're not going near them we can come and keep watch, too,' said Mandy triumphantly.

'Oh, please, Michelle,' James said. 'I've got to see if Blackie's there.'

Michelle looked doubtful. 'What would your parents say?' she asked them.

'They know we'll be safe enough with you and Simon,' said Mandy, with a winning smile.

Michelle suddenly grinned back at her and lifted her hands in a gesture of submission. 'I can't deny that,' she said. 'Come on!'

* * *

Michelle didn't want to go straight along Landmere Lane in case they met up with the men in the white van, so Mandy guided Michelle along the little twisting back lanes. Eventually they found themselves edging cautiously along a narrow, stony track with a steep drop on the driver's side.

'I don't like this very much,' said Michelle, through gritted teeth. 'Are you sure your dad comes this way, Mandy?'

'It's all right, you can stop there.' Mandy pointed to a flat ledge which jutted out above Landmere Lane. 'We'll be able to see everything that happens from here.'

'There doesn't seem to be much happening just now,' James muttered, peering down at the empty road. 'Even the white van's gone.'

'They must have moved off since Ted got that report,' answered Michelle.

'I wonder if they've taken Blackie with them,' James said anxiously.

'Even if they have, they'll come back here,' Michelle assured him. 'Ted thinks they're going to use this place for the fight. Apparently the barn have been rented by a certain Mr Bonser.'

'Bonser! I knew it!' Mandy exclaimed.

'That man's not getting his hands on my dog,'

said James angrily. 'We've got to get him back!'

'Don't panic, James,' said Michelle. 'The police will be here soon, and then we'll put those villains away where they can't do any more harm.' She opened her door and stepped out on to the path. 'I'll have to find a better place for filming. We're too far away up here,' she observed, surveying the scene below.

Mandy and James got out of the Jeep and joined Michelle. They could see the barn quite clearly from there, set up against the old quarry face, with ramshackle outhouses projecting at each end.

'It seems an odd place to build a barn,' said Michelle.

'They used to herd the sheep down there in winter, to shelter from the blizzards up on the fells,' James explained.

Mandy tried to imagine those hardy old shepherds, driving their animals down this very track, battling through the icy wind and the snow, to bring them here to safety. But if the badger-baiters had their way it would soon be a place of terrible danger for animals. The warning shriek of a jay suddenly interrupted Mandy's thoughts and she jumped. 'Listen!' she said. 'Somebody's coming!'

They all stood quite still as the sound of heavy footsteps crunched up through the undergrowth. Mandy tried to think up a credible excuse for their being up there – bird-watching? Michelle's binoculars were still in the Jeep. Badger-watching? Not in broad daylight . . .

'It's Simon!' said James joyfully.

But Michelle was less pleased. 'Simon – what are you doing here on your own? I thought you were bringing Janie and all the gear?'

'I've got it all,' he assured her. 'There's no room for two cars up here so I parked further down. Janie's scouting around looking for a

good spot for filming. You go down and check it out. We'll stay up here and watch the road.'

Michelle nodded. 'The binoculars and the phone are in the Jeep,' she told him, before heading off down the track.

Simon, Mandy and James climbed back into the Jeep. Below, they could see Janie, stepping cautiously towards the back of the barn, with a large, professional video camera on her shoulder. Michelle joined her and they disappeared from view, around the other side of the barn.

'I hope nobody sees them,' said Mandy anxiously.

'No – the back wall of the barn is close to the quarry face,' said Simon. 'They're well hidden.'

'Come on, let's have a closer look at the place.' Simon reached into the glove compartment for the binoculars, and found a chocolate bar.

'Trust Michelle to carry vital supplies,' he grinned, breaking it up and passing the pieces round. 'You'd better eat while you've got the chance,' he ordered.

Mandy was surprised at how hungry she felt. It seemed a long time since her lunch with Mum. She looked out across the valley, and noticed that the sun was dipping behind the hills. Dad would be getting back home now, she thought, and Mum would have found the note she'd left on the kitchen table. The football match would be over, so the police and Ted Forrester should arrive very soon. But where were the supposed badger-baiters and their stolen dogs? Mandy munched her chocolate and sighed deeply, wishing she could do something more than just watch and wait.

Suddenly Simon nudged her and pointed down to the lane below. When Mandy looked she saw the dirty white van lumbering into the yard and pulling in by the ramshackle outhouses.

'It's them!' breathed Mandy, peering forwards to get a better view.

She saw the two men from the Fox and Goose get out and look all round, apparently to check that no one was watching them. Then they made their way to the barn doors, flung them open and disappeared inside.

As the doors slammed they heard the sound of yelping and yapping, and several mournful howls coming from the white van.

'That's Blackie!' whispered James angrily. 'I'm sure it is.'

'You don't know that,' said Simon reasonably. 'There are several dogs in there. We don't even know that they've taken Blackie. Labradors aren't fighting dogs.'

'The one that's howling is Blackie, I just know it is,' said James desperately.

Simon shook his head. 'It could be any dog,' he said, trying to keep James calm.

But James was sure he had heard his dog. He pushed his door open. 'I'm going to get him out!' he cried.

'No!' Simon leaped out of the driver's seat and grabbed James by the shoulders, blocking his way. 'If we're seen they'll call the whole thing off.'

'Good,' said James. 'I don't want Blackie to fight.'

'I know you don't,' said Simon. 'But unless we allow them to set the fight up we're not going to get the evidence we need.' Simon put his arm round James's shoulders. 'You're not going down there. Those are dangerous men and you might get hurt.'

'Blackie will get hurt if he has to fight the badger,' muttered James desperately. 'You've got to let me get him out before those men come back.'

'Too late,' Mandy interrupted, pointing down at the barns. 'They're coming back now.'

They all watched as the two men walked to the back of the van and unlocked it. They reached in, each grabbing a couple of dogs, pulling them along by the ropes round their necks. Mandy saw a black Labrador hanging back, refusing to shift, so that the men had to drag him along on his bottom, howling all the while.

'Blackie!' whispered James. 'I've got to get him!'

'No!' repeated Simon, gripping James hard. 'We've got to wait and see what happens.'

Mandy longed to rescue poor Blackie but she knew they had to wait for Ted Forrester and the police. Her eyes filled with tears, and, as she blinked them away, she saw a big blue van pulling into the yard.

'Look!' she said, pointing downwards. 'Who do you think that is?'

James pushed up his glasses and peered down to the barn. 'It's Bonser!' he whispered.

They crouched down at the edge of the path, watching as Bonser went round to the back of his van and struggled to pull out a heavy sack full of something that squealed and struggled as he dragged it roughly across the yard to the barn.

'He's brought the badger,' breathed Simon triumphantly. 'Now we've got them!'

Six

For a moment Mandy's spirits rose. They had caught Bonser and the two dog-thieves red-handed with the dogs and the badger. Surely that would be enough evidence to get them prosecuted? But she suddenly realised that they still couldn't confront the men on their own. If they tried, the badger-baiters would just get away in the vans.

And there was still no sign of Ted Forrester or the police.

'What are we going to do?' she asked Simon.

'Let's get down there and stop them!' James hissed. He was crouching at the edge of the track, almost quivering with rage, looking as if he'd throw himself down the hillside any moment.

'No, get back into the Jeep before anyone sees us,' Simon said, looking hard at James. Before they could protest he opened the Jeep door and pushed James into the back seat. Mandy followed, flopping down beside her friend.

Simon was already calling the police on Michelle's mobile phone. 'Yes, yes, I understand,' he was saying. 'Just get them here as soon as possible – please!'

'What did they say?' Mandy asked Simon.

'The crowds are still leaving after the football match. Some of them will be along soon,' he told her.

'So, what do we do now?' asked James.

Simon sighed heavily. 'I don't think there's anything we can do. We've just got to sit it out and wait.'

The three of them sat in glum silence, looking across the quarry. Mandy tried not to think about Blackie, down there in the barn with those other dogs, all waiting their turn to fight the terrified badger. She stared out of the window of the Jeep, wishing that the police or Ted Forrester would arrive.

Suddenly she heard the noise of an engine!

But instead of a police car she saw a red van edging cautiously up the track towards the barn. Mandy sat up straight and looked again. A battered black car was following the red van – and then another van, and another car, all following on, sticking close to one another.

'What's going on?' she whispered.

'Is it Mr Forrester and the police?' asked James, leaning across Mandy to look out of the window.

'I don't know,' said Mandy, 'It's difficult to see down there and they haven't got their lights on.'

Simon had found Michelle's binoculars and he turned them on the trail of vehicles now approaching the barn. 'No, it's not the police,' he said. 'It's the spectators.'

Mandy looked at the men emerging from the parked vehicles. They strolled up to the barn door, laughing and chatting just as if they were going to a play or a concert in the village hall! 'You mean all these people have come to watch?' she asked incredulously.

'And to bet,' said Simon.

'On what?' James asked anxiously.

'On the outcome of each fight,' Simon told him gently. 'A great deal of money changes

hands at these events. That's something else
we can get them for – illegal gambling.'

'Who cares about that?' said James fiercely. 'I
just want Blackie back safely!'

'Of course you do,' said Mandy. She looked
anxiously at Simon, who was still peering
out of the window, binoculars pressed to
his face. 'Any sign of the police?' she asked
him.

Simon lowered the binoculars and shook his
head. 'I'm sure they'll be here quite soon,' he
said, glancing at James's white face.

But would it be soon enough? Mandy
wondered. What if Ted Forrester or the police
didn't arrive in time to stop the fighting? What
if Blackie was the first dog to fight? She glanced
at James, who looked sick with worry. Unable
to think of anything to say to comfort him,
Mandy turned to the window and jumped back
in surprise as she realised that someone was
standing close by.

'Michelle!' She wound the window down.
'What are you doing back here?' she asked.

'I've come back to get my camcorder,'
Michelle explained. 'I think I can get a few extra
roving shots of the spectators. They'll be useful
evidence.'

'Are you and Janie all right down there?' Simon asked.

'Yes, everything's fine,' Michelle reassured him. 'We found a series of vents in the back wall of the barn and Janie's going to film through those.'

'Isn't it too dark?' asked Simon, sounding surprised.

Michelle shook her head. 'There are a couple of floodlights set up in the barn,' she explained. 'Janie's already got footage of the pit.'

'The what?' asked James sharply.

'They've dug a shallow pit in the earth floor so that the animals . . .' Michelle was stopped by a fierce glare from Mandy.

'. . . can't run away,' James finished. He reached across Mandy and pushed his face through the window. 'Why don't you stop them?' he asked Michelle. 'You're going to all this trouble just for your stupid television programme when you could be rescuing those poor dogs.'

Mandy pulled him back. 'They can't do that,' she said. 'It isn't safe.'

Michelle nodded. 'That's right,' she said. 'There's a lot of men there now and they won't want us reporting what we've seen . . .'

'All we can do is to film them in action,' said Simon, 'and leave the rest to the police.'

'But what if it's Blackie's turn to fight before the police get here?' James demanded. 'He might be killed!'

'They were getting a couple of terriers set up when I left,' Michelle reassured him. 'Blackie should be safe for a while.'

'And the police should get here soon,' Simon comforted him.

James turned away and buried his head in his arms.

'Can't we do anything to stop the fighting?' Mandy asked desperately. She couldn't bear to think of the badger having to face those two fighting dogs.

'Ring Ted Forrester and tell him to get a move on!' Michelle suggested. 'I'll take my camcorder and get back down there now.' She headed towards the back of the Jeep, collected the camera and disappeared back down the track.

Simon rang Ted Forrester's mobile number while Mandy and James sat silently in the back of the car listening to one half of the conversation.

'. . . things are moving quickly now,' Simon ended, after briefly recounting their progress so far. 'We need to get someone here fast if we're to stop them.'

He listened gravely to some instructions.

'I see,' he replied. 'Well, if that's what you think we should do . . .'

He turned off the phone and sat for a moment, deep in thought.

'Is he on his way?' asked Mandy tentatively.

To her relief Simon nodded. 'He's still a few miles off,' he said. 'But he's spoken to the police and they seem to have got things under control. I left a message at Animal Ark, Mandy. We might need a vet.'

Mandy turned to touch James's shoulder. 'You see, it won't be long now,' she said.

'But will it be soon enough?' James replied. He twisted restlessly about in his seat. 'I'm fed up with waiting and watching.' He thumped his fist uselessly on the Jeep door. 'We've got to do something,' he muttered.

'OK – let's do something,' said Mandy. 'Have you got a pen?'

James stopped hitting the door and stared at her. 'Of course,' he said, scrabbling in the back pocket of his jeans and producing a chewed-up old ballpoint. 'What do you want it for?'

'I thought we could collect all the car

registration numbers,' said Mandy.

'That's a great idea,' said Simon enthusiastically. 'It may be too dark down there for Michelle to film them.'

'It's too dark for us to see many of them from up here,' James pointed out. 'Some of them are parked right under this bank.'

'We'll start with the ones we can see,' said Mandy. At least this would give James something to do, she thought.

But Simon was pointing to a clump of bushes lower down the track. 'You'll get a better view from there,' he said. 'Just make sure nobody sees you.'

'OK,' agreed Mandy, looking at James. 'We promise to keep out of sight.'

Simon turned to James.

'Yes, OK, I promise,' James said, hastily. 'Come on, Mandy, let's get on with it.'

'Remember – you report back here in ten minutes,' said Simon, as they clambered out of the car.

They made their way silently down the track to the hiding-place.

'I'll read the numbers and you write them down,' Mandy told James, as they settled down in the bushes. They had a good view of the

derelict outhouses now, and Mandy got a glimpse of Michelle creeping behind some bushes on the edge of the yard, taking shots of a few late arrivals. *Collecting evidence*, thought Mandy, *just like we're doing*. She peered forwards and whispered the first number to James.

As she peered down she noticed someone emerging from one of the doors at the side of the derelict outhouses. With a shiver of recognition Mandy saw it was Bonser. She could just make out his sharp, narrow features. He strode out of the doorway, dragging a big dog behind him. It was Blackie!

Mandy hoped that James wasn't looking in

that direction. But of course, as soon as he heard Blackie's protesting whimpers, he was on his feet. 'He's getting him ready to fight!' he cried. 'My Blackie!'

He called the dog's name in a hoarse whisper, and, for a moment, Mandy panicked as Blackie turned and appeared to look up at them. Bonser cursed and pulled Blackie's head back down to the ground.

'Get down, you stupid animal!' they heard him say, as he dragged Blackie into one of the other buildings. 'What's this thing doing here, you idiots?' he roared. 'Where's the other terrier?'

'No, James!' whispered Mandy, frantically tugging at his arm.

For a moment she thought he would plunge into the undergrowth and go hurtling down into the yard but James turned and ran up the track to Simon. 'Bonser's got Blackie down there,' she heard James pleading. 'I've got to do something.'

'I know,' agreed Simon. 'Here – you ring Ted Forrester and find out what's going on.' He handed James the mobile phone. 'Tell him it's urgent, a matter of . . .'

'Life and death,' muttered James, already pressing buttons.

Mandy was frantic with worry and there was so little she could do to help. Well, she decided, at least she could go on collecting evidence. She shuffled back into the clump of bushes and tried to concentrate on registration numbers. Even as she looked and scribbled she could hear terrible sounds coming from the barn now: the raucous screeches of the badger, the yapping and squealing of a dog, and the men's shouts urging them on to fight. Mandy's hand shook and she had to pause to take a deep breath, forcing herself to concentrate on the job in hand. Gritting her teeth, she worked her way steadily along the row of vehicles.

She'd just written the final number when she saw the barn door open and a couple of men came out, carrying something between them. They went to the now-familiar dirty white van, opened up the back and threw their load inside. Mandy realised, with a sickening shock, that it was a dog. The wounded animal now lay whimpering and twitching, on a sack in the back of the van.

'Lost a bit on that, didn't yer?' she heard one man say.

'Aye,' agreed the other man. 'I thought I'd got her trained, but she's none so keen.'

By the light flooding from the open barn door, Mandy could see the first man's stringy ponytail hanging from the back of his baseball cap and she recognised him as the dangerous driver of the white van who had stolen Blackie. The two men slammed the van door and turned to go back into the barn.

'I shouldn't put yer money on this next 'un,' the first man was saying. 'That's no fighter either.'

The other man grinned. 'Better than that daft Labrador,' he said. 'What did you bring that up 'ere for? Bonser was none too pleased. It won't last two minutes if you put it in to fight.'

The man with the ponytail shrugged. 'He wanted six more dogs. The lurcher got away. I thought it might be a bit of fun. Come on, let's get back!'

Mandy crouched in the bushes, trembling with anger, but glad that James was too busy talking to Ted Forrester to have heard that. Blackie was in danger and there was nothing they could do!

Seven

Mandy stood for a moment, peering down into the barnyard. Dusk was creeping across the valley now; soon it would be too dark to see anything. Or anyone, she realised, an idea dawning: if the dogs were kept in the old stable between fights she could sneak in and set them all free. With luck, she might even be in time to rescue poor Blackie and the other dogs before their turn came to fight the badger. Taking a deep breath, she plunged through the undergrowth and scrambled down the bank, landing neatly on top of a car bonnet. *So far, so good*, she thought.

She crawled round the cars, making her way

through the shadows towards the stable where she'd seen Bonser with Blackie. There was no noise from the barn now. What if they were about to start the next fight? Forgetting all about keeping hidden she raced across the yard and flung the stable door open.

Suddenly the yard was flooded with a brilliant light. Mandy turned and was almost blinded by the headlights of vehicles pulling into the yard. She shaded her eyes with a hand and saw the RSPCA Land-rover. Ted Forrester had arrived at last!

And not only Ted Forrester, but several police vehicles and . . .

'Mum!' called Mandy joyfully, as she saw a slender figure emerging from the Land-rover.

Mrs Hope turned. 'Mandy! What on earth do you think you're doing down here?'

'Oh, Mum, I was taking down car numbers, but I heard them – they've got Blackie and – oh, quick . . .' Mandy was almost incoherent with worry and relief.

'It's all right, love, it's over now. Come on, let's get you inside!'

Mrs Hope took Mandy by the arm and led her towards the stable. Just then, two of the policemen flung open the double doors of the barn and a couple of spectators rushed out, almost knocking Mandy and her mother down. The policemen gave chase and soon pulled both men down.

'Come on, Mandy,' said her mother. 'I think we'll be safer inside.'

Just as they reached the stable door, a small figure overtook them and swept past.

'James!' cried Mandy. 'Where are you going?'

'Blackie,' he called back, and rushed into the barn.

'No, James, wait for us!' called Mrs Hope.

James stopped. A large crowd was milling around inside, some people trying to get to the doors, others being lined up against a wall by the police.

'Where's Blackie? James asked, peering through the crowds as Mandy and Mrs Hope caught up with him.

'Don't worry,' Mandy told him. 'Ted Forrester will find him – look!' She pointed to the left of the crowd where Ted was bringing a string of dogs from the outhouses into the barn.

'Blackie!' cried James, as he tore across the barn. Mandy watched him hurl himself towards Ted and the black Labrador, who was covered in dust and grime from the abandoned outhouse.

Blackie gave a sharp yelp of recognition and desperately pulled at his rope. Ted Forrester let him loose and, once released, Blackie bounded up to James, wagging his tail happily. James hugged his pet as if he would never let go.

'Thank goodness he's safe,' Mandy said to her mother.

'Well, let's hope so – I'd better go and check that he's all right,' said Mrs Hope.

They went over to the dogs and Mrs Hope quickly ran her hands over Blackie's coat and checked his eyes and mouth.

'Apart from being a bit dirty, he's come to no harm,' she said, wiping her hands on some paper towels she always carried in her bag. 'You two take him and wait in the car. I've got to help Ted Forrester with the badger.'

As Mandy watched her mother walking briskly across the barn she suddenly caught sight of Bonser. He was backing away from the crowd in the centre of the barn, eyes darting everywhere.

Mandy grabbed James's arm. 'Quick – get back into the shadows!' she ordered.

'I thought we were going to take Blackie to the car,' he protested.

'Bonser's over there,' Mandy told him. 'Look, he's getting away!'

She nodded in the direction of Bonser, who was edging his way along the wall towards the doorway now. Mandy looked around for help but everyone was too busy, and it was so noisy no one would hear if she shouted a warning. She pressed back against the doorpost and gestured for James to pull Blackie into the shadow of the wall. The three of them stood, waiting for Bonser to reach the door.

As he got close to the open door, Bonser started to run. Mandy quickly stuck her leg across the doorway and the heavy man crashed to the ground, pulling her with him. Mandy tried to grab hold of his coat, but Bonser roughly shoved her out of his way. Mandy heard him cursing and scrabbling as he tried to pick himself up. He was going to escape, she thought despairingly, and nobody had even noticed!

But a sudden outburst of barking proved her wrong. Blackie pulled away from James and stood over Bonser, looking terribly fierce.

'Well done, Blackie!' Mandy murmured, scrambling up. 'Hold him there, boy!'

'Don't worry, Mandy,' grinned James, picking up the rope lead. 'We'll both hold him here all right!' Bonser cautiously stood up, pressed against the wall. Blackie snarled at him in a very convincing manner. Mandy suddenly remembered the man who'd been carrying the injured dog, the man who laughed at the idea of Blackie fighting.

'You can fight, can't you, Blackie?' Mandy said. 'When you need to.'

'Yes, he can,' said James proudly, 'but you'd better get a policeman to come and see to him.' He nodded in Bonser's direction.

When the policeman arrived he led Bonser off to join his two friends, the men with the dirty white van. From the shelter of the barn doorway, Mandy and James watched as they were arrested and cautioned.

'Good riddance!' said a cheerful voice behind them. 'And we've got enough evidence to keep them all shut away for quite some time.'

They turned to see Michelle, still carrying her camcorder.

'Did you get shots of the spectators, too?' asked Mandy.

Michelle shrugged. 'Unfortunately, I don't think the light was good enough,' she said.

'Well, we got some car numbers.' Mandy held up her arm, which was covered in ballpoint jottings from knuckle to elbow.

'Great! That'll help us identify the drivers,' said Michelle. 'And Janie's got some footage of that first fight. She says it's quite horrific.'

Mandy shuddered at the thought of the fight that had already wounded one little dog – the one which had been flung in the back of the dirty white van. Then she realised that the dog must still be in there, cold and frightened and maybe bleeding badly!

'I've got to find Mum,' she muttered, leaving James and Michelle to comfort Blackie.

The police had taken most of the men away now, and Mandy soon found her mother down in the badger-baiting pit with Ted Forrester. Ted was just shutting the badger into a carrying-cage as Mandy slid down into the shallow pit and went over to them.

'I've set her jaw. She'll need to rest for a while,' Mrs Hope was saying, as she closed her vet's bag.

'Aye – that's a nasty bite on her throat,' Ted said.

Mandy peered down and saw that the badger lay shivering on the floor of the cage. Her neck was bound up, but blood was already seeping through the bandage. Her eyes flickered and twitched, even though they were closed.

'Oh, poor thing!' cried Mandy. 'Is she unconscious, Mum?'

'She's in deep shock,' Mrs Hope told her. 'I've injected a mild tranquilliser to help her rest.' She turned to Ted. 'Make sure she's kept warm, and give her plenty to drink when she wakes up.' Mrs Hope checked the cage once more. 'I've cleaned her wounds but they'll need watching in case they go septic.'

'Don't worry, we'll take good care of her,' Ted promised.

'Good, I'd rather not use antibiotics if I can help it.' Mrs Hope looked round the barn. 'Now, what about those stolen dogs?'

'They're coming back with us,' Ted told her. 'There was only one fight and according to Janie only one dog got injured.'

'OK, let me have a look at it,' said Mrs Hope, clicking her bag shut.

Ted Forrester shook his head. 'Unfortunately we can't find her anywhere,' he said. 'Probably run off somewhere by now. We'll never find her in the dark.'

'Oh, I know where she is!' exclaimed Mandy.

'I should have thought about her sooner . . .'

'Where is she?' asked her mother.

'Outside in the back of the white van,' Mandy said, urgently. 'I think she's badly injured. Please, Mum, you must come and see – quickly.'

'The lass is right, you'd best take a look,' nodded Ted Forrester. 'You go on up there. I'll see to the badger.' He lifted the cage up out of the pit.

'Will she be all right?' asked Mandy anxiously.

'She's in good hands with Ted,' said her mother. 'Now, where's this van and the little dog?'

Mandy led her mother outside, where she saw the van clearly in the police car headlights. 'There it is!' she cried. 'Come on!'

They both rushed across to the van but stopped when a young policeman stepped out of the shadows.

'Nobody's to touch this vehicle,' he announced, indicating the blue and white police tapes which were tied around the door handles.

'But there's an injured animal inside,' protested Mandy.

The policeman shook his head. 'Sorry, young lady,' he said. 'I've got my orders. This van is going to be examined for evidence.'

'Yes, of course it is,' said Mrs Hope. 'But you see, I'm the local vet and I believe there's an injured dog in there.'

'Oh, sorry, it's Mrs Hope, isn't it, I didn't recognise you . . .' In his confusion, the young policeman turned to open the van doors – and then turned away again very quickly.

'Phew! It's a bit nasty in there,' he muttered, pulling out a handkerchief and holding it over his mouth.

'Don't worry,' Mrs Hope assured him. 'I'll deal with it!'

The policeman stood aside as Mandy and her mother looked into the van. Mandy saw that the terrier lay on the filthy sack, eyes closed, blood seeping from a deep neck wound and oozing on to the floor of the van.

'Oh, you poor, poor dog,' cried Mandy, her eyes filling with tears.

Her mother quickly examined the mangled little body. 'We'll have to get her back to the surgery quickly,' she said. 'Mandy – fetch a fleece and a sling from the back of the Land-rover.'

'Can I help?' asked the policeman, without looking into the van.

'Go and find Ted Forrester, the RSPCA inspector,' said Emily Hope. 'Ask him to phone

Animal Ark and tell my husband to be ready to receive an emergency.' She clambered into the back of the van. 'Go on, both of you!' she commanded.

Leaving the man muttering into his handset, Mandy raced round to the Land-rover, collected a sling and a fleece for the poor dog, and ran back to the van.

'Here you are, Mum,' she said. 'How is she now?'

Her mother shook her head. 'She's in a bad way, I'm afraid, love. Can you get in here and help me lift her on to the sling?'

Swiftly Mandy scrambled into the van.

'Lift her head,' said her mother. 'Gently now.'

The dog was shivering violently and was obviously unconscious. 'Easy does it,' murmured Mrs Hope, tucking the fleece around the dog and sliding the sling towards the edge of the van. 'Come on, Mandy, we'll carry her to the Land-rover.'

As they emerged from the back of the van the policeman came back. 'Ted Forrester's ringing your husband right now,' he told Mrs Hope. He looked in at the little dog now she was neatly tucked under the fleece. 'I'll help you carry it to your car,' he said.

'Thanks – take her head,' said Mandy. 'I'll go and find James and Blackie.' Now that she knew the little dog was in safe hands, Mandy wanted to check that James and Blackie were OK. Leaving the other two lifting the sling out of the van she headed back towards the barn where she found James, sitting on the ground, cuddling Blackie.

'What's all this about a missing dog?' James asked Mandy.

'We've found her now, but she's badly injured and we're taking her to Animal Ark,' she said.

'I'm going back with Mum right now.'

'I'll go with Simon, then,' said James. 'I can use his mobile to ring home.'

As soon as Mandy and her mum pulled in to Animal Ark, Mr Hope came out of the surgery, already wearing surgical gown, cap and rubber gloves. He took one look at the terrier and shook his head doubtfully. 'She's in a bad way,' he observed, quietly.

'I know,' sighed Mrs Hope.

'I should have told you about her sooner,' moaned Mandy. 'I'm so sorry!'

'It's not your fault,' her mother told her. 'You had to help James with Blackie and I had to see to the badger.'

'And she's here now,' said Adam. 'The sooner we get to work on those wounds, the better.'

But before they could move the dog, Simon pulled on to the drive.

'I thought you might need a hand,' he said, as he got out of his car.

'I do,' smiled Mr Hope. 'Take the other end of this sling, will you?' Together they carried the unconscious dog up to the surgery.

'Aren't you going with them?' Mandy asked her mother. Somehow she felt the more people helping the little dog, the better her chances would be.

Mrs Hope shook her head. 'I'm far too dirty for the surgery,' she said. 'I'll go and get cleaned up and then join them.'

James and Blackie emerged from Simon's car just then, both of them standing begrimed and rather miserable on the drive.

'And Blackie needs cleaning up too,' smiled Mrs Hope. 'Put him in the animal shower, Mandy, he'll feel much better after a wash.'

James and Mandy took Blackie off to the showers. Mandy put Blackie under the showerhead while James fetched a towel. Blackie sat under the spray, turning accusing brown eyes on Mandy as she approached with the shampoo bottle. Blackie wriggled and squirmed away from her, determined to escape from the dreaded shampoo. He looked so tragic that Mandy could only bring herself to dab a little here, a little there. As James came up with the towel, Blackie lunged forward to greet him again.

'No, Blackie – sit!' James commanded, putting the towel aside. 'You'll feel better when we've finished.'

Blackie looked doubtful, but for once he

obeyed. Holding him by the scruff of the neck, James quickly rubbed in the shampoo and Mandy rinsed it off with the shower. They had to repeat the operation twice over before all the grime came out and by that time Blackie crouched under the spray, looking utterly miserable and resigned to his watery fate.

Blackie was happier when James rubbed him all over with the towel and Mandy groomed him with the big dog-brush. 'You're beautifully smooth and glossy again now,' James told him.

'But not very dry,' Mandy added, as Blackie shook himself for the hundredth time, still spraying them with the last few drops of water from his thick coat.

'Quite right, Blackie,' said James. 'After all, we need a wash, too!'

Blackie's thick, dark coat took a long time to dry out properly, so they took him into the house and sat him by a radiator in the kitchen. Mandy fetched some dog-food and a bowl of milk and Blackie gobbled up the lot, as if he'd missed a dozen meals instead of only one.

'Steady on, Blackie,' Mandy scolded him. 'You'll make yourself sick!'

'I could do with a snack myself,' said James, looking hopefully around the kitchen.

'We'd better clean ourselves up first,' Mandy reminded him. 'Then you can put the kettle on while I make a few sandwiches. Mum and Dad are always ready for something when they've finished in the surgery.'

They had just made a pile of sandwiches when Mr and Mrs Hope and Simon came into the kitchen.

'I've fixed up the terrier,' Mr Hope told them, as Mandy and James passed round mugs of tea and cheese sandwiches. 'Luckily the wounds haven't become infected – yet.'

'She'd have no chance if they did,' declared Simon. 'She looks as though she's never been properly fed in her whole life!'

'She's lost a lot of blood,' Mrs Hope told them. 'Her test showed a very low count.'

Mandy's heart sank. She'd thought that once they got the little dog to the surgery she'd soon get better but now it seemed even her dad wasn't sure she'd pull through. Surely there was something more they could do?

'Can't you give her a transfusion?' she asked.

Her mother sighed. 'Dad has tried phoning the owners of all of our regular donors, but a lot of people are out on a Saturday night,' she said.

'We'll just have to wait for tomorrow morning,' added Mr Hope. 'If we still need them by then, that is.'

He exchanged serious looks with Simon, and Mandy knew he was thinking the dog might not live that long. Her eyes filled with tears and suddenly she wasn't hungry any more.

The others sipped tea and munched sandwiches, the silence punctuated only by Blackie's heavy sighs as he slept by the radiator. His coat had dried out now, back to its usual glossy sheen, and he looked the very picture of canine contentment.

'Well, at least there's one healthy, happy dog here,' smiled Simon, looking down at him.

James smiled and leaned over to stroke his beloved pet. Mandy was really pleased to see James looking so happy again, now Blackie was safe and sound. But she couldn't help thinking of that other dog, across in the residential unit, battling away for her life. It simply didn't seem fair that while Blackie was so well-fed, so beautiful, so loved, that poor tattered, neglected little terrier was fighting for survival. Mandy couldn't bear to think of any animal suffering, especially when she couldn't do anything to help. If only that terrier were strong and healthy like Blackie, she thought sadly.

Suddenly she had an idea. 'Dad!' she cried. 'Didn't you say you can use any blood type for a first transfusion in dogs?'

'Well, yes,' he agreed. 'But that's not the point, Mandy, we don't have a donor just now.'

'Yes we do!' Mandy pointed at Blackie. 'We've got a perfectly healthy dog right here!'

Everyone turned to look at Blackie, who sat up and blinked at them all, sleepily.

'She's right, you know,' said Mr Hope, looking at James. 'If we could just take half a litre it would make all the difference.'

Everyone turned to James, who had turned rather pale. 'Will it hurt him?' he asked anxiously.

'Oh, no, he won't feel a thing,' Mrs Hope reassured him.

'It's as easy as slipping in a microchip,' said Simon.

'And I could do that at the same time,' Adam Hope said.

James looked across at Blackie, who stood up and wagged his tail, obviously hoping he'd get to finish off the remains of the sandwiches. Mandy looked from one to the other, willing James to agree.

'Well, all right,' said James, at last. 'Blackie can give some blood and you can fix him with a microchip.'

'Oh, thank you, James, that's great!' cried Mandy, giving him a great slap on his back. 'I'm so glad you agreed.'

James looked embarrassed. 'I haven't enough money for the microchip right now, though,' he said.

'Oh, I don't think you need worry about the money, James,' Mrs Hope said. 'Blackie is giving this little terrier a chance to live – he deserves something in return.'

James flushed. 'Thanks,' he said, beaming all round. He turned to pat his dog. 'Come on, Blackie, you're going to save a life!'

Eight

Mandy felt a bit more useful now she had a new patient to look after. The blood transfusion had helped the little terrier to survive the night but her wounds were deep and she was still very poorly. Mandy visited her every few hours during the day, trying to feed her with the special diet Simon had recommended for her.

'The trouble is, she won't eat it,' she told Simon, vigorously mixing the sloppy scrambled egg and oats together in a feeding bowl. 'Don't you think we should give her some biscuit?'

Simon shook his head. 'She's still too weak to take solid food like that,' he said. 'That's why I've put her on a puppy diet. You can give her some of that Vita-milk over there afterwards.'

Mandy put the bowl of scrambled egg mixture into the terrier's cage. 'Come on, Puppy!' she called. 'Here's your dinner.'

'She's not a puppy,' said Simon, laughing.

'I know, but we're giving her puppy food, so I call her Puppy,' Mandy grinned.

'You're not supposed to call her anything at all,' Simon reminded her. 'It's up to her new owners to give her a name.'

Mandy had heard the Animal Ark rule so many times that she just grinned. 'She hasn't got a new owner yet,' she said. 'And anyway it's only a temporary name.'

'Yes, and just remember this is only her temporary home,' warned Simon.

'I know that,' sighed Mandy. 'Come on, Puppy, just try a bit of this.'

The little dog lifted her head and sniffed at the bowl. She took a few feeble laps of the food then flopped back, exhausted. 'Oh, she's given up again,' said Mandy, almost as distressed as her patient. 'Shall I feed her by hand?'

'I think it's best if we wait till she's ready to feed herself,' said Simon. 'Try the Vita-milk now.'

Mandy poured the rich, creamy milk into a clean bowl.

'Not too much,' warned Simon. 'Little and often – that's the rule with invalids.'

This time the little dog lifted up her head and sniffed at the bowl. Then, to Mandy's relief, she turned her head to the bowl and began to lap, rather feebly. But soon she put her head right in and slurped all the milk up.

'Good dog!' said Mandy. 'Look, Simon, she's taken it all!'

'That'll help,' said Simon, 'It's full of vitamins and minerals. Put the eggy stuff in the fridge. You can try it again in a couple of hours.'

Mandy spent much of the day coaxing the terrier to eat, and by evening the little dog staggered up on her wobbly legs and lapped up all the scrambled egg mixture.

'I think she's on her way to recovery now,' said Mr Hope after he'd checked the little dog over next day. 'Thanks to the Mandy Hope TLC treatment.'

Mandy laughed. 'I think it's thanks to Simon's puppy diet,' she said.

But her father shook his head. 'If we'd just left her with bowls full of the stuff, she probably wouldn't have taken it,' he said. 'Unlike cats, dogs need human contact and extra attention when they're ill.'

'Well, I'll give her all the contact she needs,' Mandy promised. She stroked a little velvety ear and the dog's tail thumped feebly on her fleecy blanket.

'And she's responding already,' her father observed. 'That's a good sign.'

'You'll soon be ready for a little run around the yard, won't you?' said Mandy, smoothing the dog's head gently. The terrier looked up at her with bright, intelligent eyes.

'And as soon as she is, she'll have to go,' her father warned. 'So don't get any ideas, Mandy.'

But, of course, Mandy was already getting ideas. A few days later the little dog was jumping to her feet as soon as Mandy rattled her bowl. She was eating so well now that Simon had put her on three normal meals a day, and stopped the Vita-milk altogether. Even so, Mandy visited her a lot more than three times a day, so the little dog soon knew her voice. She would limp to the door of her cage, ears pricked, tail wagging, greeting Mandy with a feeble, high-pitched bark.

Mandy peered into the cage and waggled her finger at the terrier. 'She sounds just like a little puppy, doesn't she, Simon?' she said.

Simon came over and listened to the little dog, who was snapping and yapping at Mandy's finger. 'That's because her ribs and chest are still weak,' Simon explained. 'She'll get her voice back properly once she gets stronger.'

Mandy began taking the terrier for gentle walks around the yard, to exercise her muscles.

'She's coming along well, now, Mandy,' Mrs Hope said, stopping to watch them as she crossed the yard. 'By the end of the week she'll be back to normal.'

'And what then?' asked Mandy, though she already knew the answer.

'I'll ring Ted Forrester in a day or two – the RSPCA kennels will find a place for her until she gets a permanent home.'

An awful thought struck Mandy. 'They won't send her back to that horrible man, will they?' she asked, bending to stroke the little dog.

Her mother shook her head. 'He'll never be allowed to keep a dog again,' she said. 'Don't you worry.'

But Mandy did worry. She knew that Puppy wouldn't get nearly as much attention in the RSPCA kennels as she'd given her. She might even pick up a virus in their crowded conditions. What if she got kennel cough? It was harmless in a normal, healthy dog, but very dangerous for a weak little terrier only just recovering from life-threatening injuries.

'We ought to find a new home for her,' Mandy muttered at breakfast, her mind still on the little dog.

'For your mother, you mean?' smiled Mr Hope. 'I agree – she never gets up in time to make the breakfast!' Mrs Hope pulled a face at him and they both laughed.

'No, for Pup— for the terrier,' Mandy said, impatiently. 'She's not well enough to go into kennels.'

'No, she's not,' agreed her mum. 'But she soon will be.' Mandy sighed and stirred her cornflakes gloomily.

'Don't worry, Mandy,' Adam Hope said. 'That dog is going nowhere until she's fully fit.'

'When will that be?' asked Mandy, wishing the little dog didn't have to leave at all.

'Sooner rather than later, thanks to all your care,' smiled her father. 'We'll see how she is early next week and then I'll ring Ted Forrester.'

But it was Ted Forrester who rang them first.

The badger injured in the fight was now fully recovered and Ted was planning to set her free in Piper's Wood that evening. He invited Mandy and James to come with him.

Mandy and James were only too eager to go. 'Michelle's coming over, too,' Mandy told James when he arrived that evening.

'Not with her video camera, I hope,' he said, looking alarmed.

'It's a pity she can't film us releasing the badger. It would make a great feature for *Wildlife Ways*,' said Mandy.

'And she might ruin Mr Forrester's plan to settle the badger in,' James reminded her.

When Michelle came over to join them, she admitted she had wanted to bring her camera but Ted was worried that too much attention might distract the badger from settling back into the wild again. 'And Janie's away this week so I couldn't get a film crew together anyway,' she said regretfully. 'I don't think my efforts with the camcorder would have been good enough.'

'Hard luck,' said Ted Forrester, smiling.

As dusk was falling in Piper's Wood, Ted drove his RSPCA Land-rover slowly and carefully along a forestry track. Michelle sat beside him, James and Mandy behind, and in the back the badger shuffled uneasily in her cage. They both turned to make soothing noises to quieten her down but the deeper into the wood they went, the more restless the badger became. Eventually she was scratching at the cage, and emitting strange squeaking noises.

'She knows she's going home,' said Mandy.

'Well, that's more than we know,' said Ted. 'The police have been questioning Bonser and he claims he doesn't know where she came from. He says he bought her off some chap in a pub.'

'A likely story,' sniffed Michelle.

'More likely than you'd think,' said Ted gravely. 'Some folk will dig a badger out to order. They don't want to be involved in the fight, but they're happy to supply the animals.'

'Like those two men who stole the dogs,' said James.

'Aye,' Ted agreed. 'Only they claim they were picking up strays to rescue them!'

'Blackie isn't a stray!' protested James.

'He certainly won't stray again,' said Mandy. 'He's been chipped,' she told Ted and Michelle.

'Does that mean we can have him for tea

with a bit of fish?' smiled Ted.

'You mean microchipped, Mandy,' James corrected her, laughing.

'Hush, now,' Ted warned, as he pulled into a clearing in the woods. 'We'll try this spot. There's an old deserted sett close by. She'll have a roof over her head at least, while she looks around for somewhere better.'

'But maybe she'll like this place so much she'll decide to stay,' said Mandy, looking round at the fringe of silver birches and the daisies lining the glade. 'It's so beautiful,' she breathed.

'Aye, but badgers aren't interested in beautiful scenery,' said Ted. 'It's all a matter of food supply.'

They all clambered out of the Land-rover and Ted opened up the back. 'Come on, lass,' he said, gently, to the badger. 'Let's be having you!'

The four of them took a corner of the cage each and carried it to the base of one of the old trees, where a grassy bank had formed in its roots.

'Steady on,' murmured Ted Forrester. 'Let her down – now!' They stooped and gently put the cage down in the grass.

'You lot get in those bushes back there,' Ted

said, softly, nodding across the clearing. 'I'll open the cage up and let her come out in her own time.'

Michelle, James and Mandy moved quietly over to a clump of brushwood, downwind of the badger. They crouched down in the damp grass and watched Ted unfastening the cage. He stood and watched the motionless badger for a moment then turned and came over to join them.

Mandy held her breath, watching out to see what the badger would do. Surely she'd be eager to run out into the woods now she was free? But at first nothing happened. In spite of all her restlessness in the Land-rover, the badger seemed to be in no hurry to be free. James and Mandy fidgeted and muttered, trying to settle themselves comfortably among the spiky brushwood and dew-damp grass.

'She's taking her time,' whispered James.

'She's bound to be cautious, after all she's gone through,' Michelle said.

'That's right,' agreed Ted. 'It's best if we keep quiet now and stay ever so still.'

They watched in silence, peering through their binoculars, but for a while there was nothing to see, except for the cage, perched on the grassy bank under the tree.

Mandy sighed as the badger stayed hidden inside the cage. It seemed that she preferred her cage to her new home, after all. What would they do with her, she wondered anxiously. Would Ted have to take her back, or could they try another sett in another wood? Mandy didn't want that to happen; after all, the two orphan badgers she'd found on the bridge had been set loose in Piper's Wood, and there was just a chance that . . .

Interrupting her thoughts, Ted Forrester nudged her. 'Look!' he breathed.

The badger was emerging now, head up, snout quivering, as if checking the air. Through the binoculars, Mandy watched as she snuffled and sniffed suspiciously, still lingering by the cage. Would she enter the old sett, Mandy wondered. Or would she dive back into the cage?

Mandy glanced at James and noticed him holding his breath with excitement as he focused on the badger. A full moon had risen behind the trees, and Mandy found she could see quite well, even without binoculars. She watched the badger take a hesitant step, then another and another towards the entrance to the sett. 'She's going in!' she whispered to James.

James put a finger to his lips, reminding her to be quiet.

Sounds of the badger grumbling and groaning to herself were carried across on the still night air. Just as Mandy became convinced that the badger was going to dig her way into the sett, she turned away and began to nose around the opposite bank, all the time grunting and muttering. 'What's she doing?' Mandy whispered to Michelle.

'She seems to be looking for something,' Michelle replied. She sounded as excited as Mandy.

The badger paused on top of the bank to gaze all round the clearing. Then she opened her mouth and gave a great rumbling bark. Mandy was so startled she almost dropped the binoculars.

'Why is she doing that?' she whispered. Michelle shrugged her shoulders. 'It's as if she's calling somebody,' Mandy muttered to herself.

'Look over there!' whispered Ted Forrester. 'There's your answer.'

Mandy followed his gaze and focusing on the other side of the glade she saw something silvery white flash in the long grass. At first she thought it was just a trick of the moonlight, but then she saw another silvery flicker, and another, as two young badgers came bursting out of the undergrowth, running and rolling and tearing around.

'The badgers from the bridge!' Mandy gasped.

'I don't know about that, young Mandy,' Ted Forrester said, taking his binoculars back. 'I set them free miles away from here.'

'Well, something's brought them back here.' Mandy refused to believe these were not the same badgers they had taken home that day.

'Look!' Michelle pointed back to the large female badger. 'She's coming over!'

The female badger was running towards the young badgers. As soon as she reached them they stopped playing and ran round her, squeaking with excitement. Moonlight flooded the glade and Mandy could see the youngsters hurl themselves at the female badger, who raised her snout and gave a great cry of welcome. For a few magical moments they all jumped and skipped and trotted around one another, as if performing a joyful dance.

Mandy watched entranced, as the female badger stopped and gathered the young ones

round her, drawing them close to her with her powerful front legs and nuzzling them with her snout.

'I was right,' she murmured to Ted Forrester. 'They *are* a family.'

'Wait and see!' he warned her. 'It depends on what she does next.'

What she did next was to groom them, licking and sniffing and combing their coats with her great claws. Finally she gave each one a little cuff on the head, as if to show them she was boss, and trotted off back to the deserted sett. The little ones followed obediently, and waited at the entrance while she flicked out the loose earth with her powerful claws, opening up the sett and shoving the cubs down under the grassy bank. Mandy caught a final glimpse of a flash of white in the shadows, as the female badger stood for a moment, glancing round before diving down after them.

'Phew!' breathed James, sitting back on the damp grass and rubbing at his glasses. 'Wasn't that magic?'

'They must be her own cubs,' said Mandy with satisfaction.

'Possibly,' said Ted Forrester cautiously, 'although female badgers have been known to take care of orphan cubs, you know.'

'You mean she might have adopted them?' asked Mandy, with interest.

Ted Forrester nodded. 'They make good foster-mothers,' he told her.

'I'm with Mandy,' said Michelle, smiling. 'I still prefer to think of it as a family reunion.' She stretched herself and groaned. 'Can we stand up now, do you think?' she asked.

Ted Forrester nodded. 'You three go back to the Land-rover,' he said. 'I can manage the cage now it's empty.'

'I'll help,' offered James.

'Thanks, but I don't want too many footsteps around that sett,' Ted explained.

'Come on, you two – we'll open up the Land-rover,' Michelle said.

Michelle, Mandy and James walked to the Land-rover while Ted, treading silently across the grass, picked up the cage and brought it back.

Mandy snuggled sleepily into her seat, half dreaming of the badger family, now united in their new home, safe and sound at last. Even if the young badgers from the bridge *weren't* the female's own cubs, she'd shown she was prepared to take care of them. *She's adopted them,* thought Mandy smiling, *just like my own mum and dad adopted me all that time ago.* 'I hope they live happily ever after,' she murmured.

'They'll be quite safe, now that Bonser and his friends are all locked away,' smiled Michelle. 'Nobody will dare come badger-digging in Piper's Wood once the story's on television.'

A happy ending for all the local dogs and badgers, thought Mandy, dreamily. But then she remembered the little terrier back at Animal Ark. Any time now, she'd be banished to the RSPCA kennels to wait for a new owner.

'If only we could fix a happy ending for

Puppy, too,' she yawned. 'Any ideas, James?'
But James was breathing heavily, his glasses halfway down his nose. He was already asleep.

Nine

After such a late night, Mandy was not up and about very early next morning. She lay in her bed, half-dozing, half-listening to the familiar sounds of the house drifting up to her bedroom. Her dad was still washing up in the kitchen, singing loudly; her mum was opening up the back door and calling across the yard to Simon, who had just arrived for work. She heard the murmur of their voices as they discussed the day's routine.

'I hope he remembers Puppy's extra vitamins,' she thought, sleepily. 'She's so much better now . . .'

She sat up, suddenly wide awake. The little

terrier was so much better that Ted Forrester was coming round to collect her sometime that very day! This would be the last morning Mandy could spend with her. She scrambled out of bed and into her tracksuit, and raced downstairs.

'Morning, Mandy!' Simon glanced at her ruffled hair and crumpled tracksuit as she came into the food store. 'Had a late night badger-watching, I hear?'

'Yes, we did,' replied Mandy. She took a pile of metal bowls from the dishwasher. 'The female has taken those two youngsters we found by the bridge and settled in an old sett. Isn't that wonderful?'

'It is,' Simon agreed. 'One big happy family, eh?'

'Well, rather a little one, actually,' smiled Mandy, 'But I think they're going to be very happy.'

'I'm sure they are,' said Simon. 'A happy ending for everybody – except for Bonser and his friends.'

'And for Puppy,' Mandy reminded him, her face clouding. 'Ted Forrester's coming to take her to the RSPCA kennels today.'

'It's for the best, Mandy,' Simon told her.

'She'll have a better chance of finding a new owner there.'

'We could keep her here until we find her a new owner,' said Mandy stubbornly.

'This is a surgery, not an animal hotel,' Simon pointed out. 'She's a healthy dog now and we'll be needing that cage for our recovering post-ops next week.'

Mandy sighed deeply and filled up the bowls with dry food. 'I just wish I knew she was going to a nice, friendly home,' she said.

'I expect she just wishes you'd get on with the breakfasts,' grinned Simon.

But who was going to give her breakfast tomorrow, Mandy wondered.

'Come on, little Puppy!' she called, opening the wire-mesh door. The terrier – who was not really a puppy at all – came trotting out eagerly. She was kept in one of the outdoor runs now, with a warm kennel at one end. Mandy went inside and put the food bowl down.

'I'll take you for a nice little walk very soon,' she promised, patting the little dog's back. Puppy's tail wagged furiously, though she didn't stop to look up from her breakfast.

Shutting the cage door securely, Mandy decided it was time for her own breakfast. And she had better clean herself up before her mum and dad caught sight of her. But before she could reach the house she saw her mother coming towards her – and with a visitor, too. Mandy wiped her biscuity hands on her tracksuit trousers and tried to smooth down her hair.

'Mandy, I thought you were still in bed,' said her mother, looking hard at her dishevelled daughter.

'I just popped down to help Simon feed the dogs,' Mandy said. 'I'm just off for a shower now . . .' She started off to the house without even looking at their visitor but her mother stopped her.

'PC Wilde has come to see the little terrier,' she said, smiling.

'Oh?' Mandy looked up now and recognised the policeman who'd been guarding the white van after the badger-baiting. She knew he had phoned once or twice since, to ask how the dog was progressing, but he'd never been to see her.

'She's just having her breakfast,' she told him.

'Well, you can still take PC Wilde down to see her,' Mrs Hope said. She turned to the policeman. 'I've got to get back to the surgery. Come up to the house when you've finished here and Mandy will make some coffee – after she's cleaned herself up.' Mrs Hope grinned at Mandy and rushed off.

Mandy looked at the constable, who seemed much younger and smaller out of uniform, and certainly much friendlier.

'I'm Bill Wilde,' he said, sticking out a hand towards her. 'I'm so glad the dog pulled through.'

Mandy shook his hand. 'Mandy Hope,' she said.

'I've been wanting to see her ever since . . .' The young man's voice faded. 'Well, since that night she was injured.'

'Why didn't you come to visit, then?' asked Mandy, surprised.

'Well, your dad said she was too ill to be disturbed at first,' he explained, 'and after that I went away on a training course. This is my first free day.'

Mandy smiled at him. If he'd come to see the dog on his first free day he must really care about her, she decided. And suddenly Mandy was struck by one of her great ideas.

'This way – come on!' She led him to the dog-run, taking a lead from the hook by the door as they passed.

'Come on, little Puppy!' she called, opening the cage. 'Walk time!'

As soon as she heard Mandy's voice the little dog ran forwards, eyes bright, tail wagging, and making short, sharp yapping noises, just like a young puppy.

'Her ribs are still a bit stiff and sore,' Mandy explained. 'So I take her for a bit of gentle exercise now and then.' She unfastened the cage, clipped the lead on and turned to the policeman. 'Would you like to take her?' she asked.

'I'd love to,' Bill Wilde replied, taking the lead and bending to stroke the dog. 'Hello, little 'un,' he said, softly. 'Are you feeling better now?'

Mandy watched the young man gently lead the dog out. The little terrier walked beautifully to heel, not pulling at the lead at all. Now and then she turned and fixed the man with a bright eye, as if to check that he knew what he was doing.

'She's a very bright dog,' PC Wilde observed. 'You know, I never thought she'd pull through. She looked half dead that night up in Piper's Wood.'

'Well, she did make it,' Mandy smiled. 'Did Dad tell you about the blood transfusion?'

'Yes – lucky that Labrador was handy!' the constable replied. 'And now you're quite well again, aren't you?' He crouched down to stroke the little dog, who leaped up to lick his face.

'Yes, she's so much better that she's off to the RSPCA this morning,' said Mandy casually.

And just as Mandy had hoped, PC Wilde looked quite shocked. 'This morning? Surely that's a bit soon, after all her injuries?' He picked up the terrier and stood holding her snuggled in his arms.

'I know,' Mandy sighed heavily, 'But you see, we haven't found a home for her and we need the kennel for another patient.' She crossed her fingers, telling herself it was almost true. 'Would you like to walk her around again?' she asked him.

PC Wilde shook his head. 'I think she's had enough for now,' he said. 'She might need a rest . . .'

Mandy smiled at the idea of the energetic little dog needing a rest already. She didn't want him to take the dog back to her kennel just then. She wanted Bill Wilde and the little dog to get to know each other better.

'Let's go up to the kitchen,' she said. 'You can look after her while I make the coffee.' She watched him fondling the dog's ears. 'She won't get many cuddles at the RSPCA kennels,' she added craftily. 'They have so many dogs to look after.' And she felt pleased with herself as she saw the frown of concern on PC Wilde's face grow even deeper.

Once in the kitchen, the terrier snuggled down on PC Wilde's knee and sat gazing up at him intently. The constable sat quite stiff and still, gently stroking the dog's ears and hardly daring to breathe for fear of hurting her.

It's as if she's already chosen him, thought Mandy. All I need now is for him to choose her! She went about making the coffee very quietly, so as not to disturb the two of them. Their peace was soon disrupted, however, when Mr Hope came bustling in from morning surgery.

'Any chance of a coffee, Mandy?' he called breezily. 'We're almost done out there.'

'Shh, I'm just making it, Dad,' Mandy replied. 'And PC Wilde is just looking after the terrier.' She stared hard at her father, hoping he'd take the hint. But he didn't.

'Hello, Constable,' he said. 'I see you're making friends with our miracle terrier!'

'Yes, she's lovely,' said PC Wilde shyly. 'I think she likes me already.'

'I'm sure she does,' agreed Mr Hope. 'Does that mean you're going to take her, then?'

'Dad!' Mandy protested. After all her careful preparations her father had come blundering in, spoiling it all!

PC Wilde looked surprised. 'Do you think I could?' he asked, eagerly. 'I mean, just like that?'

'Well, not quite,' said Mr Hope. 'We've already arranged for Ted Forrester to collect her. But he can check both you and the dog over and, if he thinks you're an acceptable owner,' he grinned at the young man, 'the dog could be yours!'

'She could?' PC Wilde beamed at the little terrier. 'Do you think you'd like that?' he asked her. As if to reassure him, she suddenly leaped up and licked his face.

Mandy let out a great sigh of relief. 'I'm so glad you came,' she told the constable. 'I never wanted her to go to the RSPCA. It's not that they're unkind or anything, but she needs a lot of love and attention just now.'

'And she'll get it,' PC Wilde promised her. 'I've got a couple of weeks' leave – and now I know how I'm going to spend it!'

Mandy ruffled the dog's ears and smiled happily. 'What will you call her?' she asked.

'I thought she already had a name,' he said,

looking puzzled. 'When we went to get her out you called her . . .'

'Mandy!' Mr Hope sighed. 'How many times must I tell you not to give names to stray animals . . .'

'I didn't, Dad, honest! I just called her Puppy – you know, like a joke, because she was so helpless when she came in and she barks in that high-pitched voice just like a puppy.'

'Oh, *puppy*!' Bill Wilde said. 'I thought you said Poppy!'

Even Mr Hope laughed at that. They were still laughing when Simon came in, bringing Michelle with him.

'We need a good final shot of that little dog for the end of the *Wildlife Ways* feature,' Michelle explained. 'Janie's just setting up the camera outside. Emily said it would be OK.'

'Fine, come and have a coffee while she gets ready,' Adam Hope said.

Once she was settled at the kitchen table with her coffee, Michelle looked round. 'I was hoping maybe James and Blackie would be here,' she said. 'It would be nice to get some footage of them too.'

'I'll ring him,' said Mandy, getting up hastily. 'And you'd better meet – er – Poppy.' She grinned at PC Wilde as she went over to the phone.

'Poppy,' he nodded, and the little dog looked up at him.

'She's quite a star,' Mandy told Michelle. 'She's going to look great in your film.' She picked up the phone.

'It's hard to believe this is the poor little dog who was nearly killed,' Michelle said quietly.

Simon nodded.

'I can't believe it, either,' Bill Wilde said, 'not after seeing your video of the fight.'

'You've already seen it?' asked Michelle.

'I watched the rough copy you sent to the station,' he explained. 'It wasn't pleasant viewing.'

'But useful, I hope?' Michelle asked.

He nodded. 'It certainly was,' he agreed. 'Those villains should be put away for a few years on that evidence. And the spectators will get quite a shock when their local police officer pays them a visit.'

As if stirred by the mention of her past, Poppy gave a lurch, jumped off PC Wilde's knee and ran across to Mandy, who was talking to James on the phone. Michelle picked up the little dog and stroked her shiny coat.

'Oh, you're a little darling, aren't you?' she said. 'I'm so glad you're better, thanks to Mandy – and Simon.' She smiled across at her friend.

'And Blackie, too,' added Mandy, putting down the phone. 'It was his blood that saved her life.'

'Blackie, the hero,' laughed Michelle. 'That's a great idea for the end of my film!'

Mandy went off to get washed and changed. By the time she came down, James and Blackie were there and Ted Forrester was just pulling up so they all went out to the garden ready for the video session.

'Do you think PC Wilde will make a good dog-owner?' asked Mandy anxiously.

Ted grinned. 'Seems to me he already is one,' he said. 'That terrier's made her mind up and I haven't the heart to disappoint her.' They looked at Poppy, who was sitting at Bill Wilde's feet, her tail wagging.

Ted turned to PC Wilde. 'I shall have to ask you to accompany me to the station,' he said gruffly.

'The police station?' The constable looked so startled that everyone laughed.

'He means the RSPCA station,' James explained.

Ted Forrester nodded. 'Just so that we can complete all the paperwork,' he said, smiling.

'Oh, yes, of course,' PC Wilde replied. 'And you'll be able to keep an eye on Poppy in future, Ted,' he added. 'I'm joining the Police Wildlife Unit just as soon as I finish my next course.'

'Well, you've certainly got the right name for the job, lad,' Ted Forrester laughed.

'And the right dog, I hope,' smiled Mandy, bending to stroke the little dog, who had curled up with Blackie under the garden bench.

Janie began to organise some group shots that Michelle explained she would edit into the film later. There was Bill Wilde and Poppy, walking through the rose-arch as if they were setting out on a long journey together, Blackie sitting nobly at attention with James blushing alongside him, and a beautiful shot of Poppy and Blackie playing together, as if they'd been friends all their lives.

'I hope they will be friends for a long time yet,' Mandy whispered to James. 'If PC Wilde is joining the Walton Police Wildlife Unit, we're bound to come across him now and then.'

'I hope so,' said James. 'That's just the kind of work I'd love to do, one day.'

'Come on, everyone,' called Michelle. 'We want the whole group now – everyone who helped to catch the Welford badger-baiters!'

After Janie had taken the final shots, Mr Hope and James got out their cameras and took some more. It was past lunch-time by the time they'd finished.

'You'd better all stay,' said Mrs Hope. 'Only soup and sandwiches, but you're all welcome.'

Mr Hope brought out a tray of drinks and Mrs Hope heated up home-made soup from the freezer while Mandy and James made a pile of sandwiches.

As they all helped themselves to lunch, Michelle told Bill Wilde how the whole story had begun when Walter Pickard had interrupted another lunch party at Animal Ark with the news of the dead badger.

'Well, at least there've been no interruptions today,' said Emily Hope.

'Except from the dogs,' laughed Mandy, pointing to Poppy and Blackie, who were chasing each other round and round the garden.

'They're only showing us how well they've recovered,' laughed James.

'Showing us it's time we were off, more like,'

said Ted Forrester. 'Come on, Bill, we'll get down to the office and make you the legal owner of that little terrier.'

Mandy kneeled down to say goodbye to the little dog. She was both very happy that she was going to a good home and a bit sad that she was leaving Animal Ark. 'You will bring her back to see us, won't you?' she asked PC Wilde.

'I'm bringing her in next week,' he replied. 'She's coming to be microchipped. Aren't you, my lovely?' He picked Poppy up and put her gently into the back of his car.

He got into the car and then, driving very carefully, so as not to disturb Poppy, he followed the RSPCA Land-rover down the road.

Mandy gave a great, satisfied sigh. 'I'm so glad she's found a good home so soon,' she said.

'And a good friend, too,' said James, pointing at Blackie, who was sitting by the gate staring after the cars. 'Come on, Blackie,' he called. 'You know what happens if you hang about the gate!'

'But it won't happen again,' Mandy told him. 'Blackie's safe now – and so are all the badgers around Welford.'

That evening Mandy stood in the garden

thinking of the badger family, newly settled in Piper's Wood. *I hope they're as pleased with their new home as Poppy is*, she thought, turning to go back to the house. Just then she heard an animal's cry in the distance. For a moment she wondered whether it was her badger, but it was too early in the evening, she reminded herself. The young badgers would still be snug in their sett, safe and sound and fast asleep . . .

'Mandy?' her mother's voice floated across the garden. 'Come on in, love,'

'It's early to bed for you, after last night,' called her father.

'All right!' Mandy called back. 'I'm coming.'

Mandy walked across the lawn, smiling happily to herself: the young badgers had their foster-mother and little Poppy had her new owner – they were all safe now, in their new homes. She gave a contented sigh and ran across the lawn, to her own home, Animal Ark.

Deer
– on the –
Drive

One

'What do you think, Mum, shorts or trousers?'
Mandy Hope came into the kitchen holding a
pair of brown shorts in one hand and a pair of
khaki trousers in the other. 'I can't decide.'

Emily Hope stopped buttering toast and
turned her head to look.

'Hmm. Difficult,' she answered. 'I know we're
having a hot August, but if you're trekking
through woods up at Glisterdale, you'll need a
bit of protection from thorns and nettles. I'd
go for trousers.' She blew a wayward red curl
off her forehead. 'Ask Dad what he thinks.'

'Ask Dad what he thinks about what?'
Adam Hope said, coming into the kitchen from

the garden, carrying a bowl of freshly-picked loganberries.

'Trousers or shorts?' Mandy held them both up.

'Oh, of course, I'd forgotten, my TV presenter daughter is off on location today,' Mr Hope teased. 'Definitely trousers, more professional. So, Mum and I have got to manage without you again, have we?'

'Da-ad,' Mandy groaned. 'You're just trying to make me feel guilty. You know I've made a deal with Simon while this project is on.' She made a face. 'I promised I'll do all the jobs he wants me to when the filming is finished.'

Mandy's parents were both vets and their practice, Animal Ark, was housed in the modern extension built on to the back of the old stone cottage that was their home. Simon was their practice nurse. Usually Mandy helped out after school and during the holidays but Simon had agreed to do her chores while Mandy and her best friend James Hunter helped Michelle Holmes, the presenter of the TV programme *Wildlife Ways*, to make a film about deer.

'I'm only joking, love. What's the plan for today?' Adam Hope sprinkled a handful of loganberries over his breakfast cereal.

'I'm meeting James outside the post office and Michelle's picking us up there, on her way to Glisterdale,' she looked at her watch, 'in ten minutes' time!'

'Mandy!' called Mrs Hope, as Mandy headed for the door. 'Eat some toast.'

'And that's an order,' laughed her dad. 'Then you'd better scoot, you don't want to keep the others waiting.'

Mandy grabbed a piece of toast, then rushed upstairs to get dressed. With seconds to spare she raced down the lane and across the green, arriving at the post office just as Michelle's Jeep pulled up by the bench where James was already waiting. Janie Doyle, the *Wildlife Ways* camera operator, was in the front seat, polishing a camera lens.

'Hi there, you two,' Janie said, turning round to face Mandy and James as they scrambled into the back of the Jeep. 'Can you fill me in on Glisterdale Grange?' She ran her hand through her short blonde hair. 'Michelle said you released a fawn there once.'

'Yes, we found a fawn in the forest behind the Old School House in Welford,' Mandy began. 'Her mother had died and we needed somewhere safe to release her.'

'Mr Dickenson owns the Grange,' James continued. 'He's got a herd of fallow deer and a tame doe called Honey-Mum. She adopted Sprite.'

'So did you already know Peter Dickenson?' Janie asked.

'No,' Mandy replied. 'We met Mr Dickenson after I found his dog, Rosie, stuck down a rabbit hole. It was just after we found Sprite and we were desperate to find a place to release her that would be safe.'

'That's when Mr Dickenson offered us Glisterdale Grange,' James finished off.

'I must say, Mr Dickenson sounded extremely helpful and friendly on the phone,' Michelle said, looking in the rear view mirror and signalling to turn left. 'He was very keen for us to film his herd.'

'You know, Glisterdale Grange is open to the public. I bet loads of people will visit once they've seen the deer on television,' said Mandy, as they left the main road and drove towards the entrance.

'Sprite might be a star!' James added.

'I really hope we see her today,' Mandy said enthusiastically.

'It would be great for the film to see how the little fawn is getting on,' Michelle grinned. 'And if, as you say, the deer go very near the house, that will make our job much easier.' She turned the Jeep between the big gates and on to the wide gravelled drive that curved in a semicircle around the house. The house was enormous, built of honey-coloured stone that shone in the sunlight. It had a big forecourt with an information office and a place where the public could park. To the side of this was an area with wooden tables and benches for picnics.

Michelle drove around the house, past the office and into a small car park marked: Private – Estate Personnel Only.

'I called in and saw Tony Morris, the estate manager, yesterday and he said we could park here,' she told them, as she turned off the engine. 'He thought that Peter Dickenson might walk around the estate with us and show us the best places to see the deer. We'll just decide where we want to film today, and then start work tomorrow.' Gathering up her notebook, Michelle got out of the Jeep. Like Mandy, she wore khaki trousers and a khaki shirt. She had a brown sweatshirt with *Wildlife Ways* emblazoned across the front slung around her shoulders.

'Mr Dickenson is really friendly,' Mandy told them, as she scrambled out of the Jeep.

'He always gives us an update on Sprite when we visit,' James added, climbing out of the back seat after Mandy.

While Michelle was locking up the Jeep, three men wearing bright yellow hard hats came around to the front of the house.

'There's Mr Dickenson!' Mandy waved at one of the three men and was about to run over to him, but he just smiled at her and then looked away.

'That's Tony Morris with him,' said Michelle. 'They look pretty busy.'

They watched as the third man flicked through pages and pages of notes on a clipboard, and pointed up at the roof. 'I don't think we should interrupt him now,' Michelle decided. Mandy nodded. She could see that Mr Dickenson looked worried.

'Why don't we take a look around the estate on our own?' Janie suggested, gathering up her bag and a light meter. 'We can catch up with them later.'

Mandy and James led Michelle and Janie down towards the paddocks at the far side of the house where a path led into the forest.

'Look!' whispered James. 'Over there!' Stepping slowly along the path were five fallow deer. They watched as the group, three adult females and two fawns, made their way daintily across the paddock, their spotted coats glossy in the sunlight.

Mandy gasped softly. 'Aren't they beautiful!' she breathed.

Suddenly, the doe at the head of the group stopped and jerked her head in their direction. She gave a sharp little bark, stamped her feet and raised her tail to show the white fur underneath, warning the others of danger. All five deer froze.

Then, just as quickly, the deer decided that the humans were not a great threat and continued picking their way across the paddock, nipping at bushes and shrubs as they passed by. Mandy could hear the soft tap of their hooves as they crossed the drive and disappeared back into the forest on the other side of the house.

'They are very trusting,' Michelle observed. 'Most deer would be extremely nervous to be this close to humans. It shows how safe they must feel here.'

'Oh, they are safe,' Mandy said happily. 'Mr

Dickenson wouldn't let *anything* happen to his deer.' She grinned.

Michelle, Janie, Mandy and James spent the next couple of hours walking along the nature trail through the estate. In the forest there were lots of glades and patches of open grassland where deer would gather.

'I'm not surprised the deer are doing well here,' Michelle observed. 'This is exactly the sort of forest that fallow deer love.' She gestured with her arm. 'Lots of shrubs and bramble patches, and long grass, perfect for hiding a newborn fawn. Did you know that when a fawn is born it has no scent at all for twenty-four hours?' She laughed at the surprise on Mandy and James's faces. 'So when the mother leaves it to browse, as long as the fawn keeps perfectly still, it need have no fear of predators.'

'So if you find a newborn fawn you should leave it alone?' Mandy asked.

'That's right.' Michelle nodded emphatically. 'Except of course when, like with Sprite, you know the mother is dead. But under normal circumstances, if you touch it you will give the fawn your smell. That will really upset the mother.' She waited while Janie took a reading from the light meter. 'And if the mother comes back while humans are around, that will frighten her off.'

'So the mother might abandon it, even though you haven't touched the fawn?' James asked.

'It's possible,' Michelle replied. She looked up at the sky and stretched out her hand. 'Uh, oh, I think we're in for some rain.' As they'd been walking, the sky had turned a dark yellowy-grey and now thunder rumbled in the distance.

'I think we'd better make a run for it,' Janie said. 'I don't want to get this light meter wet.'

By the time they made it back to the house, the rain was bucketing down. Mrs Dickenson was waiting with the kitchen door open, holding Rosie, the Dickensons' Lakeland terrier, by the collar. 'Come in, quickly,' she called.

Above the kitchen door a cracked gutter had come adrift and water was pouring straight down the wall. In her excitement at seeing Mandy, Rosie lurched forward. Mandy dodged sideways to avoid stepping on Rosie's paws and was hit by the stream of rainwater.

'Ugh, Rosie! I'm soaked, thanks to you!' Mandy said, picking the little dog up and giving her a hug. Mrs Dickenson passed her a towel and then turned to Michelle. 'You must be Michelle Holmes?' she said.

'That's right,' Michelle smiled. 'And this is Janie Doyle, my camera operator.'

Mandy rubbed at her wet hair. 'We've been looking for places to film, Mrs Dickenson,' she said. 'But we didn't see Sprite or Honey-Mum.'

Mrs Dickenson smiled, but Mandy thought her mind seemed to be on something else. While she was pouring them mugs of steaming tea, she kept glancing at the door that led to the hallway. Suddenly they heard footsteps approaching, and Mrs Dickenson tensed. James shot Mandy a puzzled look and she realised he had noticed that something was wrong too.

'OK, Tony, I'll see you later at the bridge and we'll check on the sheep.' As Peter Dickenson pushed open the kitchen door, his voice sounded weary and dejected. 'Hello, everyone,' he said, ushering another man in and gesturing for him to sit down. James shuffled round the table to make room for Mr Dickenson, who sat down, ran his fingers through his hair and gave a deep sigh. Rosie came trotting over to him and sat quietly at his feet.

Mrs Dickenson passed the two men cups of tea before asking softly, 'Tell me, is it very bad?'

'Yes, I'm afraid it is.' Mr Dickenson smiled grimly at his wife. 'In fact it couldn't be much worse.' He shook his head.

Michelle looked at Mandy and James, who fidgeted uncomfortably. 'This is obviously a bad time, perhaps we should go?' Michelle offered.

Peter Dickenson looked at her. 'My apologies,' he said. 'I'm neglecting you, Michelle. I'm so busy worrying about my troubles that I completely forgot you were coming to see us about the programme. I am sorry.'

'No problem,' Michelle smiled reassuringly. 'We can always come back another time.'

'You can if we're still here!' Mr Dickenson said bluntly.

'Oh, Peter!' Mrs Dickenson hurried over and stood behind him with her hands on his shoulders, looking at the shocked faces of the others.

'What?' Mandy exclaimed. 'Why wouldn't you be here?'

'Perhaps you'd like to explain, Charles,' Peter Dickenson asked the other man.

'Of course. My name is Charles Gregg and I'm a surveyor,' he introduced himself. 'I'll keep it fairly simple. To open a house like this to visitors you need what's called public liability insurance.' He shifted in the chair and shuffled the sheaf of papers in front of him. 'So, the insurance company obviously want to know that the house is safe, that ceilings are not going to fall down on visitors' heads or floors give way. That would cost them a lot of money in claims.' He paused. 'The problem is that this house *isn't* safe,' said Mr Gregg. 'And in a nutshell, without the necessary repairs, the house will have to be closed to the public.'

Mandy gasped. She couldn't believe it.

'What's the actual problem?' asked Michelle, with a frown. 'The house looks pretty sound from outside.'

'That's just it, Michelle,' Peter Dickenson explained. 'You don't always know a problem exists. We tend to live mostly down here in what used to be the old servants' quarters. It's nice and cosy. But the big rooms in the rest of the house, the ones we open to the public, are damp and full of wet and dry rot.'

'What *are* wet and dry rot?' James asked.

'Basically, they are both caused by fungi,' Mr Gregg told them.

'Fungi, like mushrooms?' James said, surprised.

'Yes, that's right.' Mr Gregg explained. 'Both

wet rot and dry rot are caused by a fungus that thrives in damp places. This house has internal gutters that have been slowly leaking. Good York stone, like the stone this house is built of, can absorb a lot of water and still dry out with no harm done. But all the timbers in the west wing are rotten and need to be replaced. The trouble is, dry rot spreads like wildfire.' He shook his head. 'I'm afraid work on the west wing will have to start immediately if the damage isn't to spread to the rest of the house.'

Mrs Dickenson swallowed hard. 'How much is it likely to cost?' she asked.

'It's going to cost a fortune,' Peter Dickenson sighed, looking up at his wife. 'It could be nearly a quarter of a million pounds.'

Mandy and James looked at each other, stunned. No wonder the Dickensons were worried.

'Why do you need to have Glisterdale Grange open to the public?' Mandy asked.

'We depend on the money, Mandy,' Mr Dickenson told her. 'People pay to see the gardens too, but that's only in summer. In order to keep the estate going we need to keep the house open for most of the year.' He put his hands together and leaned his chin on them.

'Nowadays, Mandy, estates and houses like this have to pay for themselves.'

'And anyway,' added Mrs Dickenson, 'we couldn't let this beautiful house simply fall down around our ears. This is our home.'

'Quite right!' Mr Dickenson said in a positive voice. 'We'll have to find a way.'

'Could I make a suggestion?' Charles Gregg asked, taking a plan of the estate out from among his papers. 'You have quite a lot of land here that doesn't produce any income. Have you considered selling any of it?'

'No!' Peter Dickenson was adamant. 'The last thing I'd want to do is break up the estate.'

'Suit yourself,' Mr Gregg said, 'but if you change your mind I happen to know a buyer who would take that woodland there,' he pointed to Glisterdale Forest on the plan he had in front of him, 'off your hands for well above the market price.' He folded the plan and put it away. 'It would be a perfect solution to your problem.'

James was frowning deeply. Mandy guessed he was thinking the same as she was. Surely Mr Dickenson wouldn't sell the deer wood. He couldn't! She thought of Sprite and Honey-Mum, and a lump came into her throat.

'I'm sorry, I just couldn't do it.' Mr Dickenson shook his head. 'I couldn't sell Glisterdale Forest.' Mandy let out a huge sigh of relief as he said, 'We'll just have to find another way round this problem.' He smiled at Mandy and James. 'Now, if you'll excuse me, Charles, these people have a film to make in that very woodland and I've held them up long enough.'

'Don't forget,' Charles Gregg said, as he got up to leave. 'If you change your mind about the woodland, just let me know.'

'I won't.' Mr Dickenson opened the door to see him out. 'I'm sure of that!'

He closed the door behind Mr Gregg and turned back to where Mandy and her friends were sitting at the kitchen table.

'I've seen enough of the woodland to have a good idea of what we want to do,' Michelle said brightly. She looked over at Janie who nodded. 'If it's all right with you, we'll start first thing in the morning?'

'Fine,' Peter Dickenson said, sounding more cheerful. 'The film might help bring more visitors to the grounds of Glisterdale Grange. That will be a help.'

Mandy was thoughtful as they walked back to Michelle's Jeep.

'What's wrong?' James asked quietly.

'It's just that everything seemed so, well,' Mandy hunted for the right word, '*safe* here a little while ago and now it all seems in danger.'

'I know what you mean,' James agreed. 'But Mr Dickenson won't sell the deer wood. You heard him say so.'

Mandy nodded but she was glum and quiet on the way home.

That evening, after Mandy had spilled out her worries about Glisterdale Grange, Adam Hope tried to reassure her. 'Don't get too upset, Mandy. Peter Dickenson loves his land, he won't sell it if he can possibly avoid it,' he told her. 'If there is any way at all of sorting things out, he'll find it.'

Mandy sighed. She knew her dad was right, but what if there *wasn't* any other way to raise the huge amount of money? What would happen to the deer then?

Two

The next morning, as soon as Mandy opened her eyes, she sprang out of bed and leaned out of the window. The sun was shining and the still air was already warm. Everywhere looked fresh and green after yesterday's rain. A perfect day for filming deer, Mandy thought to herself. She dressed quickly and set off to meet the others.

When they arrived at Glisterdale Grange, Peter Dickenson was standing on the drive next to his car. He looked hot and uncomfortable in a dark suit with a green and white striped tie. 'I'm off to see the bank manager,' he announced. 'I thought I'd better dress the part! I only wear this suit on special occasions.'

'Well, saving Glisterdale Grange is pretty special,' Mandy said. 'We'll keep our fingers crossed for you all day.'

Mr Dickenson laughed as he climbed into the driver's seat and started the engine. 'That will make filming a bit difficult, I should think,' he said. 'See you later, with good news, I hope.' He waved as he drove off.

Mandy and James helped Janie to unload her equipment.

'Mandy, could you put this spare cassette of film in that bag in the back of the Jeep, please?' Janie asked, as she slotted a cassette into the camera. 'And could you find a filter in that case for me, please, James?' She nodded her head towards a square aluminium case.

James opened the lid. The case was full of camera equipment. 'That's it, in the flat box,' Janie said, as James picked it out.

'We'll start with the paddock and the gardens,' Michelle said, gesturing towards the paddock where all the new young trees had metal guards around them. 'I want to show how the new trees and the formal gardens are protected from hungry deer.'

They opened the gate and entered the paddock.

'Why do the tree guards have to reach so high?' James asked. 'They must be at least two metres in height and the deer aren't that tall.' He stretched his arm up but couldn't reach the top. Janie began filming with James alongside the trees to show the height of the guards.

'Good question, James,' Michelle said. 'You'd be surprised how high a deer can reach when they stand up on their hind legs. If the guard isn't high enough they can get to the bark and eat it, and that kills the tree.'

'So once the tree has hardened up, they won't be able to harm it?' Mandy asked.

Michelle nodded. 'Deer don't do any damage to the bark of an established tree. But they can strip the bark completely from a young tree or even trample it down. Let's move a bit closer to the gardens.' She led them up on to a wooden bridge, over a ditch, and through the deer-proof gate into the formal gardens. Brilliantly-coloured roses grew beside red and pink geraniums. In the middle of one of the flowerbeds, an old man in green overalls and a straw hat was pruning bushes.

Michelle introduced herself, Mandy and James. Janie turned her camera on again.

'We're here to film the deer,' Mandy told the man.

'An' I'm here to do me job, so I won't stop. Me name's Albert, by the way.' With a series of efficient snips, he cleared a floribunda rose of all its dead blooms. 'But you can call me Bert.'

'Do the deer ever get into the gardens and damage the flowers, Bert?' Michelle asked.

'What!' Bert looked aghast. 'Never!' he declared. 'They'd strip 'em down as fast as you could say Jack Robinson.'

'But how do you keep them out?' James asked, waving away a wasp that was dangerously close to getting behind his glasses. 'There isn't a fence.'

'Don't need no fences, the ha-ha keeps 'em out,' Bert told them, carrying on with his pruning. 'Works a treat.'

'The what?' Mandy said, puzzled. 'What's a ha-ha?'

Bert put down his secateurs. Then he walked over to the bridge and pointed at the ditch, waiting as they gathered around. 'You digs a ha-ha,' he explained, pointing at the ditch, 'all around the gardens. And what you digs out of the ditch you makes into a steep bank. Deer don't get down there.'

'It's like a moat without water,' James exclaimed.

'And it's much better than building a wall,' Michelle said, 'because it doesn't hide the view.'

'Look now, over there,' Bert said, pointing to a patch of shrubs near a copse of trees. As they watched, a herd of about twenty deer pranced out from among the trees into the open and ran fleetly across the grass to the sheep paddock. When they reached the paddock they swerved and changed direction, now running up the hill towards the forest. They stopped in the shade of a massive oak tree.

Through her binoculars Mandy searched for Honey-Mum and Sprite, but the spotted does all looked similar and the fawns were all jumping about, playing together. She could see that some of the deer were black and one was creamy white, but most were spotted, although some had light-coloured coats and others were much darker.

'Do you know if one of those is Honey-Mum?' Mandy asked Bert eagerly. 'We're hoping to film Sprite, the fawn she adopted.'

'The fawn'll be running with the herd now,' Bert told them. 'You'll not pick that fawn out, 'cept if you tagged it.' Bert raised an eyebrow quizzically at Mandy.

Mandy shook her head frowning. 'But I'm sure I would recognise her by her coat,' she said. 'She's a golden chestnutty colour with rows of spots on her back and sides.'

'So she's a common, then,' Bert observed, looking at Michelle who nodded.

'Sprite's a fallow deer,' James said, puzzled. 'Like those ones.' He pointed at the herd.

'Aha!' said Bert wisely. 'All them deer are fallow. Fallow deer come in four types, you see.' He looked from Mandy to James to check that they were paying attention. 'There's *black* 'cause they're black, *menil* – that's pale spots, *white* 'cause they're light with light-coloured hooves instead of black, and *common* 'cause they're . . . well . . .' Bert paused.

'Common?' suggested Mandy, and they all laughed.

'Been fallow deer here for years and years,' Bert told them. 'Lovely creatures. Have to be well managed, though, else they get out of hand.' He turned back to his roses. 'I've got to get on now. If you find your fawn, ask Mr Dickenson about tagging her.' He was interrupted by a wailing cry that sounded like a cat miaowing.

'Whatever's that?' James asked.

'That's a peacock,' Bert chuckled. 'Sounds like a banshee, he does.'

A splendid peacock, followed by several peahens, came strutting from behind a hedge down to the ornamental pond in the middle of the gardens. While the others were drinking, one of the peahens turned and came bounding down, flapping her wings excitedly. She made a beeline for James and lay down in front of him, fixing him with a beady eye.

'She's taken a shine to you, lad,' Bert said, laughing, as James blushed and backed away.

'I wish she would take a shine to someone else!' James muttered, as the peahen tried to follow him.

They had lunch at one of the wooden tables in the picnic area at the side of the house. There were slices of vegetarian quiche, and cheese and tomato sandwiches, but Mandy found that she wasn't hungry. She was too busy thinking about Sprite. 'Why didn't we think to tag her?' she wondered aloud.

'Don't worry too much, Mandy,' Michelle advised. 'After all, you say Mr Dickenson has been giving you progress reports, so he must be able to recognise her.'

'Of course!' exclaimed James. 'Perhaps he can point her out to us.'

'Why don't you ask him,' Michelle laughed. 'Here he comes now.'

They watched as Peter Dickenson got out of his car. He went around to the other side and gathered up his crumpled jacket and sheaf of papers from the passenger seat. Slowly and wearily, he walked towards the little group at the picnic table. Mandy's heart sank. She looked at James and could see that he sensed Mr Dickenson's dejection too. Peter Dickenson stopped to wait for his wife who was hurrying over from the house, Rosie bounding joyfully ahead of her. They exchanged a few words, then joined Mandy and the others at the picnic table.

'I just don't know how to tell you this,' Mr Dickenson sighed, dropping the papers on the table. Mrs Dickenson was looking at him anxiously. 'I have seen *everybody*,' he said forlornly, 'and it's hopeless.' Mandy stared at him in horror. 'Everybody I spoke to said the same thing,' he told them, looking at his wife. 'Sell some land.'

'Oh, Peter, does it have to be that?' Mrs Dickenson's eyes were bright with tears.

'There's no other choice. I've tried everything else.' With a deep sigh he rifled through the papers and pulled out several typed sheets of thick cream paper. 'Charles Gregg kindly worked out the cost of the work for me.' He passed it to his wife.

'But Mr Dickenson,' Mandy asked quietly, biting her lip. 'Which bit of land are you going to sell?'

'Mandy, I'm afraid I don't have a choice. The only land that it's feasible to sell is Glisterdale Forest,' said Peter Dickenson, shaking his head. 'The buyer Charles Gregg knew of is so keen to get it that he's coming over this afternoon to discuss terms.'

'But what about the deer?' Mandy felt herself go cold. 'What about Honey-Mum and Sprite?' she asked.

'Well, I hope that nothing will change too drastically. I've asked that the deer herd be left alone.' Mr Dickenson managed a weak smile. 'I'm sure you can carry on with your film. The possible purchaser is coming over later to have a look so you can ask him then, but I can't imagine he'd raise any objections.'

'Thanks,' Michelle said, standing up. She nodded at Mandy and James. 'Perhaps we'd better get on,' she suggested tactfully. 'I'm sure Mr and Mrs Dickenson have lots to discuss.'

Mandy gathered up the leftovers and put them in the bin. She didn't want to hear any more about the forest being sold. The whole thing was awful. She and James silently followed Michelle and Janie back through the paddocks and into the woods. Noticing how miserable they looked, Michelle took charge. 'Now, look at it this way,' she began brightly. 'The best thing we can do for the deer, for Honey-Mum and Sprite, is to make a really good film about them.'

'You mean, show people how interesting they are?' James said thoughtfully.

'And encourage them to come to Glisterdale,' Mandy exclaimed.

'Exactly!' Michelle said, smiling. 'Look at it as a challenge. We've only got a few days to do it. Let's make this the best film we can.'

Mandy nodded. 'Right!' she said, in her most positive voice, 'Come on, James, let's get cracking!'

'Good,' said Michelle, handing Mandy a microphone to carry. 'Now, let's find ourselves some deer.'

*   *   *

By the end of the afternoon they were all feeling more cheerful. The deer seemed undisturbed by the filming and Janie had got some wonderful close shots of them feeding and plenty of footage of the fawns playing.

'I bet we'll see Sprite soon,' James said, optimistically.

'I'll ask Mr Dickenson about her when we get back,' said Mandy, taking off her trainer to tip out a stone. 'But I'm still sure I'll know her when I see her.'

They were tired as they made their way back to the house, but pleased with the day's work. As they stepped out of the wood and into the sunshine Mandy screwed up her eyes. A Landrover was parked outside the house, and Mandy recognised the registration number at once.

'Oh no,' she moaned to James. 'What's *he* doing here?'

Michelle shaded her eyes with her hand and stared at the man who was getting out of the passenger's door. 'Isn't that Sam Western?' she asked.

'Too right,' James agreed glumly, 'and Dennis Saville.'

Michelle made a face. 'Let's walk slowly,' she said. 'Then perhaps by the time we reach the house they'll have gone. I have no wish to meet that awful man again.'

Sam Western was a local farmer who had recently tried to introduce a foxhunt in Welford. Dennis Saville, his estate manager, had shot the vixen Michelle and Janie had been filming for another *Wildlife Ways* programme. Neither of the men were popular in the village. But as Mandy watched, she saw Mr Dickenson come out of the house and shake Sam Western's hand.

Mandy couldn't believe it. Suddenly, she felt a cold grip of fear in her stomach. 'Are you thinking what I'm thinking?' she said to James, fearfully.

'Uh-huh,' James nodded.

'Michelle?' Mandy asked.

'We'll have to wait and see, Mandy,' she replied, grim-faced. 'But it doesn't look good.'

Peter Dickenson, Sam Western and Dennis Saville began walking down through the paddocks towards them.

'Michelle, Janie, Mandy, James,' Mr Dickenson said, smiling half-heartedly, 'meet Mr Western, he's to be the new owner of Glisterdale Forest.'

Mandy and James were horrified. Their worst fears were realised. Sam Western completely ignored them and strode past, followed by Dennis Saville who was clutching a clipboard and a metal ruler.

'I'm sure he didn't mean to be rude,' Mr Dickenson said, watching Sam Western head off towards the forest. 'He seemed quite a charming man on the telephone. I'd better catch them up.'

'Wait!' Mandy called, catching Mr Dickenson's sleeve. 'Sam Western is a horrible man. He *hates* wildlife. He tried to start a foxhunt in Welford, and we saw him shoot a vixen bringing food to her cubs.' Mandy was almost in tears.

'He tried to poison our friend's goat,' James added, 'and he set traps to kill foxes which nearly caught Mrs Ponsonby's dogs.'

Mr Dickenson was visibly shocked. He looked to Michelle for confirmation and she nodded. He put his hand on his forehead. 'What have I done?' he muttered, shaking his head.

'You weren't to know what Sam Western was like,' Michelle said gently. 'And don't forget, you haven't much choice. But it could be very bad news for the wildlife.'

'What will happen to the deer now?' A tear slipped down Mandy's face as she spoke.

'Look, I *have* asked for a clause to be put in the contract that protects the wildlife.' Peter Dickenson reassured her. 'And as for the deer, because the whole of my estate is unenclosed they are free to go anywhere. Fortunately, they choose to stay. Deer are wild animals and as such have no owners. In open land like mine the deer are protected by wildlife acts.'

'But what if the land *is* enclosed?' Mandy worried, blowing her nose.

'If an estate is fenced they become the property of the landowner,' Mr Dickenson conceded. 'But don't worry, Mandy, I'll never enclose my land. As far as I'm concerned the deer can roam freely.' He managed a grin. 'I'm sure the deer will be fine. Look, Mr Western's coming back.'

'I think we'll have to tell him about the film we're making,' Michelle said, drumming her fingers on her binoculars.

Sam Western drew level with them on the way back to his Land-rover. 'Nice doing business with you,' he called to Mr Dickenson as he strode past. 'My lawyer will talk to yours.'

'Mr Western,' Michelle called, 'can I have a word please?'

Sam Western turned, looking annoyed.

'Hurry up, then, I'm a busy man.'

'It's just that I thought I should tell you we're making a film about the deer in Glisterdale Forest,' Michelle said. 'I wouldn't want you to think we were trespassing.' She laughed.

Sam Western stared at Michelle. 'That's out of the question,' he said curtly. 'My men will be down shortly to carry out a few jobs. You'll be in their way.'

Mandy looked at Peter Dickenson.

He was frowning now, and he stepped forward. 'Hold on just a moment, Mr Western,' he said crossly. 'It is still officially *my* land you know, and I gave these people permission to film the deer.'

Sam Western looked hard at Mr Dickenson. 'I don't want to jeopardise our arrangement,' he said cautiously, 'but I can't have people walking about willy-nilly. I've got plans for that forest.' He looked at Michelle. 'You can carry on until the work starts, young woman, and then I want you out!' He turned and strode off.

'Well!' Michelle exclaimed. 'He doesn't change.'

Mandy and James exchanged grim glances. 'What do you think his plans are?' Mandy asked Peter Dickenson.

'I don't know, Mandy, but we have to presume he'll want to make money out of it somehow,' Mr Dickenson answered. 'He hasn't told me his plans.'

'Then it's up to us to show everyone the importance of the forest in our film,' Michelle said firmly.

'And its value as a home to all the wildlife, especially the deer,' Mandy said.

'*Especially* the deer,' Peter Dickenson echoed softly, as he turned and walked back to the house.

Three

'Under the circumstances,' Michelle told them,
'I think we should do some more filming today.
Let's get as much footage under our belts as we
can before the workmen begin. Agreed?'

Mandy, James and Janie all nodded. 'OK.
Let's go,' Michelle said, leading them back to
the edge of the forest.

While Michelle and Janie discussed technical
details, Mandy leaned against a huge oak tree
and tried to calm down. She wished there was a
way to persuade Sam Western to leave the deer
alone.

'What do you think Sam Western's got in
mind?' James asked.

Mandy shrugged. 'Who knows?' she replied. 'But knowing him, it won't be good. I just wish Mr Dickenson didn't have to sell the land at all.'

'Look, you two,' Janie said softly, interrupting their discussion. 'There are some does with fawns. See, just coming into the clearing.'

Mandy looked through her binoculars. 'There's Sprite!' she exclaimed under her breath. 'Look, James, the one at the front.'

'It looks like her,' James said, as he fiddled with the focus on his binoculars, 'but I'm sure that fawn has a tag. Look at her ear.'

'Oh yes,' Mandy said, her voice full of disappointment. With Sam Western threatening the deer's home, she was more anxious than ever to find the fawn and know that she was all right.

At about half-past six they packed up and made their way back to the house.

'We got some good shots,' Michelle said, making notes as she went along. 'You know, the change of ownership of the forest will give an extra twist to the programme.'

'It will be interesting to see exactly what "jobs" Mr Western's men are going to start on,' Janie said as they neared the house.

'Look,' said Mandy, pointing at the house. 'It's Mrs Dickenson.'

Mrs Dickenson was standing at the kitchen door, waving to them. 'Peter would like a word before you go, if you've time,' she said, holding the door for them. 'He's in the study.'

Mandy led the way along the oak-panelled hall to a large wooden door with a big brass handle that stood open.

Mr Dickenson was on the phone. He looked up and beckoned them to come in. 'Well, I'd like it on the record that I am extremely angry about it,' he was saying in a cold voice. 'In fact, I almost feel like suggesting you tear up that contract. Forget selling the land, I'll raise the money another way.'

Mandy swallowed hard and looked at Michelle, who was frowning.

'I am not being hasty,' Peter Dickenson went on. 'I want protection for the deer herd. In writing.' He listened for a few minutes then said calmly, 'Fine, that will be acceptable. Goodbye.' Putting the phone down he sat back with a sigh.

'Trouble with Sam Western?' Michelle asked.

'That was Western's solicitor,' Peter Dickenson told them. 'I wanted you to know that Western has demanded that they take out the contract clause protecting the deer and other wildlife.'

Mandy gasped. 'But you can't!' She looked from Mr Dickenson to Michelle. 'You know what will happen if the deer aren't protected. We can't trust Mr Western.'

'It's all right, Mandy,' Mr Dickenson said. 'I've insisted that he gives me written assurance that the deer can roam in the forest for as long as they want to; for ever, in fact.'

'That sounds reasonable,' Michelle said. 'I mean he can't change his mind, once he's promised.'

'Can't he?' James muttered to Mandy.

'He's a businessman, James. As long as I have his word, it will be all right,' Mr Dickenson said. 'I'm sure everything will be fine, now that we've sorted out the important issues.' He stood up and walked around the desk. 'There's a company coming tomorrow to give me a quotation for the work on the house. If we can agree on the price, they can start work this week. It will be a terrible upheaval, but the sooner the repairs are done, the better.'

'At least the house will be safe,' said Michelle. 'We'll carry on filming tomorrow, then, if that's convenient?'

'Be my guest,' Peter Dickenson told her, as he walked them to the front door.

They piled into the Jeep and Michelle set off. At the gates she stopped and looked both ways. A huge, dirty truck was approaching. The driver flashed his lights to let Michelle pull out. But as they turned out of the drive, Mandy saw the driver of the truck clearly.

'It's Dennis Saville!' she gasped in alarm.

'And his workmen,' James added, looking back.

Mandy turned to watch and her heart

thudded as she saw them turn into Glisterdale Grange. James shook his head.

'I hope they're not planning to start work already,' Michelle said, concern in her voice. 'The contracts haven't been exchanged yet.'

Mandy frowned. The deer were at Sam Western's mercy and now it seemed that the *Wildlife Ways* programme was too.

'See you tomorrow, Mandy,' Michelle called, as Mandy jumped out of the Jeep at Animal Ark. 'And try not to worry too much about the deer. Sam Western's giving Mr Dickenson a written guarantee, don't forget.'

Mandy nodded and gave a weak grin. But as she entered the cottage she couldn't shake off a feeling of impending doom.

Adam Hope was sitting in the armchair in the kitchen reading some veterinary papers. 'What's up love?' he said, putting down the papers. 'I can tell you're worried. Has something happened at the Grange?' He patted the arm of the chair. 'Come on, come and tell your old dad all about it.' He gave her one of his lopsided grins.

'Dad, it's awful!' Mandy said, going over to perch on the edge of the armchair. 'Mr

Dickenson *has* sold the forest, and guess who's bought it?'

Adam Hope looked shocked. 'I really didn't think he would sell,' he said. 'Things must be pretty bad for him. So who *is* the new owner?'

'Sam Western,' Mandy said in a miserable voice.

'Oh, I see.' Her dad frowned. 'Not the sort of person I would imagine wanting a deer forest.'

'That's what I'm worried about, Dad,' Mandy said urgently. 'He's sent some workmen up there already. What do you think he's up to?'

'I don't know. What does Peter say about it all?' he asked. 'I'm sure he wouldn't do anything to endanger the deer.'

'Mr Dickenson's made him put it in writing that the deer can stay in the wood,' Mandy said doubtfully.

'There you are then, love,' Adam Hope smiled. 'That sounds fine. Like I said, Peter will look after the deer. He enjoys having them there so much that he doesn't even like it when they have to cull them.'

'Cull them?' Mandy asked warily. 'What do you mean?'

Her father sighed. 'Well, to start with, did you know that deer have no natural predators in

Britain, now that wolves have been wiped out?' he began. 'Apart from dogs and the occasional road casualty, there's nothing to keep down the deer numbers,' he continued.

'But why *should* their numbers be kept down?' Mandy asked, shocked. 'They're beautiful animals, why can't they grow old and die naturally?'

'Even a forest as big as Glisterdale can only support so many deer,' her dad explained. 'If the deer population grows too big, then you get too many animals competing for too little food. That's not good for the deer or the land.' Mr Hope looked up into Mandy's face. 'Think about it, love. the deer at Glisterdale are very successful. But you have to remember all the other wildlife in the forest. The deer can't keep breeding out of control, can they?'

Mandy knew her dad was right, but that didn't mean she had to *like* it. 'So how do they cull them?' she asked.

'They shoot any obviously old or sick animals, although it's quite hard to pick them out,' Adam Hope explained gently. 'And they usually shoot some of the does.' He put his hand up to stop her interrupting. 'It has to be done, Mandy, even if we don't like it.'

'Does Mr Dickenson do the culling at Glisterdale Grange?' Mandy asked.

'No,' Mr Hope said. 'It has to be done in season and by a professional using a rifle. As Glisterdale Grange isn't large enough to have a deer-keeper, Tony Morris does it.'

Mandy didn't like the thought of it one bit, but she knew her dad was right. You couldn't let the herd get too big. She was glad that Mr Dickenson didn't have to shoot them himself, though.

'What happens to the dead ones, Dad?' Mandy asked quietly.

'I thought you might ask that,' Adam Hope said, looking at her seriously. 'In an ideal world, Mandy, deer would be able to run free. But you have to think of it as harvesting a food source, like any other. Just like Mr Masters has chickens, Glisterdale Grange has deer.' He looked at Mandy to make sure she understood. When Mandy nodded, Adam Hope continued. 'A game dealer will buy the deer from Peter. It's my bet that any money he gets, Peter Dickenson ploughs back into the herd.'

'What do you mean?' Mandy asked, puzzled.

'Well, deer can be expensive to keep. They may be wild animals but they still need extra feed in the winter, to keep up their strength through the cold months.'

'So Mr Dickenson might use the money to buy hay or something?' Mandy asked, feeling sure that Mr Dickenson was doing something to help the deer.

'Well, I imagine he probably buys in some concentrates, food pellets and carrots, things like that,' Mr Hope told her.

'Dad!' Mandy said as the thought struck her. 'What do you think Sam Western will do about culling the deer?'

'If he's said the deer can stay, I would imagine things will continue much as they are.' Mr Hope stood up and ruffled Mandy's hair. 'There may be no reason at all for you to worry,' he told her. 'Sam Western's a greedy businessman, he probably just can't resist buying up any land that's going. He might not even have any solid plans for it yet.'

There was a crunch of gravel as the Animal Ark Land-rover pulled up outside. Mandy and her dad heard the car door slam and Mrs Hope's key in the lock. 'Hi,' she called. 'I'm just popping into the surgery, I'll be back in a minute.'

'Whoops!' Adam Hope said, striding over to

the fridge. 'I promised to make a start on dinner.'

'I'll lay the table,' Mandy offered, jumping up. 'Shall we eat indoors or in the garden?'

'Inside, Mandy, I still haven't mended that table-leg and I promised Mum I'd do it today!' Adam Hope said guiltily, giving her conspiratorial look.

By the time Emily Hope had come back from unpacking her vet's bag in the surgery, the kitchen was a hive of activity. Adam Hope was mixing oil and vinegar to make a salad dressing and Mandy was slicing tomatoes. The smell of warm bread filled the air.

'Hi, you two,' Emily Hope said, dropping a kiss on Mandy's cheek. 'How did the filming go?'

Mandy told her mum all about Sam Western buying Glisterdale Forest.

'I expect,' her mother said, taking a quiche from the fridge and removing the foil, 'he probably sees it as an investment to sell on later.'

'That's just what Dad said,' Mandy said, surprised.

'There you are,' Adam Hope told her with a grin. 'Great minds think alike!'

'So don't worry too much about the deer, Mandy,' her mum said. 'I know you where animals are concerned.' She sat down at the table. 'It's a beautiful evening, why aren't we eating outside?' she asked, glancing sideways at Mr Hope. 'Adam?'

'We decided it was too cold, actually,' Mr Hope said innocently. 'Didn't we, Mandy?'

Mandy nodded, trying to suppress a grin. The warm evening sunlight was streaming through the kitchen windows.

Mandy loved evenings like this when they were all together, and nobody was out on a call. Maybe Mum and Dad were right and everything at Glisterdale Grange was going to be fine. Maybe Sam Western *had* had a change of heart when he agreed to protect the deer. She couldn't wait for the next day to carry on with the filming.

Mandy and her dad offered to clear away after supper, so Emily Hope could go and relax with the paper. They washed up in silence, both deep in thought. Mandy's mind wandered to Glisterdale Grange and the beautiful deer they had been watching that day. But then an awful thought struck her. Her dad had said 'usually they shoot some of the does'. Sprite was a doe!

Mr Dickenson would recognise Sprite but Sam Western's men might shoot her!

'Dad!' she exclaimed, dropping the tea towel she was holding. 'What about Sprite? If there's a cull, I mean?'

'They usually cull in November, Mandy. Sprite's much too small, so don't worry,' Mr Hope told her.

'But what about next year?' Mandy asked, anxiously. 'She'll be much bigger then.'

Adam Hope looked at his daughter's pale, worried face. 'Even next year, Mandy, they'll still be able to tell last year's fawns. Why don't you ask Peter Dickenson first thing in the morning?' he suggested.

'OK,' Mandy agreed, hoping her dad was right. She picked up the tea towel and carried on drying the plates. Her dad had made her feel a bit better but she still couldn't help worrying. If only Peter Dickenson had been able to keep Glisterdale Forest. She was sure Sprite would have been safe with him.

Four

'*All things bright and beautiful, all creatures great and small . . .*'

The words boomed through the air. Mandy turned over in bed and smiled to herself. It was her dad's favourite hymn from the church choir and he loved singing it. But he could only remember the first verse, and after that he always got in a muddle. She listened as he continued singing.

'*The purple-headed mountain, the river running by . . .*'

Mandy giggled softly. This was the bit he always got wrong.

'*The sunrise and the morning that lightens up*

the sky.'

Mandy jumped out of bed, ran across the landing and banged on the bathroom door.

Adam Hope opened the door wearing his dressing-gown, toothbrush in hand.

'I know, I got it wrong!' he said grinning. 'One day maybe I'll get it right.' Mandy's dad sighed with a staged grimace.

'It's *sunset*, not sunrise,' Mandy told him, as he turned back to the basin. 'Dad, do you mind if I give Mr Dickenson a call?' she asked. 'I can't wait until we get over there later.'

'All right, Mandy,' Adam Hope said, grabbing a towel. 'I don't suppose we'll get any peace until you do.'

'Thanks, Dad,' Mandy called, as she ran down the stairs two at a time. Her dad knew her too well.

'Good morning, Glisterdale Grange,' Peter Dickenson said, answering the phone.

'Mr Dickenson, it's Mandy Hope here.' Mandy took a deep breath. 'Bert told us that Sprite would be running with the herd now and Dad's told me all about deer culling, and I wondered how . . .' she didn't have to finish her sentence.

'How we can recognise Sprite, do you mean?'

Peter Dickenson cut in. 'I'm really sorry, Mandy, didn't I tell you? In all the confusion yesterday, I completely forgot.'

'Tell me what?' Mandy pleaded.

'Well, some time ago when the herd came near the house, Tony and I caught Sprite and I tagged her,' he explained. 'Sprite has a neat little blue ear tag in her right ear to identify her. There's no other way you'd know her once she's running free.'

Mandy felt relief flood through her. She was now certain that the fawn they'd seen with an ear tag *was* Sprite.

'Oh, I'm so pleased, Mr Dickenson,' Mandy said. 'I thought I spotted her yesterday but I didn't know she was tagged.'

'I'm sure it was her, you'd probably still recognise her,' Mr Dickenson replied. 'Aren't you coming over today?'

'Oh yes,' Mandy said. 'I just couldn't wait any longer to find out.'

'That's OK, Mandy,' Mr Dickenson told her. 'See you later on then. Goodbye.'

'Bye,' Mandy said, putting the phone back.

'Well?' said Adam Hope coming down the stairs. 'You look happier now. I gather Sprite is tagged.'

Mandy nodded as they walked together into the kitchen. Emily Hope was just rinsing her cereal bowl in the kitchen sink.

'I heard the good news, too. Mandy. That's great.' Mrs Hope put her bowl on the draining-board, then picked up her keys and went to the back door. 'I promised to pop up to the animal sanctuary. The cat that had the breech birth last week isn't doing too well. When are you off to meet Michelle?'

'In about twenty minutes,' Mandy said, pouring her dad some orange juice. 'I said I'd walk down and meet the others in the village.'

'I'll see you tonight then.' Emily Hope blew them both a kiss and went out.

After breakfast, Mandy cleared the table and washed up. She stacked the dishes in the cupboard and popped into the surgery to say goodbye to her dad.

Simon had just arrived and in reception Jean was busy answering the phone. Just for a moment, Mandy regretted not being able to stay. While she loved helping out on *Wildlife Ways*, she *did* miss the patients at Animal Ark.

'We'll still be here next week when the

filming's finished,' her dad said, noticing the wistful look on her face.

'And so will all your jobs, Mandy,' Simon said, '*and* all the extra jobs you've promised to do for me!'

'I'm gone!' Mandy laughed, racing out of the door and sprinting up the lane.

In the Jeep she told the others about Sprite.

'Phew, that's a relief,' James said. 'So that fawn we saw *was* Sprite.'

'With luck you might see her again today,' Michelle said. 'I'm hoping to get some footage in the open today.'

'Could you bring that tripod for me, please, James?' Janie asked, as they unloaded the equipment.

They set up the camera between the paddocks and the forest, weighting down the feet of the tripod with three large stones to hold it steady. Janie pointed the camera towards the path that led into the forest and they settled down to wait.

Mandy was the first to spot the herd of deer emerging from the forest, browsing on oak leaves as they passed. She and James counted them.

'Fourteen!' Mandy said, softly. 'One male with enormous antlers—'

'And two with little dumpy stubs,' James noted.

'The male with the large antlers will be quite old,' Michelle explained. 'You see the broad, flat parts on the end of its antlers? They're called the "palms", and only moose and fallow deer have them. Each year the bucks grow bigger antlers.' She looked through her binoculars. 'He's still got some velvet hanging on the right antler, can you see it?'

'Yep, I can see it,' James said, studying the buck. 'Why *do* deer shed their antlers, Michelle?' he asked. 'Why don't they just grow bigger and bigger?'

'Once an antler is fully-grown and has shed its velvet, what's left is actually dead bone,' she replied. 'Every year, around May and June, the bucks start to shed their antlers. Each year they grow a bigger set, sort of in line with how old they are growing.'

'And do they start growing another set immediately?' Mandy asked.

'Yes, and they grow covered with the velvet,' Michelle told them.

'What's the velvet for?' quizzed James.

'The antlers need air and food to grow,' Michelle said. 'The velvet is a special sort of skin that helps to supply everything the bone needs.'

'And you said once the antlers are fully grown the velvet comes off?' James asked.

'That's right, James, and then the blood supply is cut off. The antler can't grow any bigger and it dies,' Michelle said, laughing at his expression.

'It seems a complicated way of growing antlers.' James grinned.

'How absolutely fascinating!' exclaimed a voice behind them.

They spun around to find Mrs Ponsonby standing there, Pandora, her Pekinese in her arms, and Toby, the little mongrel, dancing at her feet. 'You must be Michelle Holmes, from *Wildlife Ways*. My dear, *such* knowledge. I am delighted, no, *honoured* to meet you,' she announced, holding out a gloved hand.

Michelle looked rather shocked. They had all been so absorbed in watching the deer that none of them had heard Mrs Ponsonby coming. Michelle took her hand and shook it. 'And you are . . . ?' she asked.

'Amelia Ponsonby, dear, and this is Pandora

and that is Toby,' Mrs Ponsonby told her, putting the Pekinese on the ground. Mandy noticed that both dogs had bright new collars. Toby's was red and yellow tartan and Pandora's was pink and studded with tiny sparkling stones.

'Hello, Mrs Ponsonby,' Mandy said, bending down to stroke Pandora.

'Good morning, Mandy and James,' Mrs Ponsonby replied. 'I'm pleased to see you are hard at work making your film.'

Mrs Ponsonby was rather over-dressed for the woodland setting. She wore a flowered dress with a little matching jacket and the brim of her straw hat was pinned up at the front with a bunch of deep red plastic cherries. 'Now, dear, you just carry on as before and we will watch quietly,' she told Michelle. 'We'll be as quiet as mice, won't we, precious?' she cooed, gathering up Pandora and shuffling over towards Janie.

'What is happening here?' Michelle asked Mandy in a low voice. 'What does she think she's doing?'

'She probably wants to be in the film,' Mandy guessed.

'Huh!' Michelle exclaimed. 'We'll see about that.' She turned towards Janie who was standing with a bemused look on her face while

Mrs Ponsonby peered through her camera.

'Utterly fascinating,' Mrs Ponsonby was saying. 'How very exciting it all is,' she said. 'Now don't let me get in your way,' she added, standing back.

For several moments she stood quietly behind them, while they watched a young doe approaching. Then, as the deer drew very near to them and Janie began to film, Mrs Ponsonby announced, 'I loved your programme last week, dear,' in a loud voice. 'And we always listen to your radio slot too, don't we, precious?' she said to Pandora. The doe fled in panic.

Michelle turned to Mrs Ponsonby, frowning,

and put her finger to her lips.

'Oops, sorry,' Mrs Ponsonby whispered, shaking her head so that the cherries on her hat wobbled precariously.

Mandy and James exchanged glances as Janie began filming again.

In the forest a deer barked and another answered. The buck with the big antlers and his group were just coming into view again when, suddenly, Janie switched off the camera and turned to Michelle. 'It's no good, I'm picking up a strange noise on the sound recording,' she said in a worried voice. 'It sounds like someone breathing heavily. I think we'd better move position.'

Together Janie and Michelle carried the camera and tripod nearer the forest and resumed filming.

But after just a few seconds Janie stopped again. 'It's no good, I'm still getting that noise.'

'Right,' Michelle decided, 'we have to find out what it is. Everybody keep absolutely still.'

Mandy and James, Michelle and Janie and even Mrs Ponsonby froze like statues. They all heard the panting noise.

'Herh, herh, herh.' Eyes wide, Pandora puffed

away, getting faster now that everyone was looking at her.

'Pandora, darling, do be quiet,' Mrs Ponsonby hissed under her breath.

'Oh, poor Pandora, she can't help it,' Mandy exclaimed, stroking the little dog's head.

'Don't worry, I'll make sure she stops,' Mrs Ponsonby promised confidently.

'I'd appreciate that. Otherwise, I'm afraid I shall have to ask you to take her away,' Michelle replied apologetically.

But Mrs Ponsonby's attempts to silence Pandora by rocking her gently in her arms didn't work. In fact, it made Pandora's noisy breathing worse. Just at a crucial moment came a loud 'hic' followed shortly by another one. As well as panting, Pandora now had hiccups.

Michelle turned and looked at Mrs Ponsonby.

'I'll take her for a little walk, shall I, dear?' she asked Michelle.

'What a good idea!' Michelle said with a firm nod. 'Keep the dogs on leads though, we don't want them chasing the deer,' she called after Mrs Ponsonby.

Mrs Ponsonby looked as if she had been struck in the face. 'My dogs would not *dream* of chasing deer. They are far too well brought up,' she said with a haughty expression.

Mandy and James turned away to stifle their laughter as Mrs Ponsonby flounced off. But she hadn't given up yet. When she reached the forest, she walked the dogs up and down, up and down, peering every so often in the direction of the camera.

'Oh no, what's she playing at?' Janie complained.

'She's trying to get in the film,' Mandy told her with a grin. 'She's very determined.'

'Not as determined as me!' Michelle exclaimed. 'Stop filming and swing the camera round, Janie,' she ordered. 'OK, everyone, let's turn around and pretend to film in another direction.'

Mandy peeked over her shoulder. After a few minutes, Mrs Ponsonby gave up and disappeared into the forest.

'She's gone,' Mandy told them, stretching her arms above her head.

'I think we'll take a break now anyway,' Michelle said. 'We need a volunteer to go back to the Jeep for the picnic.'

'I'll go,' James offered, taking the keys Michelle held out to him.

'I'll come with you.' Mandy was eager to

stretch her legs a bit. 'Trust Mrs Ponsonby to turn up like that!' she said, as they walked up the path toward the paddocks. 'Hey, look, James, what's that?'

Stacked in piles beside the gate to the paddocks were huge rolls of chain-link fencing, wrapped in thick polythene.

'Mr Dickenson must be planning some work,' James said, as they climbed over the gate. 'Race you to the car park!'

They were neck and neck as they neared the car park but James surged ahead and touched down just before Mandy. 'That's the second time I've beaten you,' he told her. 'I must be getting faster.'

James unlocked the Jeep and between them they carried the refreshments back to the others.

Michelle poured coffee for herself and Janie, and handed Mandy and James cans of soft drinks. Janie opened a packet of chocolate digestive biscuits that were beginning to melt and stick together. They were all munching the biscuits when James spotted Mrs Ponsonby heading back towards them with the dogs.

'I won't disturb you,' she said. 'I'll be taking my two darlings home soon, they're getting rather hot.' She was red-faced and puffing from the effort of her walk. 'I just wanted to show you what we found in the forest. Look, a bird has picked it clean. I thought you might want to take a picture of it for your programme.'

'May I see?' Michelle asked. Mrs Ponsonby handed her the remains of a pine cone. 'That's a squirrel's work,' Michelle told them. 'Squirrels eat pine cones rather like we eat corn on the cob. They strip it bare.' She held up the cone to show them all. 'A bird would have just pecked out the seeds and left it looking rather ragged.'

Mrs Ponsonby looked very impressed. 'Such knowledge, dear,' she said approvingly.

At that moment Peter Dickenson came striding down the path. 'How are you getting on here?' he asked. 'Seen lots of deer?'

'Loads,' Mandy told him, 'and Mrs Ponsonby found a pine cone that the squirrels have eaten.'

Mr Dickenson's eyes lit up. 'Ah yes,' he said, 'I meant to tell you about that. Did you know we have one of the few surviving pockets of red squirrels here?'

'Really?' Michelle exclaimed. 'When did you last see them?'

'Let me think. I haven't actually seen them for a few months,' Mr Dickenson said, scratching his head. 'But I saw them back in the spring.'

'They're really rare, aren't they?' Mandy asked, her voice full of excitement at the thought that they might spot a red squirrel.

James nodded. '*Really* rare!' he agreed, 'I'd love to see one.'

'Well, the pine cone proves they are still here, surely?' Mrs Ponsonby said.

'Sadly it doesn't,' Michelle said, shaking her head. 'It could mean that grey squirrels have moved in. We don't know why exactly, but the reds always move out when the greys move in.'

'There are definitely grey squirrels in Welford,' James told her.

'Ernie Bell's squirrel, Sammy, is a grey,' Mandy said. 'And we get lots in the garden.'

'Well, I suggest we all keep our eyes peeled to see if the red squirrels are still at Glisterdale,' Michelle decided. 'I'd love to get some shots of them for the programme and it might help us to protect the forest.'

'In that case, I shall come back tomorrow, dear,' Mrs Ponsonby told Michelle. 'To help you look. Bye-bye for now.'

As Mrs Ponsonby headed back towards the house, a group of workmen in overalls and hard hats were coming down the track carrying the rolls of chain-link fencing between them. Two men pushed wheelbarrows loaded with tools and bags of sand and cement, and another carried long, sharply pointed metal poles. 'Mind your backs, ladies and gentlemen,' a voice called out.

'Would you mind telling me where you are going with all that fencing?' Mr Dickenson asked, sounding puzzled.

Mandy frowned. If the men weren't working for Mr Dickenson they must be working for Sam Western – and that might mean the end of the filming . . .

Five

'Sorry if we disturbed you,' one of the workmen said, putting down his load. 'We're starting work fencing off the forest.' He gestured to Glisterdale Forest with his arm.

Peter Dickenson's face went white. 'On whose instructions, might I ask?' he said angrily.

'Instructions from the foreman,' the younger man replied, shrugging his shoulders. 'The foreman wants a fence, we make him a fence.'

'But this is *my* land,' Mr Dickenson said, 'and I don't know anything about this. I insist that you wait until I've found out what's going on. I am sure there's been a mistake.'

The workman looked doubtful. He glanced

back the way he'd come. 'Here comes Harry now, sir, he's the foreman. You'd best speak to him.'

'Good afternoon,' Peter Dickenson said, stepping out to greet the foreman.

'Afternoon, sir.' Harry was a big man with a dark suntan and his bald head was shiny and as brown as a conker. He stopped and shook Mr Dickenson's hand. 'What can I do for you?' he asked courteously.

'Perhaps you can tell me what's going on,' Peter Dickenson said, with a smile. 'I own Glisterdale Grange.'

'Ah!' Harry said. 'Then you'd be,' he looked at the worksheet pinned to his clipboard, 'Mr Western.'

'No, I'm Peter Dickenson,' he exclaimed. 'The owner of Glisterdale Grange.'

'Just a moment, sir,' Harry said, determinedly. 'I have been hired by a Mr Western to supervise the fencing of this forest. Are you telling me it doesn't belong to him? I wouldn't want to get involved in anything dodgy.'

'Well yes, Sam Western is buying the forest,' Peter Dickenson grudgingly had to admit. 'But I didn't know he intended to fence it off.'

'With all due respect, sir,' Harry said politely. 'If it's his forest, he can do what he likes with it.' He nodded to the startled group and started walking off towards the younger workman. 'Come on, Steve, let's get to work.'

Mandy couldn't bear it any longer. She was determined to find out what was going on. 'Excuse me,' she said, stepping forward. 'But *why* is he fencing it?'

'To keep people out, I expect. That's the usual reason,' Harry answered, turning back.

'Good Lord, the man doesn't waste any time,' Peter Dickenson said in a cold voice.

'I'm to fence all the areas where the public can get into the forest,' Harry told them. 'According to Mr Saville, he wants to keep out all the busybodies, all the "Nosey Parkers" who might start complaining when the work begins.'

'What work?' Mandy asked in a tense voice. At least Harry seemed happy to tell them anything, even if Sam Western wasn't.

'The tree felling. From what I've heard, he's going to start taking out the prime timber first,' Harry began.

'What's prime timber?' James asked, puzzled.

'Prime timber is the big old oaks and the fine beech trees,' Peter Dickenson told them quietly.

'The big trees that make up most of the forest.'

Mandy was shocked. She looked at James. Like her, he seemed to be having trouble taking it in.

'That's right,' Harry continued. 'He's got a mate who owns timber yards, apparently. Shame really.' He looked around. 'It looks like a nice forest for bird-watching. I'm partial to a bit of that.' He shrugged and said, 'Still, once the work starts with chainsaws, and the trucks and heavy machinery come in, you can't have people walking about. It's too dangerous. See you later!' And with a cheery wave he strode down the track.

'Sam Western has *got* to be stopped,' Mandy declared, horrified at the idea of the forest being felled. 'But how?'

'We'll have to find a way to change his mind, Mandy,' Peter Dickenson said. 'But first, I have to check on that fencing.' He strode off after Harry and Steve.

'You two go with him,' Michelle told Mandy and James. 'See what happens. Did you get all that, Janie?' she asked, turning to face her.

Janie nodded. Mandy turned to look at Janie and realised that, without any of them noticing, she had filmed the whole episode.

'Come on, James,' Mandy said, dashing after Mr Dickenson with James hot on her heels. When they caught up with him, he was inspecting the fencing. The workmen, with their hands on their hips, stood in a line behind it.

'Look, I know you are working for Sam Western,' Mr Dickenson was saying, 'but believe me, this fencing is nowhere near high enough.'

'It's nearly two metres high,' Harry said in a reasonable voice. 'People won't get over that too easily.'

'I'm not worried about people,' Peter Dickenson explained. 'There's a large herd of deer in the forest and they'll try to jump that. If it's not high enough the danger is that they will get caught on it. The fence *must* be at least two metres, preferably two metres thirty,' he said. 'I'm afraid I have to insist on it.'

Harry the foreman looked as if he was going to argue, but then changed his mind. 'I see, sir,' he said with a sigh. 'It's going to raise the cost a lot. I don't think Mr Western will wear it.' He looked at Peter Dickenson, who showed no sign of giving in. 'All right, sir, leave it with me,' he said, taking out his mobile phone.

Mr Dickenson turned, and with Mandy and

James in tow, walked back up to where Michelle and Janie were waiting.

'But if Sam Western fences the forest and the deer are trapped inside,' James asked, 'won't that mean they will belong to him?'

'Strictly speaking, yes,' Peter Dickenson said. 'But he's not allowed to trap them in on purpose, and they may leave of their own accord before the job is finished. They won't like the noise and disruption of the fence being built.'

'But what if they *don*'t leave,' Mandy said, worried. 'I mean, if he wants to cut the forest down, what's he going to do with the deer?'

'Well, he could have them caught and sell them off as live animals, or he could have them all shot,' Mr Dickenson said bluntly. 'Unfortunately, if deer become enclosed, you have to rely on the benevolence of the owner.' He gave a bitter laugh. 'Sam Western, benevolent! Somehow that seems unlikely.'

'But if the deer leave the forest, they'll be safe from Sam Western, won't they?' Mandy asked hopefully.

'The problem is, Mandy, where will they go?' Mr Dickenson ran his hand through his hair. 'Glisterdale has been a deer park for over nine hundred years. But once the noise starts they'll probably flee the forest.'

'Where do you think they will go?' Mandy asked with a catch in her voice.

'The most likely prospect is that many will run on to the roads and get injured or even killed by traffic,' Michelle said solemnly. 'Others will get on to the surrounding farmland and if they start eating the crops, that won't please too many farmers.'

'Any farmer has the right to shoot deer on his own land if they cause problems.' Peter Dickenson sighed.

'So the only answer is to stop Sam Western from fencing the forest,' Mandy said fiercely. 'We *have* to find a way of saving the deer *and* the forest.'

'I have one idea, Peter,' Michelle said thoughtfully. 'If the forest is that old, then some of those oaks and beeches must be very old indeed.'

'I can look in the estate archives,' Peter Dickenson said. 'They would mention any preservation orders.'

'And we can ask around for more information about the forest,' Mandy offered. 'Lots of families have lived here for years and years. My grandad was born in Welford, he'll know something about the forest, I bet!' she said.

'We could look in the library at Walton as well,' James suggested. 'We *can* do it can't we? Find a way to save the deer I mean,' he said, turning to Michelle.

'We can certainly try,' Michelle agreed. 'And we can cover all this on *Wildlife Ways*. People will be very interested in the fate of the deer.'

'It would be awful if Sam Western got away with destroying the forest,' Mandy said. 'I bet that's why he's started work so quickly, before all the people he calls "Nosey Parkers" can stop him.'

'And by "Nosey Parkers" he means bird-watchers, ramblers, wildlifers and anyone else who enjoys the forest,' Michelle said angrily. 'Like us. The sort of people who would rightly complain.'

'There is another way I can stop him,' Peter Dickenson told them. 'At the moment, the only way he could bring heavy machinery in would be over my land.'

'And you could refuse him access!' Mandy was getting fired up now. 'But is there any other way he could get in?'

'There is a place where he could make a drive

from the main road,' Mr Dickenson said, 'but it would involve a lot of work and slow them down.'

'And he'd need to get planning permission, wouldn't he?' Janie added, dismantling the camera. 'That's not easy,' she pointed out.

'It is if you're Sam Western!' Mandy said darkly.

'He has *friends*,' James said. 'In high places.'

'We'll just have to block his every move,' Mr Dickenson said. 'I'm sure we'll find a way.'

They started back up the track towards the house. Michelle had decided that with the workmen making so much noise in the forest, there would be no more filming today. Mandy and James hung back. 'That horrible man wants to ruin everything!' Mandy said, her voice a mixture of anger and sadness.

'Just when we thought Sprite was safe,' James said. 'I can't even think about her running out on to the road.'

Mandy stopped abruptly. 'We can't let him do it, James,' she said firmly. 'We just can't!'

James nodded. 'Whatever it takes, we'll stop him,' he agreed.

They were quiet on the journey back to Welford,

each trying to think of ways to stop Sam Western from destroying the deer forest.

'I'd like to get to Glisterdale very early tomorrow,' Michelle said as she dropped them off. 'Before the workmen start. Say about seven?'

Mandy nodded. They might have a better chance of seeing Sprite early in the morning, she thought to herself.

'How about you, James?' Michelle asked. They all knew how he hated getting up in the mornings.

'Yep, fine,' James agreed immediately. Mandy smiled at her friend. She knew he would do anything to help the deer.

When Mandy got home, both her parents were out on call. She went and sat in the residential unit and picked up a Jack Russell puppy with an injured ear. He had a special collar round his neck to stop him scratching his wound. As she sat stroking the little dog, Mandy started telling him all about Sam Western and his terrible plans for the forest.

'And,' she said, putting the little dog back in his bed, 'James and I are going to stop him!' She bent over and settled the dog down.

'*Whoooo!*' Mandy looked up when she heard

the strange quivery noise. There was nobody about but it hadn't sounded like an owl. She leaned through the open door and went to investigate.

'*Whoooo!*' Mandy heard the noise again. 'Are *yooo* going to stop?'

Mandy folded her arms and grinned. 'Come out, Dad, I know it's you!' she called.

Adam Hope stepped out from behind the hedge. 'I thought it sounded very realistic,' he said, looking disappointed.

'It would have been the world's first talking owl, then!' Mandy exclaimed.

Adam Hope laughed, then frowned. 'Let me

guess,' he said. 'Might it be Sam Western who's upsetting you?'

'Dad, he's *awful*,' Mandy declared. 'He's fencing off the forest and cutting down all the trees. There won't be anywhere for the deer to go! But James and I have decided to stop him.'

'You know, Mandy, some people have no feeling at all for the countryside,' her father told her. 'Sam Western probably hasn't given the deer a thought. His main concern will be business. There's so much pressure to produce an income from the land.' Mr Hope shook his head. 'And there's a lot of money to be made. Sam Western won't care about where the deer go or what happens to them. I'm afraid it's down to people who care to worry about that.'

'People like us, you mean?' Mandy asked.

'That's right,' Mr Hope replied. 'People who are willing to stand up and fight for what they believe is right. To challenge what they think is wrong. Like you do, love.'

'Me?' Mandy said, eyes wide with surprise.

'Yes, you,' her dad said. 'Mum and I are very proud of the way you stand up for animals.'

Mandy linked her arm in her dad's as they walked down the garden. 'Mmm,' she wondered aloud. 'Who do you think I get that from? I can't think of anyone around here who might be passionate about taking care of animals.'

Mr Hope laughed. 'You're a chip off the old block all right, Mandy Hope,' he said.

The light went on in the kitchen and Emily Hope waved to them from the window.

'You'll find a way to beat Sam Western,' Mr Hope told Mandy, opening the kitchen door. 'The battle has only just begun!'

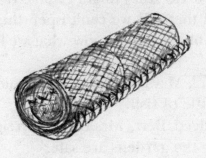

Six

Early next morning, as Michelle's Jeep pulled into Glisterdale Grange, Mandy could tell immediately that something was wrong. Estate workers were dashing about all over the place and there were deer wandering about in the car park.

Mrs Dickenson came running out to greet them. 'I'm glad you're here,' she told them. 'The deer have begun leaving the forest in quite large numbers. They don't like the disturbance. Most of them are in the paddocks but one or two came up on to the drive.' She looked over her shoulder at the sound of footsteps crunching on the gravel. 'Good, here comes Bert. I'm terribly worried they might get into the gardens and spoil them. If we can't open the grounds to the public, I don't know what we'll do,' she went on.

'Mornin', Mrs Dickenson,' Bert said. 'This is a nice kettle of fish!'

'It is indeed, Bert,' Mrs Dickenson sighed. 'Do you think the gardens are safe?'

'I reckon as I'd better walk around the ha-ha,' Bert said, 'just to be on the safe side.' He rubbed his back. 'Trouble is, me back's playin' up today. I might be a mite slow.'

'We could help,' Mandy offered quickly, looking across at Michelle. 'That's if you can spare us.'

'Of course, Mandy, that's fine,' Michelle said, glancing at Janie. 'We'll spend some time just filming the results of the night's events. Come down to the paddocks when you've finished.'

Mandy and James followed Bert to the gardens. A little way off they could see the paddocks. The lower one was dotted with deer mingling among the sheep. Mr Dickenson and Tony Morris were both standing by the fence watching. They waved to Mandy and James.

'Mr Dickenson's right worried,' Bert said, scratching his chin thoughtfully. 'And Mrs

Dickenson too. If them deer get into the gardens, we've had it. There'll be nowt for the visitors to see. Fact is, if they can't visit the house, nor walk in the woods, the garden's the only thing left.'

'When will the work start on the house?' James asked.

'Well, that's a bit of good news,' Bert said. 'Mrs Dickenson said they'll start spraying the east wing today, so the dry rot won't destroy the timbers. They can open that while the work's being done on the west wing.'

Bert stopped by a bridge that led over the ha-ha to the gardens. 'Right then, James,' he said. 'If you go inside the gardens and walk around checking the edge of the ha-ha, me and Mandy will check the inside wall.'

'What exactly am I looking for?' James asked.

'Look to see if the bank is crumbling anywhere,' Bert told him. 'Any place that a deer could use to get across.'

'What do *we* look for, Bert?' Mandy asked, looking at the steep inside wall of the ha-ha. It was built of bricks and looked solid and strong.

'We look to see if anything has fallen in,' Bert replied. 'You see up the back of the gardens, under those big trees?' He pointed at a stand of oak trees. 'A long time ago, some branches and leaves and debris fell down and almost filled the ha-ha to the top. I found a big old buck trying to climb across.'

Slowly they walked all around the gardens. Sure enough, at the far end, there was a pile of branches in the ha-ha and Mandy and James clambered down to clear it out.

'A deer might be tempted to try to cross on that,' Bert told them. 'Then it'd be in a pretty pickle.'

They continued around the garden and, when they reached the last bridge, they realised they had a serious problem.

'Look!' James cried. 'Someone's tried to break down the gate.'

'That's the deer that's done that,' Bert declared. 'They throw 'emselves at it, trying to break it down.' He tutted, shaking his head. 'They must have been in a panic to get away. It don't seem like they got in, though. It'll have to be fixed today.'

'What shall we do?' Mandy asked anxiously.

'We'd best get back and tell Tony Morris,' Bert replied, crossing the bridge into the gardens. 'He'll get someone up here to fix it. We'll go back through the gardens and check on my roses.'

They had just reached the pond when there was a loud screech. A peahen came hurtling down the path and stopped in front of James. She lay down at his feet and fixed him with one glinting eye.

'That's the same hen bird as before,' Bert said, grinning. 'She's after you, me lad.' The peahen wriggled and stared at James.

Bert was laughing fit to burst. 'Eh heh,' he gasped, wiping his eyes. 'You'll have to put a foot on her, lad, like the peacock 'ud do!' That sent him off into more fits of laughter.

Mandy couldn't help laughing too. James was blushing to the roots of his hair.

Suddenly there was a wail and a whoosh, and a big peacock ran up behind James and threw itself at his back.

Startled, James staggered forward, almost treading on the peahen at his feet.

'He's jealous!' Bert announced, grabbing James before he fell. 'What have you got that the hen likes so much?'

'Nothing!' James said, pushing his glasses back on and looking nervously around. 'I didn't do anything.'

They walked around the pond where the peafowl were drinking.

'Look out, lad!' Bert yelled as the big peacock fixed James with a menacing eye and started towards him again.

'Run, James!' Mandy cried.

James ran. The peacock followed him for a few paces. Then, as if it was content that James had been seen off, it strutted back to where Bert and Mandy stood. It stuck its brilliant blue chest out and lifted its tail-feathers, opening them out into a huge semicircular fan. The feathers were marked with eyespot patterns, and shimmered blue, gold and emerald green in the sunshine.

'Wow!' Mandy gasped in admiration at the sight. 'The patterns on his tail feathers are beautiful,' she said, awestruck.

'It's called his fan,' Bert told her. 'He's a beautiful bird all right.'

They walked over to where James waited at the bridge. It was still early and cool, but the sun was warm and he was taking off his jumper.

'For some reason that bird does *not* like me,' he said, falling into step as they walked back.

'But the hen bird does, young James.' Bert snorted and swallowed a laugh. 'Funniest thing

I've seen in a long time. She's taken a right shine to you!'

'James!' exclaimed Mandy. 'Your jumper. Look at the pattern on it.'

James held it out. 'Brown and blue circles,' he said wrinkling his nose. 'So what?'

'On a green background,' Mandy said with a grin. 'Look, Bert, it's just like the colours on the peacock's fan.'

'Aye, it is that,' Bert agreed. 'I reckon that peahen thinks you're a good-looking peacock,' he told James, spluttering with laughter again.

'Thanks a lot,' James said, grinning and blushing pink. 'That's just what I need!'

'There goes Mr Dickenson.' Bert noticed, pointing toward the house. 'Will you two do me a favour and tell him about the gate?' he asked. 'It'll save my poor old legs. I've plenty to do today as it is.'

'Of course we will,' Mandy said. 'Come on, James, we'll tell him about the gate and then we've got to meet Michelle.' They raced down to the house after Mr Dickenson and passed on the message.

By the time Mandy and James got to the upper paddock and met up with Michelle and Janie,

Sam Western's workmen had arrived.

'Morning,' Steve said, as he passed, pushing a wheelbarrow loaded with drums of water. 'We're cementing the posts in today.'

'Did you get the higher fencing like Mr Dickenson said?' Mandy asked.

Steve frowned and shook his head. 'Mr Western said his budget wouldn't run to it,' he told them, 'even though Harry explained it all to him. Mr Western doesn't care much for wildlife.'

'But isn't it dangerous for the deer?' asked James. 'They'll try to jump it and get hurt.'

Steve took off his hard hat and hung it on the barrow handle. 'I'll let you into a secret,' he said looking around. 'None of the lads are happy about the deer getting hurt by the fence. So, when we dig the channel that the chain link will sit in, we're going to make it a bit deeper than normal. That way we can keep the height down. I worked with deer once in Scotland,' he said. 'And they could *easily* clear a fence that was a metre and a half.'

'But the fawns won't be able to, will they,' Mandy sighed, thinking of Sprite.

'It's the best I can do,' Steve said. 'But don't forget, deer will only jump if they're under

pressure. Most of the time they'll follow the fence till they find a place to get out. In Scotland we once had a herd of deer that came across a fence too high to jump,' he said, grinning. 'A load of them charged at it over and over again until they just broke it down. I've never seen anything like it.'

'I've seen deer appear to test the height of a fence by standing up on their hind legs and touching the top with their chins.' Michelle told them.

'I've seen that too,' said Steve. 'If their chin touches the top, they'll jump it.'

'What did you actually do in Scotland?' Janie asked curiously.

'I was deer-keeper on an estate,' Steve said. 'Best job I've ever had.' He stared at the deer with a wistful look in his eyes. 'Ah well,' he said in a resigned voice, 'I'd best get back to work.' He headed off towards the forest.

'Oh no.' James glanced back towards the house. 'Look who's coming down the track.'

They all turned to look. Mrs Ponsonby was wearing a brown dress with big green swirly roses on it. On her head was a green straw hat with brown and beige silk acorns dotted around the brim. She didn't have her dogs with her and she looked very agitated.

'At least she's toned her colour scheme down,' Michelle observed dryly. 'That must be her idea of camouflage clothing!' Mandy tried not to look at James in case she started giggling.

'My dears, this is a dreadful state of affairs,' Mrs Ponsonby puffed as she hurried toward them. 'I've just heard from Mr Dickenson up at the house that Sam Western is fencing off the forest. It really is too, too dreadful.' She looked from Mandy to Michelle. 'Is there *no* curbing him?'

'We hope so, Mrs Ponsonby,' Michelle said calmly. 'We are going to do our very best.'

'Good,' Mrs Ponsonby said, nodding her head. '*I*, meanwhile, have a little idea of my own to follow up.' And she strode down the track towards the forest.

'What on earth is she up to?' Mandy asked, puzzled.

As they watched, Harry shouted something to Mrs Ponsonby and hurried over. He stood between her and the forest and held up his hands to halt her progress. But Harry was no match for Mrs Ponsonby on a mission. She marched past him, forcing him to jump out of her way. Before he had got over the shock of what had just happened she had disappeared among the trees.

'A formidable lady!' Janie exclaimed.

'Good job she's on our side, then, isn't it?' Michelle remarked. 'Oh look, there are more deer coming out of the forest. Can you film them, please, Janie?'

They stood watching in silence. First a buck with big antlers came out of the far end of the forest and looked cautiously around. Licking his nose to test the wind, he stamped first his right front foot and then the left.

'He's not too sure about being in the open,' Michelle said quietly. 'They're very unsettled by all the work going on.'

Suddenly the buck gave a series of barks. Five does, three fawns and another younger buck emerged from among the trees and joined him, jostling each other nervously. From behind them in the forest came a loud clang as one of the workmen up-ended a wheelbarrow, dumping a load of metal posts on the ground. In a flash, the deer were off. They ran straight up the paddock and then, to Mandy's amazement, one by one they began springing into the air, all four legs hanging straight down.

'That's called "pronking", ' Michelle said.

'They do it when they're alarmed. For some reason, fallow deer do it more than any other type.'

'They're running at the paddock fence!' Mandy said, clutching her hand to her mouth. Effortlessly the group of deer leaped over the low wooden fence and slowed to a stop on the far side of the upper paddock. They put their heads down and began to graze.

'Cooee!' Mrs Ponsonby's voice broke the stillness. 'I've found the evidence.'

'What evidence?' Michelle said, turning around. Mrs Ponsonby was plodding up the track to where they stood.

'*This* evidence,' she said, holding a neatly chewed pine cone in one hand and a bag of acorns in the other. 'Red squirrels!' she declared. 'There are definitely red squirrels living in the forest.'

'I'm afraid the pine cone only tells us there are squirrels here,' Michelle said patiently. 'Not which species.'

'Ah, but there's more than that,' Mrs Ponsonby said confidently. 'I was reading about squirrels last night and red squirrels don't usually eat acorns, but grey squirrels do,' she explained. 'Here, I gathered a bag of young acorns. If grey squirrels were living in the forest, these would have been eaten.' She opened the bag and showed them all.

'Well, there wouldn't be very many acorns around,' Michelle agreed, 'but I don't really think this counts as proof. I'm afraid it's not substantial enough to prove that red squirrels are here.'

'What would you say if I told you I saw one?' Mrs Ponsonby challenged her triumphantly.

'Did you really?' Mandy asked, eyes wide with interest.

Mrs Ponsonby smiled smugly to herself.

'What did you see?' Michelle asked, doubtfully.

'Well, first I looked for coniferous trees for pine cones,' Mrs Ponsonby explained. 'And then I remembered that red squirrels like deciduous trees like oaks. So I found an old oak tree,' she continued, 'and, would you believe, as I stood there a red squirrel dropped a pine cone on my head. Well, of course, I looked up and there it was, as large as life and *so* pretty! It seems to have made its home in the fork of a branch.'

'It's called a drey,' James told her.

'That's the name for the nest squirrels make,'

Mandy explained. 'They make it out of twigs and leaves, and build a little roof over the top. Then they line it with thistledown and feathers.'

'Oh, how sweet,' Mrs Ponsonby said, smiling.

'And you're absolutely certain it was a red squirrel, not a grey?' Michelle asked carefully. 'They can look quite similar in summer,' she added tactfully.

'I can see you don't believe me, but I will very soon have some undeniable proof to show you,' Mrs Ponsonby announced, opening her handbag with a flourish and taking out a camera. 'You see, I took a photograph of it.'

'Oh, excellent, Mrs Ponsonby!' Michelle said, beaming at her. 'That will be *very* useful. If we can prove there's a pocket of red squirrels here, then they will be protected by law.'

Mandy glanced at James. He grinned back and she felt her spirits lift. Things were looking up.

'Good,' Mrs Ponsonby said. 'I shall go straight into town and get the film developed.' Dropping the camera back in her bag she marched off to her car.

'What a surprise! We're not out of the woods yet,' Michelle joked, 'but we're certainly on our way to building a case for saving the forest!'

'And the deer,' Mandy reminded her, in a firm voice.

Seven

'You're home early!' Emily Hope said, when Mandy and James arrived back at Animal Ark. 'I wasn't expecting you back till tonight.'

'Michelle and Janie wanted to do some editing,' Mandy told her. 'Michelle wants the deer film to be included in next week's programme.'

'So what are your plans for now, then?' her mum asked.

'We're going to work on saving the forest,' Mandy announced, 'if that's all right with you? We need to do some research. Mrs Ponsonby saw a red squirrel there this morning, and they're protected,' she told her mum.

'We thought we'd ask around,' James added, 'see if anyone knows anything about Glisterdale Forest that might help us to protect it.'

'I suppose we can spare you for a little bit longer,' Mrs Hope said, with a smile. 'Gran and Grandad arrived home from Scotland last night. Why don't you go and see them? They might have some ideas.'

'Good idea, Mum,' Mandy said, grinning at James. 'Gran might even have been baking today.' James went pink. Mandy was always teasing him about his liking for her gran's cakes.

'She probably has,' her mum said. 'It's her Women's Institute meeting tomorrow and they've got a produce sale on Thursday. Make sure you don't eat everything!'

Mandy and James headed up the lane to Lilac Cottage. A mouthwatering smell of baking drifted up the garden path. Mandy's grandad, Tom Hope, was in the greenhouse.

'Hi, Granded,' Mandy called, peeking inside. 'How was Scotland?'

'Hello, love!' he said. 'It was beautiful, apart from the midges!' he told her, holding out his arm to show the little red bite marks.

In front of him on the workbench inside the greenhouse were rows and rows of tiny flowerpots all with a single small plant in them. 'What are all those?' Mandy asked, puzzled.

'Don't they look smart? Like little rows of soldiers!' her grandad said, putting the last rooted cutting in the last pot and giving a big sigh of contentment. 'We've only been back a day and your gran's got me working. These are herbs to take to the WI sale. This is mint, those are rosemary . . .'

'And that's sage,' James said, pointing to a neat row of grey-green plants. 'We've got a huge bush in our garden.'

'That's right,' Grandad smiled. 'I'll just put them in trays and then we'll see if Gran can stop baking long enough to make us some tea.'

'Something smells wonderful,' Mandy said, handing James a polystyrene tray and holding up one herself.

'Gran was up at the crack of dawn making lemon curd and green tomato chutney,' her grandad told her, as he tidied up. James's eyes lit up and Mandy grinned. She knew James loved her gran's fresh lemon curd.

'That's us done,' Grandad announced, rubbing the potting compost off his hands. 'Put them over there in the shade, please, and let's go inside. Thirsty work, potting is.'

Inside Lilac Cottage the air smelled of coconut. Dorothy Hope was in the kitchen brushing little cakes with jam and rolling them in desiccated coconut. 'There, that's all the madeleines done,' she said out loud, putting the last cake on a tray. 'Hello, Mandy, James, I'm just about to make your grandad some tea.'

'You haven't put the cherries on top, Gran!' Mandy accused her. 'They don't look right.'

'Or the little leaves,' James added. 'Madeleines have to have leaves!'

'There now,' Gran said, smiling. 'I was saving those jobs for you, your mum said you might be down.' Handing them a tub of glacé cherries and a box full of little green angelica leaves, she added. 'You'll stop and have some tea, will you? I'll open a pot of your favourite lemon curd, James.'

'Wow, Gran!' Mandy exclaimed. 'You *have* been busy.'

On the dresser was a tray of jam tarts, a large chocolate cake, two carrot cakes and a big slab of her gran's special, rich, sticky parkin.

'That's not all, Mandy,' Dorothy Hope said, opening the oven and letting the delicious smell of baking bread waft through the kitchen. 'This is just about done, now it needs to cool awhile,' she said, taking the tin from the oven.

Mandy was busy dipping the cherries in jam and putting them on the top of the cakes while James added two leaves beside each cherry.

'Perfect!' Mandy announced, as they finished the last one. 'Grandad, can we ask you a question?' she said as he came back into the room. He had changed out of his gardening clothes and was wearing comfortable trousers and a clean blue shirt. He sat down at the table and turned his attention to Mandy and James.

'Fire away,' he said, taking a sip from his cup of tea. 'What can I do for you?'

'Well,' Mandy began, 'you know Glisterdale Forest, near where Mr Dickenson lives?' Mandy paused as her grandad nodded. 'Sam Western has bought it and he wants to cut all the trees down. We're looking for ways to stop him before all the deer leave.'

Gran was cutting great wedges of homemade bread and spreading them with butter and lemon curd. 'Your dad was telling us about that this morning,' she said sympathetically. 'It's terrible.'

'We thought you might know something about the forest that might help to stop him,' Mandy said.

'If I remember rightly, Mandy,' her grandad told her, 'Glisterdale Grange was taken over by the army during the war.'

'That won't help us,' Mandy said. 'It's nothing to do with the army now.'

'I remember that,' Gran commented, passing them plates and glasses of fresh orange juice. 'They used it for rifle training.'

'We used to cycle past there and hear the gunfire in the forest,' Mr Hope said. 'I tell you, we used to get a move on in case any of them were bad shots!'

'What were they shooting at?' James asked, a puzzled look on his face.

'They put targets on the trees,' Grandad said. 'The soldiers crawled through the long grass, where the paddocks are today, and fired at the targets.'

'But what's that got to do with saving the forest *now*, Grandad?' Mandy said with a frown. She couldn't see any connection, but there was a twinkle in her grandad's eye.

'Now there's a thought,' Gran murmured, taking a bite of bread. She chewed thoughtfully. 'If they used those trees as targets, won't they be full of bullets, Tom?'

'Your gran's right, Mandy.' Grandad nodded

agreement. 'Those trees wouldn't be any good for timber. They probably wouldn't even be any good for pulping.' He winked at Mandy. 'I bet Sam Western won't be too pleased to hear that!'

'That's great news, Grandad,' Mandy said, taking a piece of parkin from her gran. 'What about the big oak trees? Did they shoot at those?'

'No, not that I remember. Those big oaks are very old and Mr Dickenson's grandfather didn't want them damaged,' her grandad replied. 'They were only allowed to use the beech trees, mostly the ones nearest the house at that.'

'I bet the shooting frightened the deer,' James remarked.

'It certainly did, James,' Mandy's grandad said, 'but at that time some of the land next to Glisterdale Forest was woodland too and the deer moved right over the other side,' he told them. 'When I was a lad at school we were told that Queen Elizabeth I hunted deer in Glisterdale Forest,' he said, pausing to take a drink of his tea. 'In those days you needed the Queen's permission to cut off a single branch, never mind cut down a tree,' he said.

'So those oak trees could be over three hundred years old?' James asked thoughtfully.

'Surely that makes them pretty special!'

'I'll mention Sam Western's plans at the WI meeting tomorrow,' Gran said, gathering up the empty plates. 'Our members won't like it; they won't like it at all! There's too much chopping down of trees already, it's up to all of us to stop it.'

'The workmen have only just started fencing off the forest and the work is already frightening the deer,' Mandy sighed, picking up a cloth to help her gran with the washing up. 'They obviously don't feel safe and they've started coming out of the forest.'

'I hope Peter Dickenson's keeping an eye on those gardens. It would be sad if the deer got into them and destroyed them,' Grandad remarked, shaking his head at the thought.

'We're going to save the forest *and* the deer, Grandad,' Mandy told him. 'Come on, James,' she said. 'We'd better get on.'

Gran went to the larder and brought out a big plastic box. 'Here,' she said handing it to Mandy. 'I couldn't bake without saving something for your mum and dad.'

Mandy looked inside. 'Mmm, Dad's favourite carrot cake.' She kissed her grandparents. 'Thanks for the information,' she said.

'Yes, and thanks for the tea,' James added.

'Good luck with your campaign,' Grandad said, opening the front door for them. 'Gran's right you know, we're losing too many trees. We need the woodlands for the wildlife.'

'That would be a good slogan,' James suggested, as they started to walk back to Animal Ark. 'Woodlands for Wildlife!'

'Mmm,' Mandy agreed, but she was busy thinking about the great oaks. 'I'm going to phone Mr Dickenson and tell him what Grandad said as soon as we get in,' she declared. 'Then tomorrow we can visit Ernie Bell and Walter Pickard and ask them if they know anything about the red squirrels.' As head of Welford Wildlifers, Walter Pickard knew almost everything there was to know about the local countryside.

Adam Hope was putting some tablets in a bottle as they walked past the window of Animal Ark. Mandy lifted the lid and held up the box of cake so her dad could see. He gave her a thumbs up sign and licked his lips. In the kitchen James looked up the number of Glisterdale Grange while Mandy put the cake in the fridge.

'Here it is,' James called. He read the number out and Mandy dialled.

'Hello, Glisterdale Grange,' Peter Dickenson answered, after a few rings.

James stood close to Mandy, trying to hear.

'Mr Dickenson, it's Mandy Hope,' she said. 'I've got some news for you from my grandad.'

'And I've got some news for you, Mandy!' Peter Dickenson said. 'But let's hear yours first.'

Mandy told him about the beech trees being full of bullets. 'And Grandad thinks some of the oak trees are over three hundred years old.'

'He's right,' Peter Dickenson said. 'And what's

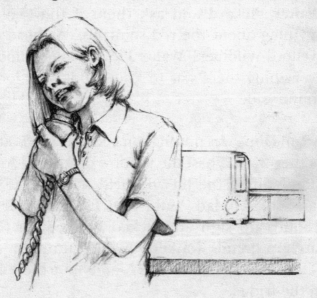

more, the County Council has confirmed that there are now preservation orders on all of them.'

'So Sam Western can't cut them down?' Mandy said, grinning at James, who punched the air with his first.

'No, Mandy,' Mr Dickenson confirmed. Mandy could hear the relief in his voice. 'He's not allowed to touch them.'

Mandy was still worried, though. 'Sam Western does exactly what he likes,' she said. 'What if he just cuts them down before anyone can stop him?'

'I don't think he will, Mandy, not this time,' Peter Dickenson told her. 'He'd be in big trouble if he went against the preservation order. The Council takes things like that very seriously. If he damages even one of those oaks, he could be liable for a massive fine. *That's* what will put Sam Western off now, the fear that it would cost him a lot of money. And if the beech trees prove to be useless to him, maybe he'll just decide to give up the idea of harvesting the timber.'

'I hope so,' Mandy said fervently. 'We've still got to make sure it's really safe for the deer, though.'

'And the squirrels,' James whispered to Mandy.

'And the red squirrels,' Mandy added.

'This is a step in the right direction,' Peter Dickenson assured her. 'Sam Western will have to change his plans.'

'But where are the deer now?' Mandy asked. 'Have they left the estate?'

'As soon as the workmen left, a lot of them made their way back into the forest,' replied Mr Dickenson. 'There's quite a large section that hasn't been fenced yet. And it's the actual work that frightens them, all that banging.'

'Then it's up to us to stop him before any *real* work starts,' Mandy said in a positive voice. 'The deer will *hate* it if Mr Western starts felling trees.' She swallowed hard.

There was a long silence on the other end of the phone. Then Peter Dickenson said in a sad voice. 'I know, Mandy. You can't imagine how many times I've been over and over the problem.' Sighing deeply he carried on. 'My only consolation is that I'm still here to care for them on the rest of the estate. Just suppose I'd had to sell the house as well, who knows what might have happened to the deer if we weren't around?'

Mandy shuddered at the thought of someone like Sam Western having the run of Glisterdale Grange. 'That's true,' she agreed.

'We'll all have to do the very best we can to keep them safe,' Peter Dickenson declared.

'Right!' Mandy agreed. 'Oh – and give Rosie a hug for me!'

'Yes, I will,' he answered, laughing. 'Bye for now.'

Mandy hung up the phone and looked out of the window at the sky. 'James, it won't be dark for ages yet,' she said. 'Why don't we go and see Ernie Bell and Walter Pickard now?'

'That's OK with me, it's on my way home anyway,' James replied. 'Mum's not expecting me back till later. I said I'd probably have tea here.' He grinned. 'I couldn't eat another thing after that tea over at your gran and grandad's.'

'I'd better just tell my mum first, then,' Mandy decided. With James following, she ran along the hall and pushed open the door to the Animal Ark reception. 'Is Mum busy, Jean?' she asked the receptionist.

Jean Knox pushed her glasses up on to her head and looked at Mandy. 'When *isn't* your mother busy, Mandy, tell me that?' she asked good-naturedly. 'She's in the examination room at the moment. One of the police dogs from Walton has got some glass in his paw.'

'Oh, poor thing!' said Mandy. 'Can we go in?' she asked, as the phone rang.

'I'm sure it will be all right,' Jean said, picking up the receiver. 'Good evening, Animal Ark. Yes, an appointment for when?' She fumbled with the appointment book. 'One moment please.' Putting her hand over the mouthpiece she scrabbled around under the desk.

'What have you lost, Jean?' Mandy said in a serious tone.

'My pen!' Jean hissed softly.

'Under that file,' Mandy whispered. How Jean ran the reception so efficiently with her poor memory, Mandy couldn't guess. She knocked on the door of the examination room.

'Come in,' Emily Hope called.

When Mandy opened the door she saw an enormous German shepherd dog sitting on the examination table. It watched Mandy and James enter with bright, intelligent eyes.

'All right, Gaffer, you'll be fine now,' Mrs Hope stroked his head.

The young policeman holding his lead grinned at Mandy. 'He thought he'd get time off work with a bad paw,' he joked. 'But Mrs

Hope's fixed him up perfectly.'

'A day's rest for that pad and he'll be fine. Won't you?' Mandy's mum said.

As Gaffer jumped down, Mandy stepped forward, looking at the policeman. 'Can I stroke him?'

'Sure,' he nodded vigorously. 'Gaffer's an old softie when he's off duty.'

Mandy and James made a fuss of the big dog while Mrs Hope gave his handler instructions on taking care of the injured paw.

'Pop back with him if there's any problem.' Emily Hope said, as the young policeman left. 'Now,' she turned expectantly to Mandy and James. 'What can I do for you two?'

'We're off to see Walter Pickard and Ernie Bell,' Mandy told her. 'To see if they know about the red squirrels at Glisterdale.'

'Fine, but make sure you're home before dark, please,' Emily Hope ordered, opening the door. 'And don't outstay your welcome if they're busy,' she added, with a smile.

'OK, we won't. Gran sent you a carrot cake,' Mandy called over to her. 'It's in the fridge.'

'Who shall we visit first, Ernie or Walter?' James said breathlessly, as they raced down the lane.

'Whoever we leave until last will be cross.' The two old men were always competing with each other, and each liked to think he knew more about the village.

'We'll decide that when we get there,' Mandy puffed, running across the green towards the pub and the row of cottages behind, where Ernie Bell and Walter Pickard lived. But as they reached the Fox and Goose, Mandy grabbed James's sleeve and stopped.

'Looks like our problem's solved,' she smiled. 'Look!'

Eight

Sitting at a wooden table outside the pub were Ernie Bell and Walter Pickard, both in shirt-sleeves with flat caps on their heads. 'Come on, let's go and see them.' Mandy said.

'Good evening, Walter, Ernie,' James said politely, hovering beside the table.

'Hello, young James, young Mandy,' Walter said in his gruff voice. 'And how's life treating you?'

'We've got a campaign on at the moment,' Mandy announced, pulling a couple of chairs over. 'That's why we wanted to see you both.'

'Oh aye,' Walter said, raising his eyebrows quizzically and pushing back his cap. 'Happen you've struck lucky then. Two for the price of one.'

'How's Sammy?' Mandy asked Ernie Bell.

'He's on a diet!' Ernie pronounced darkly. 'Some folks,' he said, looking pointedly at Walter, 'have been giving him too many treats.'

'One cream cracker won't hurt him,' Walter spluttered. 'It's all them nuts!'

'Have you ever seen red squirrels around here?' Mandy said, tactfully changing the subject.

'Not nowadays, lass.' Walter shook his head slowly from side to side. 'Happen there's still some left, but not in Welford, not where you find the grey. Never find the two together.'

'Why the interest in red squirrels?' Ernie asked bluntly. 'What's wrong with grey?'

'Oh no, nothing,' Mandy said hurriedly. 'It's just that we're trying to save the forest at Glisterdale. We think there might be red squirrels there, and if there are it might help protect the forest because they're so rare.'

'I heard Sam Western had bought the forest,' said Walter. He's causing trouble again, is he?'

'He wants to cut down the forest,' Mandy told them, and began to explain about the danger to the deer. 'We need to find a way to stop him destroying their home.'

'Protected by law, red squirrels are,' Walter Pickard said, nodding.

'Mrs Ponsonby is sure she saw one at Glisterdale,' James said.

'Pah!' Ernie Bell retorted. 'It was probably just a grey in the sunlight.'

'I'd agree with Ernie here,' Walter said. 'They can look alike in summer. Even country folk can have a job telling 'em apart.'

'That's what Michelle said,' Mandy told them, disappointed. 'But we're really hoping Mrs Ponsonby is right.' Mandy was determined to keep positive.

'You might be in luck, now I think about it.' Walter rubbed his chin. 'Glisterdale 'ud be a nice little spot for red squirrels. Have you seen any grey squirrels there?' he quizzed them. Mandy and James shook their heads.

'Then it's a possibility,' he said, nodding. 'Mebbe I should take a look sometime.' He turned to Ernie. 'How about you? You up for a trip out?'

'Aye, I'll come with you,' Ernie agreed. 'I want to see what Sam Western's about over there, anyhow.'

'Eh-up, young Mandy,' Walter said, looking over Mandy's shoulder. 'In't that the Animal Ark vehicle, over there by there by the green?'

Mandy shaded her eyes against the setting sun and peered over to where Walter was pointing, then stood up and waved as her dad got out of the driving seat. 'Da-ad,' she cried, 'Over here!'

Adam Hope looked round to see where the voice was coming from, then came across to the pub garden.

Walter shuffled along the bench to make space for Adam to sit down.

'Thanks, Walter, but I can't stop. I've been sent to collect these two,' he said as he reached them. 'Mum sent me out to find you,' he told Mandy. 'You'll be late for *Wildlife Ways*, and they've rescheduled the deer film, it's on tonight!' He looked at his watch. 'In half an hour, in fact. Come on, we've just got time to run James home.'

'We'd best finish up here and get home to see it then,' Walter announced, draining his glass, as Mandy and James jumped up and ran off towards the Land-rover.

They dropped James off at his house and headed back to Animal Ark.

'I wonder why the deer feature has been brought forward?' Mandy wondered aloud as they turned into the driveway.

'Don't ask me, love,' her dad said. 'I'd just walked in the door when Mum put down the phone and sent me back out so quickly my feet hardly had time to touch the floor.'

'Thanks, Dad,' Mandy said appreciatively. 'I'd have hated to miss it. I wonder if anyone else knows?'

'That,' Adam Hope said, turning off the engine, 'is a question you can ask Mum.'

Mandy jumped down and ran inside.

'I know what you're going to ask,' Emily Hope told her. 'And I've phoned everyone I could think of. I even phoned the Hunters, in case Dad didn't find you both.'

'Did Michelle say why the programme was brought forward?' Mandy asked.

'Yes, apparently the producer thought it was so topical, he didn't want to wait another week,' Emily Hope replied. Mandy followed her mum into the sitting-room and turned on the television. Her dad joined them as the familiar *Wildlife Ways* theme tune began. Mandy felt a shiver of excitement.

Michelle began to speak. 'We're here at Glisterdale Grange to film the herd of fallow deer whose ancestors roamed in the forest here hundreds of years ago,' she said, as the camera showed the Grange behind her. 'Glisterdale deer can wander freely about the estate, although they are not allowed in the spectacular gardens and care has been taken to protect the new young trees.'

'Look, there's James,' Mandy cried, pointing at the screen. James was measuring his height against the tree guards. And then there were the deer, running, jumping and frolicking, their coats glistening in the sunlight.

'Whose funny face is that?' Adam Hope joked, as the film showed Mandy talking to a workman.

'Do you mind, Dad? Mandy protested. 'That's me! And that's Steve I'm talking to. He's worked with deer in Scotland.'

'Take no notice, Mandy, you look fine,' Emily Hope smiled. They watched in silence as the film showed the fencing gradually going up. Peter Dickenson explained about the problems they were having and the deer coming out of the forest.

Then the camera focused on Michelle's face with the herd of deer running in the background. 'Deer have lived and bred happily at Glisterdale for hundreds of years,' she said sombrely. 'But who knows what the fate of the herd will be now?' The picture faded and the screen went black for several seconds. Then the closing credits and theme music started and Mandy's mum and dad turned to congratulate her.

'That was excellent, Mandy,' Mr Hope said. 'Hard-hitting and powerful. That should make people sit up and listen.'

'Very moving.' Emily Hope nodded. 'Michelle's watching the programme at

Simon's. I said you'd give her a ring afterwards.' She turned to Mandy who was sitting in the armchair hugging her knees. 'Are you all right, love?'

'Mandy sniffed and nodded slowly. 'Mum, Dad, what *do* you think will happen to the deer?' she asked.

Mr and Mrs Hope looked at each other. Adam Hope raised his eyebrows at his wife and she nodded.

He clenched his hands together and took a deep breath. 'To tell you the truth, Mandy, at the worst they might get so distressed by the noise and the work that they will eventually leave,' he said sadly. Mandy's face crumpled. 'Wait, Mandy. Having said that, there is always the possibility that they will adjust to the upheaval and learn to live with it.'

'Deer have been known to learn to live alongside motorways, during and after construction,' her mum added. 'So it's not impossible.'

'And if, between you, you can put a halt to Sam Western's plans,' her dad said, 'well, who knows what could happen?'

'You're right,' Mandy said, perking up. 'Thanks.' She shot her parents a grateful smile and jumped up and went off to phone Michelle.

A few minutes later she came back into the room, smiling. 'Michelle phoned the TV station and they said that the phone hasn't stopped ringing,' she told her parents. 'They've had loads of protests about the threat to the forest and the deer.'

'There you are, then,' Mrs Hope said. 'We told you it would move people, and it has.'

'People power!' Adam Hope announced. 'Nothing like it.'

'Michelle wants to meet us at Glisterdale tomorrow to see if there are any developments,' Mandy said. 'I'll ring James now; we can meet first thing in the morning.'

Over the phone, James sounded as excited as Mandy when she told him Michelle's news. That night, as she lay in bed, Mandy felt too nervous and excited to sleep. She knew how important it was that something happened *now* to save the deer and the forest. It was good to know there were other people out there who cared too, she thought, as she eventually drifted off.

Nine

'My goodness!' Adam Hope said, staring in surprise through the windscreen of the Land-rover. Mr Hope had offered to give Mandy and James a lift to Glisterdale the next morning. But as they approached the turning to the Grange, the traffic had almost come to a standstill. Cars were queuing to enter the estate from each direction.

'Your film certainly got things moving,' Mr Hope told them. Then he checked his watch. 'The trouble is, I'll be late for my call if I wait. I think I'd better go back and cut through around the back of Law Farm.'

'OK, Dad, we can walk the rest of the way,'

Mandy said, gathering her bag and sweater.

'Thanks for the lift, Mr Hope,' said James. 'Will you be calling in later?'

'I'll see how we're fixed, James. I'd certainly like to see what's happening,' Mr Hope remarked, as he reached into the back of the Land-rover and put a sign that said 'Vet on Call' in red lettering in the windscreen. 'I expect your mother would too, Mandy,' he grinned. 'See you later.'

'Bye, Dad.' Mandy waved.

At the gates of Glisterdale, they found Bert busily directing the traffic. He was wearing an orange jacket that said 'Marshall' on the back. The main car park up ahead looked almost full already.

'Well, well, well, I'll be blowed!' Bert said as he waved another car through. 'Michelle is already here,' he told them. 'She's talking to the people that arrived last night.'

'Last *night*!' Mandy and James exclaimed together.

'Aye, last night. They're camping on the lawns,' Bert said, putting his hands on his hips. 'They've got banners and the like. Never seen nothin' like it, I haven't.'

Bert was looking a bit harassed. A group of

ramblers standing at the entrance were assembling a placard that said *Save Glisterdale Forest* and waiting to speak to him.

'Mr Dickenson left these for you,' Bert told Mandy and James, handing them sleeveless white tabards with green fluorescent stripes and 'Marshall' written on the back. 'We use 'em when we have events here. Never had nothin' like this though,' he sniffed. Mandy and James slipped them over their heads and tied them at the sides.

'We ought to go and find Michelle,' said Mandy, stepping backwards as a minibus full of excited boys from the Walton Cub group tried to squeeze its way past them.

'James, lad, can you give us a hand up here for a bit?' Bert asked him. 'It needs two of us really. I'll see 'em in, you make sure they knows where to go. We'd best open up the private car park, behind the house, too.' He plodded over to the minibus holding his hand up, palm facing forwards like a policeman directing the traffic.

'You find Michelle and I'll see you later,' James told Mandy. 'When it quietens down.'

'If it does!' Mandy answered. 'Isn't it great that so many people care enough to come here?' James nodded.

'Over here, lad!' Bert shouted from the drive and James ran to join him.

Mandy made her way over to the house, looking out for Michelle. There were little groups of people all over the grounds and along the path that led to the forest. They all seemed to be holding placards and banners protesting against the plans for the forest. At the top end of the paddock the deer huddled nervously together.

'Mandy!' a voice called. 'Over here!'

Mandy turned. Beside the house Mrs Dickenson stood talking to a young woman with short highlighted hair who wore a brown suit and was holding a briefcase. Rosie, dancing with frustration at being kept on a lead, barked as she saw Mandy approach.

'Mandy, I'm so pleased to see you,' Mrs Dickenson said smiling. 'This is Sally Hudson from the Forestry Commission.'

'Hello, Mandy,' Sally Hudson said. 'I had a long chat with Michelle last night and she told me how much you've helped in making the *Wildlife Ways* programme.'

Mandy blushed. 'My friend James helped too,' she said, stroking Rosie.

'Yes, where is James?' Sally Hudson asked.

'He's not missing this, is he?'

'He's helping Bert at the gates,' Mandy replied.

'Oh good,' Mrs Dickenson said gratefully. She glanced around anxiously at the crowd. 'Where *is* Peter? He was about to take Sally to find Michelle when we realised we're going to need some way of talking to all these people. He's gone to set up the Tannoy system. The trouble is, with all the work going on he probably can't find it!' She smiled at them both. 'Mandy, would you take Sally to meet Michelle for me, please? She said she would be interviewing the people who are camping.'

'Yes, of course, I was looking for her myself,' Mandy agreed.

Slowly they worked their way past all the people. Outside the teashop there was a line of people patiently queuing for cups of tea and coffee. Mandy paused and gazed around, then she pointed towards the forest, where groups of people were standing beside a circle of small tents.

'There she is!' she exclaimed to Sally. 'Down there by the tents.'

They hurried through the crowd, who moved aside for Mandy when they saw her marshall's vest. Michelle was busy interviewing a group of people in jeans and green sweatshirts with the logo *Forests for the Future* on them. Mandy and Sally stood to one side, listening.

'So, would you please tell our viewers what made you take this stand of camping here last night?' Michelle said to one young man. 'Just tell us in your own words.'

'Well,' the young man began, then cleared his throat and looked at Michelle.

Michelle nodded her head toward Janie and the camera, and the man turned to look at the camera.

'Well, we as a group feel very strongly that

too much forest has been lost already. There's hardly a forest left in the world that hasn't been damaged by people in one way or another.' Taking a deep breath he continued. 'As a boy I spent all my spare time in the forest watching wildlife, and I . . .' He hesitated and then, holding his arms out to indicate the others, continued, '. . . *we*, want to make sure that there are forests full of wildlife left for *our* children to walk in. We're prepared to go anywhere to stop forests being cut down simply to make money.' The young man stopped and indicated the tents. 'And we're prepared to stay until the problem is resolved.' His friends were nodding agreement.

Mandy felt a shiver of anticipation run through her. These people felt like she did. Surely between them they could save the deer.

'Thank you very much,' Michelle said, as everyone clapped. She moved across to talk to another group holding a banner that said *Save Glisterdale's Deer*. 'Would any of you like to give an opinion?' she asked.

'Yes, I certainly would,' said a woman in a smart tweed suit, stepping forward. 'The deer have been here for generations. These creatures have no means of defending themselves, or the forest they live in, from money-grabbing men who wish to steal, yes, I said *steal*, their land.' She paused for breath. 'It is up to us, the people of this country to put our foot down and say no!' she concluded.

'Hear, hear!' The group cheered so loudly they almost drowned out Michelle's response.

'Sam Western's not going to like this,' said a soft voice. Mandy turned to see James standing behind her. 'Pretty hot stuff, eh?' he said.

'You're not kidding!' Mandy whispered. Michelle was talking to the Walton Cubs now. Each of the boys held a small placard with a single letter on it. As Michelle lined them up they spelled out *Save the Deer*.

'Have people stopped arriving now?' Mandy asked James.

'There are still a few, but Bert can manage on his own now.' James told her. 'Mr Dickenson wants us up at the house.'

'Why?' Mandy asked. She was loath to leave what was fast becoming the hub of activity. 'What do you think he wants?'

'I don't know,' James replied. 'He just called out that he could use our help, as I passed the house. I said I'd go back when I found you.'

They made their way up through the crowds.

'Look, there's Gran!' Mandy cried. 'And she's brought loads of people!' She ran up to the formal gardens where Gran stood, solid and straight like a soldier, holding one end of a long banner that proclaimed *Welford Women's Institute Against Deforestation.*

'Hi, Gran,' Mandy smiled. 'I didn't know you were coming.'

'Neither did I, Mandy,' her gran replied. 'But I watched your programme last night and it made my blood boil.'

'But what about everyone else?' Mandy asked, looking down the line of banner holders. 'And what about your meeting?'

'After your mum rang last night, I called all the members and told them all about the programme,' Gran replied, 'and of course they all watched. We all feel very strongly about preserving the environment around Welford, so we put the meeting off until tomorrow.' She looked around at the mass of people. 'This is a fine turnout for a protest, Mandy, I'm sure it will do some good.'

But as Mandy walked back to the house she began to wonder what good it actually *would* do.

'I know Michelle will probably put this in the

programme next week,' she said to James, 'But will it make any difference to Sam Western?'

'It would be better if he was actually here to see the protest,' James admitted, 'but at least he'll see it on the local news tonight,' he said, looking sideways at Mandy.

Mandy spun around to face him, 'James! Why didn't you say? How do you know?' she exclaimed.

'There's a team from the local news programme here filming; I let them in myself,' James told her proudly.

'Mandy and James, just the people I need,' Peter Dickenson called from outside the house, where he was talking to Harry.

They ran across the drive to join him.

'And I'm telling you, sir, if you don't keep all those people away from where we're working, there'll be an accident,' Harry was saying to Mr Dickenson in an angry voice. 'And I'll not be held responsible. I've warned you now. Like it or not, I've a job to carry out.'

'You're right,' Peter Dickenson agreed, trying to calm him down. 'I'll make an announcement asking people to stay on Glisterdale land.' He turned to speak to Mandy and James. 'Would you help me carry the sound system down to where Michelle is,' he asked. 'Most of the people seem to be down there now. And if you could help me with this platform,' he said to Harry, 'then I'll explain to everyone that we have to stick to the law. We can't trespass on Sam Western's land. This is a proper protest, and we don't want it to get out of hand. We don't want to end up looking like a bunch of rowdy hooligans.'

Mr Dickenson lifted one side of the platform, and Harry took the other. Together they set off down the drive.

James whispered out of the corner of his mouth to Mandy, 'I couldn't ever in a million years imagine Mr Dickenson looking like a rowdy hooligan.'

'Or my gran,' Mandy added, smiling at the thought. They carried the sound system down to where the two men had set the platform down. Mr Dickenson picked up the microphone and jumped up on to the platform.

'Ladies and gentlemen,' Mr Dickenson called over the Tannoy. 'I would like to thank you all for coming here today and giving your support to Glisterdale Forest and its deer. This united stand will surely show the new owner how strong our opposition is to his plans. However,

I must ask that you keep away from where the men are working and stay on Glisterdale Grange land. Thank you.' He put down the microphone and jumped down off the platform.

'It's a shame the protesters can't take over the forest and drive the workmen out,' Mandy grumbled.

'Between you and me, Mandy, I tend to agree,' Mr Dickenson told her. 'But we have to stick to the letter of the law or Sam Western could prosecute. Life's not simple any more,' he sighed.

'Mr Dickenson, Mr Dickenson, can I have a word, please?' called a workman, pushing through the crowd towards them.

'It's Steve!' Mandy said, surprised.

Still wearing the hard hat that marked him out as one of the workmen, Steve was being booed as he passed.

'Have you got a phone I could use, in private?' he asked uneasily. 'I think Mr Western should come and see what's going on here. Some of the crowd are getting a bit stroppy. There's no way they'll let us finish the fencing, I can tell. The rest of the boys don't like what he's doing much either. Most of us agree with the demonstrators, to be honest.' He looked around to see if anyone was listening, then added, 'He's going about this the wrong way. Putting everyone's back up. It's terrible to see the deer so frightened. If I wasn't so concerned about the deer, and doing the best I can for them, I'd have walked off this job long ago.'

'You can use the phone in the office; ask my wife to show you, up at the house,' Peter Dickenson told him quickly. 'I agree, Sam Western should see this.'

Steve hurried off and Mandy and James followed Mr Dickenson down to the half-finished fence. A number of people were standing where the remainder of the fence was to go, arguing with the foreman.

'You can't do this,' a smartly dressed man in a waxed jacket was saying. 'The people are against it. You can see for yourself.' He gestured towards the rest of the crowd.

'Look, sir,' Harry said, resignedly. 'It's my job. *Our* jobs.' He indicated the rest of the men but they shook their heads and sat down on the last remaining roll of fencing. They had clearly given up. 'It's what we're getting paid to do, lads,' Harry entreated them, but they wouldn't budge. As he tried to persuade them, he was interrupted by a loud voice behind him.

'Stop this work immediately! You are breaking the law and I have proof!' Mrs Ponsonby called, pushing her way through the crowd. She was waving a large brown envelope above her head.

'Oh no,' Harry groaned, his shoulders sagging. 'It's her again.'

'In this envelope I have all the proof I need that you must leave the forest immediately,' Mrs Ponsonby declared.

Harry held out his hand. 'Let's see it, then,' he said with a huge sigh.

'Oh no you don't!' Mrs Ponsonby said, glaring at him and clutching the envelope to her chest. 'I shall only reveal this in front of the television cameras.'

'Good grief,' James whispered to Mandy. 'She'll do anything to be on telly.'

'Shh,' Mandy hissed back, stifling a giggle.

There was a long silence as everybody waited to see what would happen next. Harry stared at Mrs Ponsonby who stared back unwaveringly.

Eventually the foreman turned and walked over to the men. 'Right, lads,' he said, taking a deep breath.

'There'll be trouble if he orders them to carry on,' Mandy murmured to James.

'And he'll be in trouble if he doesn't,' James answered.

Harry turned back to face the crowd. 'From now on,' he declared, 'we're off the job until it's sorted.' A big cheer went up and Harry's red face went even redder.

'Well done, my man,' Mrs Ponsonby said, with a firm nod of her head. 'We are all behind you.'

Harry looked as if he wasn't sure whether that would be a lot of help when he had to explain himself to Sam Western.

'Might I suggest that we move right back up nearer the house,' Peter Dickenson suggested over the Tannoy. 'That will leave more room for the deer, both in the forest and on my land.'

The crowd was just moving away from the forest when a car carrying Sam Western arrived. It skidded to a halt and Dennis Saville got out, followed by Sam Western, an angry scowl on his face. As he marched through the paddocks, word went around that the new owner of Glisterdale forest had arrived. A chant went up. 'Save the forest, save the deer. Save the forest, save the deer.'

For just a few seconds, Mandy had an anxious burst of trepidation, now that a confrontation was about to happen. Then she looked around at the crowds of people, all here to support the campaign for the deer, and felt confident again.

'Get off my land!' Sam Western thundered, as he drew nearer to the forest. 'This is a work site now, not a nature reserve,' he said, turning to make sure Dennis Saville was behind him. 'A bunch of namby-pamby tree-huggers won't stop the work going ahead.' He stopped in front of Michelle and Janie. 'This is your fault, young lady,' he said, wagging a finger in Michelle's face. 'And I'm going to take it up with your employers. Misrepresentation, that's what it was. You should be ashamed of yourself!'

'Everything we said on the programme was true,' Michelle told him in a clear, firm voice, 'as all these people know.'

'All these people,' Sam Western leaned toward her, glowering, 'should have better things to do than interfere in my business.'

'We can't hear what's happening,' someone at the back of the crowd called out.

'That's just too bad,' Dennis Saville shouted back. 'Why don't you all go home?'

But quick as a flash, Mr Dickenson ran over with the microphone from the Tannoy system.

'Mr Western,' Michelle spoke into the mike.

'Let's be reasonable about this. There are lots of important facts about this forest that perhaps you weren't aware of.'

'And what might they be?' Sam Western demanded.

Mandy held her breath as she watched Michelle glance round the crowd. Then Michelle's eyes met hers and she beckoned Mandy and James over. She handed Mandy the mike and urged her forward. Mandy knew that if ever they had a chance to save the deer, it was now.

Ten

Mandy took a deep breath and spoke into the microphone. 'Well, in the war lots of soldiers did their training up here and some of the trees' – she turned and pointed – 'these beech trees near the house, are full of bullets. So they wouldn't be much good as anything but trees,' she announced in a clear voice. To her surprise, Mr Western didn't shout or bluster; he appeared to be listening.

'That's true,' a voice called out. People made way as someone pushed forward. It was Walter Pickard. 'I remember that,' he said.

'So do we,' shouted Mandy's grandad and Ernie Bell. 'Those trees would ruin any machine you put them through.'

Sam Western pulled at the lobe of his right ear and frowned.

Mandy handed the mike to James.

'Some of the oak trees,' James began, but the mike made loud popping noises. He looked desperately at Michelle who mouthed, 'Hold it further away!'

James tried again. This time it was fine. 'Some of these oak trees are more than three hundred years old,' he told the crowd. 'They have preservation orders on them and they can't be cut down. It would be against the law.'

'That's right,' a man in a waxed jacket said. 'The courts would take a very dim view of such action,' he added.

'And who might *you* be?' Sam Western said, looking perplexed.

'I am here as a conservationist today,' the man responded with a faint smile, 'but I am also a lawyer. I am perfectly happy to act for these people to see fair play is done.'

'That won't be necessary,' Sam Western assured him, looking flustered.

Peter Dickenson held a sheaf of papers in the air. 'Here's the proof, if it's needed.'

'I should like to speak now,' Mrs Ponsonby

said, moving in front of the camera.

Sam Western raised his eyebrows. Taking out a handkerchief, he mopped his brow. 'Go on, then,' he said. 'Everybody else has. You may as well put your two-pennyworth in.'

Mrs Ponsonby glared at him as she took the mike from James. She was wearing the hat with the cherries on it and they wobbled as she spoke.

'In this envelope,' she said, pausing to hold it up for everyone to see, 'is positive proof, yes, PROOF, that there are red squirrels in that forest.'

Sam Western shook his head in disbelief. 'Is that all you've got to say, woman? A bunch of squirrels!' he exclaimed.

'But,' Mrs Ponsonby said smiling a little smile of victory, 'perhaps you don't realise, *man*, that red squirrels are protected by law, and nobody, not even you, can get round that.'

'She's right,' Walter Pickard agreed. 'The law's the law, Western, you can't disturb them.'

'Let's see this proof then,' Sam Western challenged Mrs Ponsonby.

Mandy and James looked at Michelle. They'd all realised together that what was in the envelope was the photograph Mrs Ponsonby had taken the other afternoon. What would it be like? An unrecognisable dot up in the canopy? Or, even worse, would it turn out to be a grey squirrel?

Mandy held her breath as Mrs Ponsonby opened the envelope with a flourish. She held up the picture to Janie's camera.

Mandy gasped. It was a large, glossy photograph of a creature that was unmistakably a red squirrel.

'I photographed this red squirrel just a couple of days ago,' Mrs Ponsonby said, turning around so that the crowd could see the picture.

'What a perfect photograph,' Michelle said. 'May I see?' Mrs Ponsonby blushed and handed it over.

'Yes, there is no mistake,' Michelle said, passing the photograph to Peter Dickenson. 'There are red squirrels here all right. What an expert photographer you are, Mrs Ponsonby. Good enough to work on a wildlife magazine!'

'Thank you, my dear,' Mrs Ponsonby said sweetly, meeting Michelle's eyes without a waver.

'Mr Western,' Michelle said seriously, 'if all these factors aren't enough, let me try to persuade you about the benefits that could be gained from a different . . .' she paused as she searched for a tactful word, '. . . *attitude* to the forest. This is Sally Hudson from the Forestry Commission.' Michelle introduced Sally and handed her the mike. Sam Western looked warily at her, as if he thought she was about to arrest him.

'Mr Western, might I suggest a couple of ideas you may not have considered?' Sally began. 'After all, this has all happened rather speedily.'

'And we know why,' James muttered to Mandy.

'Before anyone could stop him, you mean,' she whispered back.

'Perhaps you had planned to fell the forest and sell off all the prime timber, Mr Western?' Sally didn't wait for an answer. 'Why not review your felling policy instead, and manage the forest in a way that would benefit everyone?'

Sam Western looked seriously at Sally. 'Go on,' he said bluntly.

Everyone listened intently as Sally explained. 'Large parts of this woodland are made up of conifers,' she pointed out. 'Why not exploit these parts and leave the deciduous woodland alone. You could fell it section by section and replant as you go along so it would be a fast-growing, renewable source of timber.'

Sam Western raised his eyebrows and looked at Sally with respect.

'If you manage it like that,' Sally continued, 'not only will you have a constant cash crop of timber, but you won't destroy this ancient forest and its wildlife. We can help you to work out a management plan for the deer. Deer can be very useful in the management of a forest. They keep the grass and shrubs under control, and as long as the herd is kept to a manageable size the forest can support them without suffering any damage.'

While Sally was speaking, Mandy gazed at the deer milling about on the edge of the crowd. One little group of five does and a fawn were standing on the drive near the house. Mandy began edging her way towards them. She looked back to see Michelle watching her. Michelle gave her a nod and Mandy made her way over to the deer. She could still hear Sally's voice through the loudspeakers.

As she reached the drive Mandy's heart leaped and a thrill of excitement rushed through her. The fawn had a neat blue ear tag! But even without it, she would have recognised Sprite. And now Mandy could see that one of the does was Honey-Mum. Slowly she moved closer. One of the does raised her tail and stamped the ground in alarm. Another gave a sharp bark. The startled group made to run away but Sprite and Honey-Mum stood their ground.

'Maaa,' Sprite called.

Mandy kneeled down and put out her hand.

Sprite wandered slowly across the drive, stretched out her neck and nuzzled into it.

'Just like you used to,' Mandy said, feeling the soft wet nose in her palm. Sprite had grown stronger in her time with the herd. Mandy could clearly see how her muscles had developed. Her eyes were bright and her glossy coat glinted in the sun.

'What's to become of you, little one?' she breathed softly. 'Your future depends on Sam Western today.'

Mandy watched in silence as Honey-Mum came nearer. And as Sprite licked her hand, she felt a hot tear slide down her cheek. These animals were so trusting, and so beautiful. She hoped desperately that Sam Western would listen to Sally Hudson. Mandy had done all she could do to save Sprite's home and she couldn't bear it if they had failed.

'And that's my suggestion for the forest, Mr Western,' Sally finished. 'I hope you'll consider it.'

Mandy stood up and watched as Sam Western took the microphone from Sally. Her legs felt like jelly and she barely noticed Sprite pulling at her shoelace.

'I've listened to everything you've said,' Sam Western's voice boomed out, 'and now it's my turn.' There was absolute silence as the crowd waited to hear his words. 'I bought this forest as a business, just like I'd buy a factory, and I admit, I'd planned to take out all the prime timber and replace it with conifers.' He waited as a murmur rippled through the crowd. 'But in the light of what I've heard today, I've decided to leave the older parts of the forest intact,' he said. 'The beeches and the oaks can all stay. I'll not touch them.'

'And the squirrels!' Mrs Ponsonby called out.

'Yes, woman. And the squirrels!' Mr Western agreed, sounding exasperated.

Everyone was cheering. Mandy hugged Sprite, then ran as fast as she could down to where Sam Western stood shaking Sally Hudson's hand.

Mandy tried to get his attention but everyone was making too much noise. 'Mr Western, please!' she shouted, so loudly that the microphone picked it up. The crowd was silent, as

Mandy stood there white-faced.

'Don't tell me you're *still* not happy, young lady?' Sam Western said, frowning.

'Mr Western, what about the deer?' Mandy asked desperately. 'You haven't said if they can stay in the forest.'

Sam Western gave a deep sigh. 'They might as well; they live there, don't they?'

'But they need to move freely and they can't,' Mandy pleaded. 'Not with the fence there.' She glanced around quickly. Mr and Mrs Dickenson were holding their breath. James had his fingers crossed, and there were her gran and grandad, looking anxious; she could almost feel them willing her on. On the edge of the crowd, Steve winked at her.

Sam Western lifted the microphone again. 'Not only have I agreed to leave the forest and,' he said, looking at Mrs Ponsonby, 'the squirrels alone, but this young lady wants me to take down the fence. The fence that I have just had put up at great cost!' he said, raising his eyebrows.

Mandy looked at her feet. She had a sudden feeling of fear that by asking this much of him, she might have made Sam Western so cross he'd change his mind about everything. She could

hardly bear to listen as he started to speak.

'I don't suppose you want deer all over your drive, do you, Dickenson?' he asked, with a chuckle. Mandy looked up in disbelief. 'All right, Harry,' Mr Western called. 'Take the fence down along this side. Just fence the parts where work is being done.'

There were whoops of joy from the crowd.

Peter Dickenson rushed over and shook Sam Western's hand. 'You won't regret this decision,' he said, gratefully.

'You're a canny man, Dickenson,' Sam Western looked at him shrewdly. 'You got what you wanted all round. I'll be needing your keeper to manage those deer, though. Saville knows nothing about them.'

'But Steve does, Mr Western,' Mandy said, grinning. 'Steve was a deer-keeper in Scotland.' She pointed Steve out in the crowd.

'Hmm, was he now?' Mr Western rubbed his chin. 'I'll have to think on that.'

Ernie Bell and Walter Pickard came over to join them.

'It's a strong man who knows when to change his mind,' Walter said to Mr Western, who looked rather pleased. But before he could reply, a group of estate workers hoisted him up

on their shoulders and carried him forward to
where Janie was filming. For a moment Sam
Western looked flustered, but soon he was
beaming at the camera.

'And so, viewers,' Michelle said, 'this is a
better ending than we could possibly have
imagined. The ancient forest is saved, the deer
can run free again, and up above our heads, a
colony of red squirrels are safe once more.'

She switched off the mike and turned to Mrs
Ponsonby who was still hovering near the
camera. 'Even if they haven't got their winter
ear tufts like the one in your picture,' she said
with a wry smile.

'I'll tell you a little secret,' Mrs Ponsonby said,
beckoning Michelle, Mandy and James closer.
'When I got to Walton, I had an attack of nerves.
Supposing my photograph didn't come out?
All might have been lost!' she told them. 'So
I popped into the library on the way and
photographed one on a poster that I'd seen,'
she confessed. 'It came out so much better than
my other photograph, that I decided to use it
instead.'

'Mrs Ponsonby, that was very naughty of you,'
Michelle said, suppressing a smile.

'I have nothing to feel guilty about,' Mrs

Ponsonby declared. 'I know what I saw, dear, and one red squirrel is very like another.'

What with Mrs Ponsonby's trick and Mr Western's performance as the hero of the day, Mandy and James were giggling so much, they could hardly stand up.

'Well done, love,' said a voice behind them. Adam Hope put an arm around Mandy's shoulder.

'We arrived just as you started speaking,' Emily Hope told her. 'We heard it all.'

Peter Dickenson came over to the group. 'We've been hugely successful today, Mandy,' he said. 'And everyone knows that saving the deer was down to your persistence. Sam Western thinks that he's going to put Steve in charge of the herd, and he's asked if I will help out with some advice.'

'So Sprite and Honey-Mum are safe now,' Mandy said, feeling a warm glow of success spread through her.

'As safe as they'll ever be,' Michelle said, as she joined them. 'Imagine, we came to film a deer herd and ended up saving a forest. Just think how impressed the viewers will be when we show the footage on next week's programme. This will be a hard act to follow!'

While Michelle spoke to Peter Dickenson and Mr and Mrs Hope, Mandy and James walked back down to the forest. Although most of the people had started to leave now, the campers were still packing up their tents.

'Look,' James said, pointing at the groups of deer that were leaving the paddocks and returning to the forest. 'They're going home!'

'Good,' Mandy declared happily. 'It's where they belong.'

PONY IN THE POST
Animal Ark Christmas Special

Lucy Daniels

Mandy Hopes loves animals more than anything else. She knows quite a lot about them too: both her parents are vets and Mandy helps out in their surgery, Animal Ark.

A wrong delivery at Animal Ark brings a big surprise – the tiniest horse that Mandy has ever seen! The Miniature Horse was meant for Tania Benster, a newcomer to Welford. But Tania's parents have just divorced and she's too upset to care about her gift. Can Mandy show Tania how much this little horse has to offer?

CHINCHILLA UP THE CHIMNEY
Animal Ark 42

Lucy Daniels

Mandy Hope loves animals more than anything else. She knows quite a lot about them too: both her parents are vets and Mandy helps out in their surgery, Animal Ark.

When Animal Ark's receptionist, Jean Knox, returns from the shops, she brings back more than she'd bargained for: a chinchilla has crept in with her shopping! Before it can be caught it shoots off to hide. Mandy and James must find it – but there's no sign of the chinchilla anywhere!

Another Hodder Children's book

PUPPY IN A PUDDLE
Animal Ark 43

Lucy Daniels

Mandy Hope loves animals more than anything else. She knows quite a lot about them too: both her parents are vets and Mandy helps out in their surgery, Animal Ark.

When Mandy's dad diagnoses an undersize Old English Sheepdog puppy as deaf, Mandy feels sad for it. But it isn't until she finds another Sheepdog pup abandoned and in a sorry state, that she and James begin to be suspicious. Could a local breeder be to blame for the condition of these puppies?

ANIMAL ARK *by Lucy Daniels*

All Hodder Children's books are available at your local bookshop, or can be ordered direct from the publisher. Just tick the titles you would like and complete the details below. Prices and availability are subject to change without prior notice.

Please enclose a cheque or postal order made payable to *Bookpoint Ltd*, and send to: Hodder Children's Books, 39 Milton Park, Abingdon, OXON OX14 4TD, UK. Email Address: orders@bookpoint.co.uk

If you would prefer to pay by credit card, our call centre team would be delighted to take your order by telephone. Our direct line *01235 400414* (lines open 9.00 am–6.00 pm Monday to Saturday, 24 hour message answering service). Alternatively you can send a fax on *01235 400454*.

TITLE		FIRST NAME		SURNAME	

ADDRESS	
DAYTIME TEL:		POST CODE	

If you would prefer to pay by credit card, please complete: Please debit my Visa/Access/Diner's Card/American Express (delete as applicable) card no:

Signature ....

Expiry Date: ....

If you would NOT like to receive further information on our products please tick the box. ❏